DEADLY INVASION

SARAH SPILLMAN MYSTERIES BOOK 2

RENÉE PAWLISH

Deadly Invasion
A Sarah Spillman Mystery

First Digital Edition published by Creative Cat Press

ACKNOWLEDGMENTS

The author gratefully acknowledges all those who helped in the writing of this book, especially: Beth Treat and Beth Higgins.

Again, a huge shout-out to Colonel Randy Powers, retired, Chief Deputy. Any mistakes in police procedure are mine.
If I've forgotten anyone, please accept my apologies.

To all my beta readers: I am in your debt!
Renee Boomershine, Brenda Enkhaus, Tracy Gestewitz, Chris Godwin, Patti Gross, Eileen Hill, Sheree Ito, Maxine Lauer, Judi Moore, Becky Neilsen, Ann Owen, Dick Sidbury, Albert Stevens, Joyce Stumpff, Marlene Van Matre

AUTHOR'S NOTE

I have exercised some creative license in bending settings and law-enforcement agencies to the whims of the story. This is, after all, a work of fiction. Any similarities between characters in this novel and real persons is strictly coincidental.

CHAPTER ONE

He stood in the doorway, peering into the darkness. Over the sound of his own shallow breathing, he heard the slow, steady rhythm of the woman breathing. He listened for a moment and watched the form on the bed. Rays of moonlight cascaded over her long brown hair and gave her cheeks a soft glow. His nerves tingled in anticipation.

The bedroom window was open, and he heard a dog bark. Then silence. She stirred and mumbled something. He froze, then took a quiet step back and waited. Her breathing evened again. He slipped stealthily into the room, his footfalls silent on the carpet. He moved to the window, quietly closed it, and shut the blinds. The square of moonlight on the bed vanished. He gazed at the woman for a moment longer. His heart sped up, and his palms began to sweat inside his gloves. He gripped the knife tighter and stepped over to the edge of the bed. The woman's mouth was slightly open, as if she were about to say something. He put the knife blade to her face, ran the edge of the blade along her lips, then up to her cheek, not enough to cut the skin, but enough that the cold metal woke her. She blinked a couple of times, then her eyes flew open. She started to sit up. He pressed a latex-gloved hand to her mouth, and pushed the blade against her neck. She sank back into the mattress, her body trembling.

"It's okay," he said softly. "Do what I say, and you won't get hurt."

She nodded slowly, but the terror in her eyes betrayed her. She knew everything would not be okay.

CHAPTER TWO

The sound of the 1940's-style jazz quartet greeted me with gusto as I walked into the banquet hall of the Westin Hotel near the Sixteenth Street Mall. The upbeat tune was familiar. Then I placed it. "Who Can It Be Now" by the Australian band Men at Work.

"You've got to be kidding me," I muttered under my breath. It was bad enough I had to come to this event, but to have a cheesy jazz quartet softening up a great 80s tune, that was too much.

I scanned the dimly lit room, searching for Harry Sousen in the throng of guests. Practically every man in the room was wearing a dark suit. I had no doubt Harry would be similarly dressed, which made finding him even harder. I walked between round tables covered in neatly pressed white tablecloths and scanned faces. I recognized a few by name only. This wasn't my crowd. Truthfully, it wasn't Harry's either, but being the president of his own computer consulting company, he had to rub elbows with many of these people; it was good for business.

The band finished "Who Can It Be Now" and I listened to the next tune. This one I didn't recognize, but it, too, had a familiar ring. I looked to the stage. Above it hung a large banner with blue lettering: "Denver Small Business Association." A podium sat centered on the stage, surrounded by chairs, ready for the awards presentation. I shouldn't have been so down on the event, but in my mind, Harry should've been receiving the award for Business Person of the Year, not Darren Barnes. I frowned. I'd met Darren a few times at this type of event. He was smug and arrogant, and he always left me feeling as if I needed to wash away his presence. Seeming to know I was thinking about him, Darren materialized in front of me.

"Sarah Spillman." He flashed a set of gleaming white teeth at me, his salesman smile in excellent form. He moved smoothly between people and approached me, took my hand, and pecked my cheek. "I was just headed outside for a cigarette, and look who I run into. You look lovely this evening."

I resisted the urge to wipe away the subtle kiss. "Darren, it's nice to see you. Congratulations on your award." I was as sweet as I could be, which wasn't much, I admit.

The smile remained plastered on his face. "Well, this little soiree is okay, I guess." He wasn't faking the smile very well, showing too many teeth, keeping his brown eyes open. With a real smile, the eyes tend to close as the cheeks enlarge, forming the classic crow's feet around the eyes. None of that from Darren. He wasn't fooling me, though, he was loving every minute of the event. He held up a drink. "Thank goodness I started earlier. I stopped at Tres Hermanos for their happy hour, and I had a margarita. Have you been there?"

"Yes," I murmured.

He took a drink, looked at me over the glass. "I suppose you're looking for Harry."

I nodded. "I got tied up at work and got here as soon as I could." I didn't know why I was explaining things to him. He made me feel as if I had to, which was part of what I didn't like about him. Among his many negative qualities, he'd made blatant comments in the past about the police, and how he didn't think my profession as a homicide detective was commendable. In some ways he reminded me of my sister, Diane, who often implied the same. A psychologist would say I was transferring some of my frustration with her to him. Possibly. Or maybe Darren just wasn't a nice guy.

"Well," Darren said, his smile intact but his eyes cold, "a woman like you shouldn't be left alone." He appraised me. "You know, you may be a homicide detective, but that would be fine with me."

I gritted my teeth and forced a laugh. That was another thing I didn't like about Darren. He joked about my relationship with Harry. I wasn't sure whether Darren was kidding about his interest in me or not. Regardless, I would never be interested in him.

"Darren–"

"Don't say a word." He stepped back and surveyed me again. "You do look ravishing. That blue dress does wonders for your eyes."

The truth was, I felt bare without my gun and holster on my hip, but I didn't say that. I didn't reply to his compliment at all. "Have you seen Harry?" I said. Try as I might, I couldn't keep my smile.

"I just bought a Corvette. It's spectacular. Black. Sleek lines. We could take it out for a spin."

"What, are we in high school?"

He ran a hand over his brown hair. "Trust me, I'm better than any high schooler."

Was his act all in jest? I didn't want to make an enemy, but I wanted to take my handbag and smack the slimy look off his face. Instead, I made a show of rummaging in the bag so I wouldn't have to look at him. "So ... have you seen Harry?" I asked again.

"I'll give you a call." Before I could protest, he went on. "I believe he's talking to the mayor." Darren was tall and could look over the crowd. He reached for my elbow to escort me to Harry, then someone called his name. He glanced over his shoulder, disappointment in his eyes. His gaze fell back to me and lingered for an uncomfortable moment. "That dress does look good on you." The voice called again. Darren's eyes flashed hot. "Excuse me, please. I do hope to see you after the ceremony."

"Of course." It was insincere, but I don't think he caught it.

He smiled again, pointed toward Harry, and brushed against me as he stepped by.

"What a douchebag," I muttered to myself. I smoothed my dress, wishing Darren hadn't made the comment about my eyes. I took a deep breath and squared my shoulders, then made my way across the hall. Of all the people to run into the second I walked through the door, it had to be Darren Barnes. I was still silently grousing about him when I saw a tall, handsome man with steel-gray hair and dark eyes. His dark suit and yellow tie fit him perfectly, enhancing his sleek physique. He turned, saw me, and his eyes lit up. All thoughts of Darren slipped away.

"Sarah."

With that one word, Harry made me feel like a queen. He held out a hand, and *his* smile was warm and genuine. I reached out and his hand enveloped mine, that small gesture a reassurance of my love for him. Harry, ever the gentleman, introduced me to the man he was chatting with. "I'd like you to meet Mayor Carlson."

I'd been in the same room as Mayor Carlson a few times, but the circumstances had been different, dealing with a homicide investigation. This time, it was much more pleasant.

Carlson obviously remembered me, and he smiled. "It's so nice to see you, Detective Spillman. We've never met formally. I'm Boyd." He held out a hand and I shook it.

"Sarah," I said.

"I sure appreciate your hard work."

I murmured a thank-you, and he gestured at Harry. "Harry and I were discussing the upcoming elections. In general terms, I assure you. I'm not pounding the pavement for votes." Harry and I laughed. Carlson waved a hand in the air. "Boring stuff. But it's what I have to do." He smiled, as practiced as Darren Barnes in that art. And yet I didn't feel the slime as I had with Darren. "If you'll forgive me," Boyd said. "I do need to mingle. Part of the job."

"It was good to see you again," Harry said.

Carlson nodded, and we watched him move away and greet other people with precision. He knew how to make people feel comfortable, eliciting genuine smiles and laughs from everyone he spoke to.

"He's a nice enough man," Harry said in a low voice, "but I don't agree much with his politics."

"I could never rub elbows and schmooze people like that," I said. "I'm too blunt."

Harry put his arm around my shoulder. "Yes you are. And I love you for it."

I squeezed his hand. "Sorry I'm late."

"No worries. Would you like a drink?" Harry took in my dress. "You look stunning. I love that blue. What it does to your eyes."

"Thanks." I frowned.

"What?"

"Darren Barnes just said the same thing. Then he asked me out for a drive in his new car."

He tipped his head, bemused. "He did? You think he was kidding?"

"I would like to think so," I said. "I've never liked the guy. He's ... smarmy."

"In what way?"

I mulled on that for a moment. "I can't put my finger on it. His words are nice ..."

"Well, he'll be busy schmoozing with other people the rest of the night. And if he comes by, we'll dodge him."

I smiled. "I like the sound of that."

"Now let's enjoy the party."

"Right."

He caught the sarcasm. "Thanks for coming. I know you don't like these events."

"Anything for you." I meant that.

He kissed my cheek, and *that* I didn't mind. "How about that drink?"

I nodded toward the bar behind him. "I would love a martini."

He took my hand. "You got it."

We made our way to the bar, got drinks, and went to a table with several other guests. Soon everyone was taking their seats. Harry introduced me to a few people, and I played the chit-chat game. Finally a prime rib dinner was served. I had to admit, it was delicious. Unfortunately, it came with a side of awards, and that meant having to listen to Darren give a speech. He was good, though. He had a way of working the crowd, punctuating his speech with well-timed jokes that elicited plenty of laughter. At one point, Harry leaned over and whispered in my ear. "He aspires to politics."

"That explains why I don't like him."

"Yeah, I don't much care for him either." Harry caught a whiff of my perfume and whispered, "I can't wait to get out of here and take you home."

He put his hand under the table and squeezed my knee. I wanted nothing more than to go home with him right then.

Instead, we suffered through more speeches. Finally, the award ceremony was over. Harry stood up.

"Let's go home."

We said polite good-byes to the others at the table and turned to go. Out of the corner of my eye, I saw Darren Barnes making his way toward us.

"Harry," I murmured.

He glanced over my shoulder and saw Darren. "Let's get out of here. I'll talk to him later."

Darren was too quick for us. "How about this?" he said, holding up a plaque with his name on it.

"Congratulations," Harry said. He put an arm around my waist, pulling me close. "If you'll excuse us, Sarah and I need to go."

"Sure," Darren said.

We turned and hurried for the door. I felt Darren's eyes on me. Harry held me close as if to shield me from Darren. We went outside and the valet brought our car around.

"What is it with Darren?" I said as I slid into the passenger seat.

"I've never really liked him, but he throws a lot of business my way." Harry pulled onto the street.

"I know." It was part of why I was trying not to make too big a deal about Darren. "You know how he is about the police." I thought about my encounter with him. "It's like I'm somehow not worthy."

"Of being a cop? You're a great homicide detective, and you know it."

I thought about that, trying to pull together what I felt. "It's more than that."

"Wait. He thinks you're not worthy of me?"

I stared out the windshield. "Maybe."

He rested his hand on my leg. "You know that's not the case. Sarah, you're beautiful, you're smart, and I love you."

I dismissed that with a wave of my hand. "His attitude–it reminds me of Diane."

He drew in a breath, looked over, then back at the street. "What's going on here? Is this about Darren, or about you and your sister?"

"What?" I snapped. "You should've heard him."

"I'm sorry I missed it."

"Me too."

He checked the rearview mirror, then suddenly pulled over and put the car in park. He drummed the steering wheel, and I stayed silent. He finally spoke. "Sarah, I don't know what happened between you and Diane when you were in college, but you can't continue to let it overshadow things now."

"I'm not."

He twisted in his seat to lock eyes with me. "Are you sure? I get that Darren isn't a great guy, but he's not Diane."

"No," I said slowly. "He's not."

"Maybe it's time to talk to Diane, to tell her how you feel about what happened."

A long time ago I made a mistake. A big mistake. I was a sophomore in college. Diane was in med school, and she messed up, did something she shouldn't have. She was terrified it would screw things up for her, that she'd get kicked out of med school. I stepped in to help her, and even then, I worried that what I did could cost me the career in law enforcement I'd dreamed of since I was a teenager. The whole incident has been eating at me ever since.

"Maybe," I said.

"Hey." He leaned over and kissed me, long and lingering. "Let's go home and forget about both of them."

I put a hand on his chest and felt his heart thumping. "That sounds good."

He kissed me again, then forced himself back to the wheel. He pulled into the street and we drove home. And I didn't think about Diane or Darren for the rest of the night. However, I would have to deal with both sooner than I realized.

CHAPTER THREE

"That's a helluva look in her eyes."

I looked over at my partner, Ernie Moore, and nodded. "She looks terrified," I said.

He swore. "A helluva way to die, too." He subconsciously reached for a cigar stub, which was usually clamped between his teeth. He mostly just chewed on an unlit stub, but he couldn't do that at a crime scene. He put his hand down with a growl.

I stared at the body of a woman lying on a bed in a small room. The bedsheet had been pulled up around her chest, covering her breasts, but her arms were on top of the sheet. She looked a little taller than average, maybe five-six, her hands delicate, fingernails painted a bright red. Rigor mortis had set in, and the backs of her arms were darker where the blood in her body had settled.

Ernie glanced at me. "You look tired. How was the awards thingy last night?"

"Not bad," I lied. "I got home late." I bent down and studied the fingernails, breathing through my mouth to avoid the smell from the body. I've never been able to describe the odor of a dead body. It's something that stays with you, though. "There might be some skin under one of these. Maybe she scratched her assailant." Todd Siltz, a crime-scene tech, tall and thin as a pencil, was taking pictures throughout the room. Every so often, he paused to push his wiry hair out of his face. "Make sure your team scrapes under the nails," I said to him.

"You got it." Todd nodded, looking at me with his intense blue eyes that missed nothing.

I continued to study the body. Dark brown hair cascaded around the pillow. The woman's mouth was partially open, a silent scream. As Ernie had said, her blue eyes were wide open and held pure terror. Ugly black and blue bruises ringed her neck.

"Do we know who she is?" I asked.

"I found a purse in the other room." My other partner, Roland "Spats" Youngfield, had come into the bedroom. He looked slick in a dark suit and green silk tie. Only the disposable booties covering his usually polished shoes ruined the look. A former partner of his had given him the nickname "Spats" because he'd always dressed in flashy clothes and wing-tip shoes, like a gangster from the thirties. To my knowledge, Spats never actually wore spats on his shoes, but he hadn't been able to shake the nickname.

"Do you ever dress *down*?" I said to him. "Does the suit *ever* come off?"

He smirked. "Only when I'm in bed."

Todd stifled a laugh. I held up a hand. "I don't want to know about it."

Ernie hefted his pants over his ample mid-section. "You could stick with a standard suit, like me."

"A classic look," Spats said, eyeballing Ernie's old brown suit, white shirt, and black tie.

Ernie snickered. "Classic, yeah. From the guy holding a woman's purse."

Spats rolled his eyes, then used a latex-gloved hand to pull a small leather wallet from the purse. "Her name's Cherry Rubio. Thirty-two years old."

"Cherry. That's an unusual name." I bent down again and stared at her neck. A faint lavender smell drifted up to me. Or maybe I was imagining it. "What else do we know about her?"

Ernie jerked a thumb over his shoulder. "I have some officers canvassing the neighborhood, asking questions. We'll see if anyone has any surveillance cameras that might show Cherry's house." He held up a hand. "And before you ask, I checked around the house, and she didn't have any cameras set up. So far, we know she worked as an office manager at a small construction company, she wasn't married but some of the neighbors say she had a boyfriend, and I guess he's not too nice. A guy who lives a few doors down, named Blaine Sinclair, saw the boyfriend here about a week ago, says they were arguing. And he thought the boyfriend might've been around last night. He thinks he heard Cherry and the guy fighting again. Sinclair didn't like the boyfriend, that was clear." He scrunched up his nose. "Other than that, she was taking some classes at night, working on a business degree. One of the neighbors said she's got an older brother named Chris, but nobody's been dispatched to talk to him yet. He lives in the Ruby Hill neighborhood, but is probably at work now."

I straightened up. "You better get on that. Find him and deliver the news before someone else gets hold of him."

"How about you and I talk to the boyfriend?" Spats suggested to me. "In case he gets angry."

"What's the boyfriend's name?" I asked.

Ernie consulted his notes. "Manny Guerrero. I've got a detective looking into his background."

I nodded and looked around the room. "What a way to start the morning."

As soon as I'd gotten to the office this morning, I'd received a call about a homicide on the west side of town. Cherry Rubio hadn't shown up that morning for work, so her boss called the house, then called the police. When officers showed up and got no response to the doorbell or to knocking on the door, they checked around the house and found a kitchen window screen cut. At that point, they suspected something was wrong, so they entered the house through an unlocked kitchen door. Once they discovered the body, they called us. We had to get a warrant to search the house, and while we waited on that, we began talking to neighbors. After we received and read the warrant, we entered the house.

"Did anyone see or hear anything suspicious last night or early this morning?" I asked.

Spats shook his head. "Hm. Other than the neighbor saying Cherry might've been fighting with her boyfriend, everything was quiet last night. Same thing this morning. So far no one reports seeing Cherry in a day or two."

"Nothing suspicious?" I repeated.

"Not so far," Ernie said.

I tapped my chin as I looked at the body. "Who did this to you?"

The room was still, other than the muted movements as Todd worked.

"No air conditioning," I observed. "It's hot in here."

"Yep," Spats said.

"Think she was raped?" Ernie asked. "The brother's going to ask."

I shrugged, and looked up at her face and neck again. "I'm wondering about that. She obviously was placed back in this position. If you were strangled, you'd be flailing all over the place.

You don't end up neatly lying on the bed like that after you've struggled with your assailant."

"Makes sense to me." Ernie swore again as he surveyed the room. "Someone took the time to clean up after himself, or herself. Although it would have to be a pretty strong female to strangle her."

"And look at that." I pointed to the end of the bed. "The bedspread was folded and put on the floor. Did Cherry do that, or her killer?"

Jack Jamison, the Denver Police Department coroner, had entered the room. He was in a dark suit, with light blue booties over his shoes. "Let's see what we can find," he said.

He got down on one knee beside the bed and withdrew a stethoscope from a medical bag. He carefully moved the sheet, exposing Cherry's naked torso. He put the stethoscope on her chest and listened.

"She's dead," Ernie muttered, emphasizing the work "dead."

Jack eyed him. "Protocol. And yes, she's dead." He took off the stethoscope and as he did, he ruffled his steel-gray hair. He didn't notice as he studied the body closely. "We'll have a better look at those bruises when we get her on the table."

"Was she raped?" I repeated Ernie's question.

He carefully pulled the sheet down, then gestured for Todd to come over. "Help me turn the body on its side."

We watched while Jack and Todd tipped the body and examined the sheets beneath.

Jack peered at the light green fabric. "Might be some blood there."

"Shut off the light," Todd said. Spats flicked a switch, and the room dimmed. Todd shined an ultraviolet light on the bed. "Not picking up any traces of semen," he said after a minute. He nodded at Spats, who turned the light back on. "I'm not seeing any hair on the sheets, but we'll check carefully."

Jack glanced at me. "We'll do a rape kit during the autopsy."

They rested the body back on the bed, and Jack covered it. Some small dignity in death. I looked around. "Any sign of her underwear, a bra, pajamas?" I got down on my hands and knees and peered under the bed. "Ah, here we go. Underwear. Todd, get a picture of this."

He got down on his knees as well and took several pictures. "We'll get that in a bag and documented."

"Good," I said. I didn't see anything else except dust bunnies under the bed.

Jack was still examining the body. "It certainly appears that she died of strangulation, but I won't know if anything else was a factor in her death until we run a full toxicology." He gently checked the back of her head, and studied each arm and her legs. "At the moment, I don't see any other signs of trauma."

"Time of death?" I asked.

Jack pursed his lips. "Based on the rigidity, my opinion, an opinion only, is sometime during the night."

"Our killer was careful," I observed. I put my hands on my hips. "Todd, find me something. No one should get away with this. Give this room the thorough treatment. Look for hair fibers, blood, semen on any of her clothes, something that will help identify who did this to her."

"You got it," Todd said. He was joined by another tech named Nancy Zimmerman, a short, stocky woman, and they set to work in the room.

"Ernie," I said. "Go talk to the brother now, and let me know how it goes."

He hefted up his pants. "I'm on it. You two be careful with the boyfriend."

"No problem," Spats said. I had no doubt he'd pour on the charm when we talked to Guerrero.

I gazed around. The room was painted a light mauve that

matched a picture of mountain flowers hanging over the bed. Blinds over the window were drawn, and I parted them to let bright sunlight into the room. "The window's closed."

"On a night like last night?" Spats said. "In a house with no A/C?"

"The window's not locked. Want to bet it was open, and our killer closed it so no one would hear him? But he doesn't lock it–"

"–so he doesn't wake the victim," Spats finished my sentence.

A nightstand beside the bed had an alarm clock, lamp, and cell phone. I went over and opened the drawer. Fashion magazines were stacked together, and resting on top of them were a notepad with a Sheraton Hotel logo on the bottom of it, and a phone charger.

I swiped at the phone screen. "It's password-protected."

Spats nodded. "We'll need a warrant to get into it."

"Yes." The dresser drawers were closed, and I opened the top one. Inside were underwear and bras. Everything was folded. The rest of the drawers were the same, T-shirts, shorts, and slips all neatly arranged. A small jewelry box was on top of the dresser. I carefully opened it. A few rings, a necklace, and a gold bracelet.

"We need to find out if any of this is valuable," I said. "The family might be able to tell us if anything is missing."

Spats moved over to a small closet. "Very neat. Shoes lined up on the floor, no dirty clothes thrown around. Looks like there's a couple of men's shirts here, and a baseball cap on the shelf up here."

"A boyfriend's stuff?" I speculated.

He shrugged.

"I don't see anything out of place," I said. "Was anything taken from her purse? Money, credit cards?"

He thumbed through the wallet. "There are two credit cards in here, a Visa and Discover. And there's ..." he paused, counting, "thirteen dollars."

I gnawed at my lip. "Burglary doesn't appear to be a motive."

Spats looked around the room. "The killer came through a window, right?"

I stepped past him and into the hallway. "Let's look again."

We walked down a short hall of the small ranch-style home and checked a bathroom. Her toiletries were neatly arranged, with everything in its place. A small window above the shower was closed. The living room was bright, with worn flowered couches, oak coffee and end tables, and an oak bookcase against one wall packed with paperback romance novels. None of it looked expensive, probably Target or IKEA. A laptop sat on the coffee table. I checked it, it was also password-protected.

"A warrant for that, too," Spats said before I could.

"Yes. Then we'll get Tara to go through it all."

Tara Dahl is one of the department's IT investigators, and she is a technical wizard. She'd be able to get into the laptop and analyze all the data, the browser history, and anything else that might help us find Cherry's killer. In a few hours, she'd also amass all kinds of information on Cherry, her family, her friends, and anyone else who we'd want to talk to about Cherry's death.

We went into the kitchen. It was cute, with yellow walls, old cabinets painted white, and a tiny round table in the corner. A bike was propped up next to the door.

"That's a good bike," Spats said. "Specialized, a decent brand. Not cheap."

My eyes immediately went to an open window by the back door. The screen had been cut in an X pattern, its pieces hanging at odd angles. The lower part appeared to have been ripped.

Spats studied the screen. "Probably done with a knife." He motioned with a hand. "A couple of slices, and you're able to quickly get to the window. He probably tore part of the screen to make the hole bigger."

I stared at the window, then the sill. "The hasp looks okay, no sign of forced entry. Think the window was already open?"

"It was hot last night." He shrugged. "It's hot now."

"In that suit, I'll bet."

"Ha ha." He left the room, then returned with Nancy. He pointed at the window. "Make sure you check for prints on the window sill, the jambs, and the locks."

"Absolutely," she said.

The sound of a car on the street drifted in through the damaged window. How had it sounded to Cherry last night? Did she go to bed with the night sounds soothing her, with no thought of dangers? I frowned and looked at the back door.

"The officers doing the welfare check said this door was unlocked?"

"Yep," Spats said.

I squinted at the handle and deadbolt. "Hard to tell if the lock's been tampered with. We need to make sure to check for fingerprints. Maybe the murderer tried the doors before he came through the window."

He stepped back. "I'll bet our killer came through the window, then let himself out the through the door. Why bother to lock it once he'd done that?" He jerked his head toward the bedroom.

I nodded.

"I'll check for prints on all of it," Nancy said. "We'll dust all around the window–inside and out–for evidence."

"Thanks," I said.

Nancy went back into the bedroom, and Spats and I walked out the front door. An officer at the door logged us out. He'd be noting entries and exits until everyone had finished with the crime scene. Spats and I went around the side of the house and didn't find any footprints near the window. We inspected the outside of the window as well and didn't see any signs that it had been damaged.

"Let's hope the techs find something I'm not seeing," I murmured.

Spats was surveying a late-model Honda that sat in a carport. "Nothing unusual here. It's locked."

After looking around a bit more, we went back inside and searched through the rest of the kitchen. It was small, so it didn't take long. Cherry was a tidy person, dishes, cans of food, and other utensils all precisely in place. Everything was clean, the refrigerator orderly, although not much in the way of food or drinks. Another framed photo of flowers hung above the table in the corner. We tramped downstairs to a minuscule unfinished basement where Cherry had stored a couple of old chairs. A stackable washer-dryer sat in the corner. Nothing seemed out of place. Once we had gone through the entire house, Spats and I ended on the front porch. It was a hot August morning, the dry Colorado heat already stifling. A few onlookers were standing at the sidewalk, held back by one of the uniforms. A command center had been set up nearby, and detectives were already researching Rubio and her boyfriend. Spats got what they had so far, and he and I scanned the information on Manny Guerrero.

"He has a prior for domestic violence," I noted. "Other than that, he's clean."

"Yep. Here's his pic." Spats held up a driver's license photo of Guerrero.

"After we talk to the boyfriend, get everything you can from the officers canvassing the neighborhood. And don't forget, we need warrants for that laptop and her phone."

"The boyfriend works at A-plus Auto Repair on South Sheridan," he said. "Let's get over there now, deliver the news, and see what his reaction is."

"I'll drive," I said, "then swing back by here for your car."

"Go in as a united front, right Speelmahn?" Spats said with a smile. I didn't know why but he always gives my name a Jamaican flair, even though he's from Harlem.

With that, we marched down the sidewalk and headed to my car.

CHAPTER FOUR

A-plus Auto Repair is located on Sheridan Boulevard at the boundary between Denver and Jefferson counties. I took Sixth Avenue west, then drove south on Sheridan and soon turned left and parked my Ford Escape around the corner from the shop. The steady drone of traffic greeted us as Spats and I got out. We walked through a parking lot that was full of a variety of cars, some needing repairs, some waiting for owners to pick them up. The high-pitched buzz of air tools and metal clinking on metal from the nearby garage bays followed us into the office. The air-conditioning was a welcome relief from the scorching sun outside. To the right of the door, cheap plastic chairs lined a wall with framed advertisements. A lone man reading a magazine lounged in one of the chairs. Behind a counter to the left sat a man with dark hair and olive skin talking on an old phone.

I recognized Guerrero from the picture we had. He held up a finger as he continued his conversation, then he cradled the receiver on his shoulder as he typed on a computer.

"Yeah, I need that part by tomorrow, if you can get it." His voice had a deep and resonant timbre with the trace of an accent.

"Yeah, okay. I'm also going to have another order for you this afternoon. I need it for that Mazda." He paused and nodded. "All right, sounds good, thanks." He hung up the phone, wrote on a notepad that had grease on it, then looked up. "How can I help you?"

"You're Manny Guerrero?"

His eyes narrowed, any pleasantness in his face vanished. "Yeah?" Wary.

Behind me, the chair creaked. I knew the other man was listening. Guerrero glanced behind me, and I shifted so he had to meet my gaze.

I flashed my badge at him and introduced Spats and myself. "Could we speak to you for a few minutes, perhaps in private?" I smiled. "It's about an investigation we're conducting, and you might have information pertinent to it."

Guerrero stared at me, then gazed at Spats. Anger flashed in his eyes, then vanished.

"All right, hold on." He picked up the receiver, hit a number, and spoke into the phone. "Get up here. You need to cover the desk for a minute."

He cradled the receiver and frowned at me. "I gotta have someone cover this." He pointed at the counter.

Spats and I both nodded.

"Take all the time you need," Spats said pleasantly.

A moment later, the door to the garage opened. An air tool whirred, then stopped, and we heard voices in Spanish, and rock music. Another Hispanic man walked into the room, wiping greasy hands on an equally greasy blue cloth.

"What do you need, Manny?" he said.

Guerrero motioned at the counter. "Take care of things here for a minute. I gotta talk to these people." He was careful not to identify us as detectives.

"Yeah, sure, but I don't know how to operate the computer and ..."

"Just take care of it for a minute, okay?" Guerrero snapped at him.

The guy squinted at Spats and me, then nodded. "Okay."

Guerrero got up, and the man slid into his chair. Guerrero walked across the room to another door, his back rigid. We followed him into a tiny office with a desk and chair and some gray metal file cabinets in the corner. He moved around the desk and sat down stiffly, and pointed at the door. "Shut it." Then he tacked on, "Please."

Spats closed the door, turned around, and leaned against it. He locked eyes with Guerrero. Guerrero was making a point of not looking at me, so I glanced imperceptibly at my partner, letting him know that he could take the lead. If Guerrero didn't want to talk to me, that was okay.

"You know Cherry Rubio?" Spats asked him, his tone neutral.

Guerrero's eye twitched. "Is this about her? I haven't seen her in a while."

"How long?"

"A few weeks, maybe a month," Guerrero said.

Spats pursed his lips. "I thought you and Cherry were dating."

I looked at Spats. Like me, he was holding back his surprise. We hadn't heard that Guerrero wasn't seeing Cherry anymore.

"We broke up."

Spats nodded slowly. "It's been a while since you've seen her, huh? I thought one of her neighbors said you were at her house last week, and you might've been there yesterday. Am I mistaken?"

"He's lying."

Spats looked at me, one corner of his mouth up in the slightest of smirks. "I didn't tell you it was a he."

Guerrero sat unmoving and gulped. He stared at me, as if I might rescue him. I stayed silent.

Tension hung thick in the air, and Spats let it linger. Then he said, "You're sure it was three weeks ago?"

"Yes, it was." Guerrero went on. "We had dinner at a Chili's restaurant, and right during the middle of it, she broke up with me."

"At the restaurant, with everybody around?" Spats gave him a sympathetic look. "Was that a little awkward?"

Guerrero stood up. "What do you think?"

"And?" Spats prompted him.

Guerrero assessed him, as if wondering what he knew. "I think I raised my voice, and the waiter asked us to leave." He crossed his arms. "I know how this goes. You'll go to the restaurant and talk to them. Well, you do that, and they'll tell you Cherry and I were there, and we didn't finish our dinner. We left without a problem, I took her home, and that's the last time I saw her."

Spats straightened his tie, his way of giving himself a moment to think. I moved to the corner and peeked at a paper on top of the file cabinet, then back to Guerrero. He was focused on Spats. Spats glanced at me, and I knew from the gleam in his eye that he wanted me to take over. He and I had done enough of these interviews that we had a feel for each other, knew the ebb and flow of an interview and who might elicit information from someone we're talking to.

"That must've been hard for you," I said, my voice soft.

Guerrero's head jerked toward me. "You know about that kind of thing? Done that to a guy yourself? You break up with him at a restaurant, somewhere in public, because you hope nothing bad will happen."

I arched an eyebrow. "Would something bad happen? Is that how you do things?"

His Adam's apple bobbed, He knew he'd just revealed something about himself and how he might've felt about women, how he might've treated them. "That's not what I mean."

I kept my voice even. "You got in trouble for domestic violence?"

"That doesn't mean I did anything to Cherry. And not at any restaurant."

"What about when you got back to her house?" Spats asked. "The neighbors heard a fight."

Now we were keeping Guerrero off balance, not sure what might be coming next.

Guerrero put his palms down on the desk and leaned toward Spats. "I raised my voice, but it was not a fight. Nothing happened. I didn't raise a hand to Cherry then, or any other time, no matter what anybody told you." Then he lifted a hand and jabbed a finger at Spats. "Is that what her brother's saying?" He shook his head slowly. "That guy had it in for me from the start. He never liked me. But that doesn't mean I did anything to Cherry."

"The DV charge?" I asked again.

"I got in trouble, a long time ago with a different woman," Manny said. "I don't deny it. I went through classes and counseling, and I've never hit a woman since. I'm working on things, you know? I never hit Cherry."

"Were you verbally abusive? Yelling at her, calling her names?" I went on.

"No."

"Never?"

"That's right," he said.

Spats and I contemplated him. Guerrero didn't say anything.

"Have you heard about what happened to her?" I asked.

Guerrero's brow furrowed. "What do you mean?"

The volley went back to Spats. "Why do you think we're here?"

Guerrero hesitated. "I don't know. What did she say I did?"

"She didn't say anything," Spats said. "She's dead."

Guerrero went rigid again, and he took a couple of shallow breaths. He was careful not to show anything. "You think I did it?"

Spats gave me a slight look, both of us knowing Guerrero was not handling the interview well. "I didn't say that someone *did* anything to her," Spats said. "I just said she's dead."

"What happened?" Guerrero asked. His voice held no emotion.

"She was strangled," I said, my voice now without sympathy.

Guerrero glared at me. "And what? Because I got a past, I would do that to her? I haven't seen her in weeks. I wasn't over there last night, and you got no business bothering me here." He sucked in a breath. "I think I need my lawyer."

"Why do you need a lawyer, if you didn't do anything?" Spat asked calmly.

Guerrero quickly came around the desk. In the tight space, he was close to Spats. Spats wasn't fazed. He continued to lean casually against the door and waited.

Guerrero strained to stay calm. "I didn't have nothing to do with Cherry's death, and I wasn't over there last night. You can check around."

"Where were you?" Spats asked.

"I was with a woman." Guerrero got even closer to Spats. "You guys need to leave now."

"What's the woman's name?" I asked.

Guerrero's head whipped around to look at me. "I'm not saying any more without a lawyer. I know you won't believe me, no matter what I say." Guerrero reached around Spats and grabbed the door handle. Spats stepped forward and Guerrero jerked the door open. He stepped back and gave us a steely look.

Spats finally turned around and studied Guerrero with concern. "You're only making this harder. If you didn't do anything, help us find who *did* do that to Cherry."

"You want any more from me, you talk to my lawyer. I haven't been around Cherry lately, and that's all I'm saying."

"Do you know where Cherry was last night?" I asked.

He shook his head. "I don't know."

I moved toward the door. "I'm sorry you feel that way. We just want to find out what happened to her. No one deserved to die the way she did."

"Look for a guy named Rex," he muttered.

"Rex who?" I asked.

"I don't know. She mentioned him."

"When?" I fired the question at him.

"The other ni–" Guerrero stepped back to the desk, trying to put distance between himself and me. "I don't know." He didn't say another word, just pointed toward the lobby.

Spats tipped his head at Guerrero, and I thanked him again. He didn't reply. Spats and I walked into the lobby. The other employee and the customer watched us carefully. Guerrero stayed back in the office doorway, and I could feel his eyes bore into my back as we walked outside. I shielded my eyes and looked at Spats.

"That was interesting," he said dryly. "For somebody who seems worried about us assuming the wrong thing about him, he did just about everything to make us suspicious of him."

We walked around the corner, and I clicked the key ring to unlock the Escape. "Yep. Did you notice he didn't ask us why we were asking about Cherry, or how Cherry died?"

Spats opened the passenger door and got in. "I sure did. He's seen Cherry more recently than three weeks ago. He almost slipped and said "the other night." I want to double-check with the neighbor who thought he saw Guerrero there last night. We need to make sure that's accurate. And Guerrero seemed to know it was a man who saw him arguing with Cherry, not a woman."

"I caught that too." I started the car and thought for a few seconds while the A/C kicked in. "I don't know whether Guerrero really is just spooked because he's been in trouble before, or if he's got something to hide."

Spats nodded thoughtfully. "And who is Rex?"

"That's a good question," I said. "Think he threw the name out, just to throw us off track?"

"We'll find out."

CHAPTER FIVE

As I drove away, I pulled out my cell phone and put it on speaker. "Ernie," I said after I dialed his number. "How's it going with Cherry's brother, Chris?"

"About what you'd expect." I heard a man's voice in the background, and Ernie excusing himself. Then he went on in a low voice. "I'm still with him. I told him about Cherry, and he was understandably wrecked, and pissed. He called his mother and told her about Cherry, and she's understandably upset. A neighbor is with her now. We've been talking for a while, and he wants to come over to Cherry's house before he sees his mom. I discouraged that, said it's still a crime scene, but I couldn't change his mind."

"All right. If that's the case, let's have him go through the house to see if he thinks anything is missing. And I can get an impression of him."

"What'd he say about Manny Guerrero?" Spats asked.

"Doesn't like him," Ernie said. "Apparently Cherry broke up with him a few weeks ago."

I turned onto Sixth Avenue, headed back to Cherry's house. "We heard the same thing."

"Manny's been around Cherry since then," Spats said. He gave Ernie a quick update.

"Did anybody that you talked to this morning mention a man named Rex?" I explained how Manny ended our conversation by saying we should look for him.

"Nope, that's not a name that came up, but I'll double-check with Chris." Ernie went on. "On my way over to his house, I got a little more information from the officers canvassing the neighborhood. Everyone says Cherry was a friendly person, but that she stayed to herself a bit, and a couple of them said she didn't have very good taste in boyfriends. One mentioned Guerrero, said that he'd seen them fighting a few times. Another one said that she hadn't seen Guerrero around as much, and that if Cherry had broken up with him, that was the best thing she could've done for herself."

"Did that neighbor mention Cherry seeing anybody else?"

"Not Rex, if that's who you mean," Ernie said. I heard a voice again, and he cleared his throat. "I'll get the full details on Guerrero when I see you. Let me wrap up here and I'll meet you at Cherry's house."

"Sounds good." I ended the call and stopped for a red light. "I'd like to talk to the neighbor who says he saw Cherry and Guerrero last night. You think he's still available?"

"Blaine Sinclair," Spats said. "He works from home. I'll see if he can take a few minutes to talk to us again."

I nodded. "Then we need to get on warrants for her electronics. I'll let you work on that." Spats is a smooth talker and good with judges who might not easily sign a warrant, which is why I frequently give him that task. "And get a surveillance team on Manny. I want to know what he's up to."

"I'll add it to the list."

By now, I had turned onto Alcott Street and parked in front of Cherry's house. No gawkers were around; it was too hot to stand and watch nothing.

"Let me get Sinclair," Spats said as he headed down the block.

I gave him a short wave and headed up the walk to the front porch. An officer remained at the door, and once again he logged me into the crime scene. I put booties over my shoes, donned gloves, and entered the house.

Todd was in the bedroom, dusting the bed for prints. Cherry's body had been removed, and the bedsheets had been rolled up and bagged in order to gather any possible evidence. The lab folks would check them for hair or clothing fibers. The room was stuffy.

"I didn't think I'd see you again," Todd said.

"We got a tip that Cherry might know a man named Rex. Have you found notes around, anything that might tell us this guy's last name?"

He shook his head. "Not so far. We're almost finished, but look around. I'll keep an eye out too."

I gestured at the bed and the bagged-up sheets. "Find anything else there?"

He grimaced. "Not at first glance. My guess is our guy has watched too many cop shows. He knows to be careful about leaving any evidence around. We'll be thorough, but I wouldn't get your hopes up."

"I never do."

I checked all the dresser drawers again, then the nightstand. Todd glanced at me, and I shrugged and left the room. I walked through the house again, carefully looking around, but I didn't see anything that would tell me who the mystery man Rex was. I ended up in the tiny kitchen. The window where the killer had presumably entered had fingerprint dust on it. I gazed through the cut screen to the back yard. Behind that was an alley, and a large blue truck drove by. I pictured last night, the heat creeping into the little house. Who could blame Cherry for leaving the windows open? Unfortunately, it made easy access for her murderer. I heard my name being called, and I turned around and went back out the front door. Spats was standing in the lawn with a man I judged to be in his late twenties or early thirties. He was casually dressed in khaki shorts and a T-shirt with a San Francisco Giants logo on it. His lips were a thin line, his exaggerated sigh an indication that he wasn't happy to be here.

"This is Detective Spillman," Spats introduced me, then held up a hand. "This is Blaine Sinclair. He's the man I was telling you about."

"I appreciate your taking the time to talk to us again," I said. "I understand you overheard Cherry having an argument with her boyfriend–or ex-boyfriend–Manny Guerrero, correct?"

Sinclair nodded as he scratched his short blond hair. "Yeah, it was about a week ago."

"You're sure on that timeframe?" I asked.

Sinclair nodded his head vigorously, then jerked a thumb at Spats. "I told your partner that it was a week ago. I know that because I had just gone to the Rockies game, and I'd come home and seen them outside." He let out another huge sigh.

"I'm sorry you're having to go over this again," I said to defuse his seeming frustration. "We had a discrepancy on when Guerrero last saw Cherry, so I want to make sure we have things correct."

"I know I'm right. The Rockies played the Giants, my team. And I know what you might be thinking, I don't like the guy, so that's why I'm saying this. But I'm not lying about seeing them. As I drove by, they were getting out of Manny's car. It's an old Charger, so I knew it was him. I had my window rolled down, and I heard Manny yelling at her, something about 'not this time.'

I slowed down and watched in my rearview mirror. Manny grabbed Cherry's arm, and she jerked away from him. Then they went into the house."

"Did he hit her?" I asked.

His nose wrinkled. "I don't think so. Maybe."

"Maybe?"

He thought for a second. "I don't think so."

"You don't like Guerrero?" I watched him closely.

He shook his head. "Look, I liked Cherry, okay? I thought she was real sweet, and she was a knockout. I would've liked to go out with her, only she wasn't interested in me. But that doesn't mean I can't make an honest assessment of Manny. He's a jerk, and I even told her one time I didn't know why she was messing around with him."

"Did she tell you why?" Spats asked.

Sinclair snickered, and he looked uncomfortably at me. "He was a good lay." He gave Spats a knowing look. "She may have liked Manny at first, but about all that was left was the sex. She liked that part."

I cocked an eyebrow. "She told you that?"

"Yeah."

"Apparently she got tired of the sex," I said. "She broke up with him."

"Uh-huh." A car drove by, and Blaine waved at the driver, then turned back to us. "He wasn't worth the rest of it, all the fighting."

I went on. "You saw Manny here last night?"

He hesitated. "I thought I saw some guy walking out of her house, and he was talking to her. It was dark, and I'm not sure who it was."

"What'd he look like?"

"Hmm. Dark hair, I guess. Kind of tall."

"Was Manny's car parked out front?"

He shook his head. "I don't recall seeing it. Maybe it was someone else. But I know a week ago it was him."

"Did Cherry ever mention somebody named Rex?" Spats asked.

Blaine thought about that as he squinted at us. "I don't think so. I probably talked to her once a week or so, if she was outside. I haven't seen anybody else around other than Manny."

"Was Cherry scared of anyone?"

"If she was, she didn't tell me." He scratched his head again. "Hey, I need to get back to work. I'll talk to you some more, if you want to come by later."

"I think we have what we need now, but we'll certainly stop by if we have more questions," I said. "One more thing, though. Where were you last night?"

"I was here until about ten, then I went to my girlfriend's. I heard Manny–or whoever it was–as I drove away. He was talking loud. I spent the night at my girlfriend's, then came back to my house this morning. I gave you that info," he said to Spats.

"Yep, I have it," Spats said pleasantly.

"Did you see or hear anything unusual last night before you left?" I asked.

"No." Blaine looked toward the house and bit his lip. "Cherry was a nice girl. It's too bad." He rubbed his arms. "I hope you find who did that to her, and if it was Manny, he better watch out." Then he blinked hard. "Sorry, I didn't mean that."

"That's okay." Spats said.

We watched as Sinclair walked down the block, then up his sidewalk and into his house.

"The girlfriend's name is Elaine Nowicki," Spats said. "I sent a detective to go talk to her, but she's not at her office right now. I'll keep on it."

"If we can't get in touch with her by the time I'm finished

here, I'll talk to her. I'd like to hear for myself what she has to say."

"What do you think of Sinclair?" Spats said as he shielded his eyes against the sun.

I thought for a moment. "I believe him over Manny Guerrero."

"You think Guerrero is hiding something?" Spats asked.

"Maybe he was here last night. Things get out of hand and he kills her?" I speculated. "He cleans up, makes it look like a break-in with the cut window screen, and lies and says he hasn't seen her in weeks."

Spats put his hands in his pockets. "We can't check his alibi. We don't know the girl he was with."

I nodded. "I might talk to him again, see if I can get him to open up."

"Good luck with that. I'm going to work on the warrants for the electronics and set up that surveillance team."

"Great," I said. "I'll do one final pass through the house, and then I'll look into Sinclair as well. He was interested in Cherry, so ..." I didn't finish.

"Yeah, he's a suspect, too."

I stared up at the sun. "This heat is unbearable."

"That it is. I'll get to work on the warrants." He glanced up and down the street. "Ernie should be here soon with Cherry's brother."

I drew in a breath and let it out slowly. "I hope that goes okay." Dealing with distraught family members of a murder victim is a part of the job, but something I do not like.

"I'll call you when I have something," Spats said. "And I'll text you the contact information for Sinclair's girlfriend."

"Sounds good."

I watched him go to his car, then I walked back toward Cherry's house.

CHAPTER SIX

I again put on gloves and booties, and the officer at the door logged me in yet again. I went back into the bedroom where the techs were still working. I stood in the doorway for a moment and watched them.

Todd turned and saw me. "We've got some prints on the window, on the latch." He moved over to the window and pointed. "Some of them are smudged, and I'll bet those are the victim's."

I looked at the latch. "The only saving grace about cop shows is that they're often wrong, so maybe our killer slipped up and left us a good print." I put my hands on my hips. "Still nothing on Rex?" He shook his head. I pursed my lips. "Maybe she wrote a note with a phone number somewhere. If this guy exists, I want to find him."

Todd called out to Nancy, who was working in Cherry's closet. "You find anything about someone named Rex?"

"Nothing so far," she yelled back.

I shrugged, moved to the nightstand, and opened the drawer. I stared at the magazines, notepad, and phone charger that I'd seen before, then pulled out the notepad. The top page was blank. I held it at an angle up to the light. "I don't see any imprint of writing on a previous page."

Todd shook his head. "We younger generation put everything on our phones."

I studied him. "You can't be that much younger than me."

"But I feel so old," he said with a mock sigh.

I laughed and put the notepad back. "It was worth a look."

I glanced in a wicker trash can next to the nightstand. It was empty. "The trash can was like that? You didn't take anything out of it?" He shook his head again. "Nothing there."

"Has anybody gone through the kitchen trash?"

"I was going to do that soon," Nancy called out from the closet. "You want to look at it?"

I needed a tech to go with me so that there was no question a detective might've tampered with the crime scene. I went to the doorway. "Leave no stone unturned."

"Or piece of trash." She was on her hands and knees, checking Cherry's shoes.

"Can you interrupt what you're doing?"

"Sure." She got up and waved a hand at me. "The trash is my favorite part. Especially the kitchen trash." I laughed at her sarcasm. Working crime scenes will give you a dark sense of humor.

We went into the kitchen, and Nancy surveyed the room. "The country kitchen look," she said, noting the yellow walls and sheep decorations. I glanced at her, and she gave me a warm smile. "My sister likes this style. The cutesy farm animals and country décor. Not saying I do."

I grinned. It wasn't my style either. I favored white walls, not a lot of decorations. My life is chaotic; I want my home simple. I opened a cabinet underneath the kitchen sink and pulled out a small black trash can that was partially full. I waved a hand in front of my face. "Something in there is ripe."

Nancy backed up, and I put the trash can on the floor. "You get pictures of this?"

"Just the can itself, so I'll take more now." She snapped several more pictures. "Just so everything we do is documented."

I carefully started taking things out of the can. A banana peel, some dried orange rind. A plastic bag with something moldy in it.

"There's our culprit," I said as I scrunched up my nose. "I don't want to guess what's in there." I peeked inside anyway, just in case. "Rotten vegetables."

I held the bag open and she took a picture. Nancy took the bag, closed it up, and set it away from us, the smell not seeming to bother her as much as it did me. I kept pulling things out of the trash, and she kept snapping pictures. An empty spritzer bottle. A grocery store receipt. Some torn pieces of paper. I studied one closely.

"There was some writing on this." I took the pieces and tried to fit them together. After a moment, I had the paper together. Coffee grounds smeared most of it, but I could make out, "Call at 7."

"Does that mean anything to you?" I asked.

Nancy shook her head. "Maybe somebody was supposed to call somebody at seven?"

"Ha ha."

She laughed and took a picture of the paper puzzle. I set it aside. Cherry had torn up some mail, along with a brochure for Littleton Chevrolet. I emptied the rest of the trash can, and nothing seemed like a clue to me. I put everything back, and Nancy went back into the bedroom. I perused the house again, checked all the trash cans, and searched around the coffee table and end tables in her living room. No clue to who Rex might be. I ended up back in the master bedroom.

"Sorry, I don't think the kitchen trash was helpful to you," Nancy said.

"Maybe not now, maybe later."

Todd held up a hand. "All of this will go to the crime lab, and we'll give you a full report on everything as soon as we can."

I nodded. "I appreciate it. Then we'll see what we come up with."

I thanked him for his time and walked out of the bedroom.

CHAPTER SEVEN

I went outside and the officer logged my exit. What a tedious job.

"It's hot out," I said to him.

"Yes ma'am."

Ma'am? I was getting old. "Have you been watching the onlookers?" I motioned at the street, where, earlier in the day, curious neighbors had been hanging out.

"Yes. I didn't see anyone acting strangely. They'd stay a few minutes, talk to each other, and move on." He peeked toward the sky. "It's too hot to stand around for too long, if you don't have to."

"Amen to that."

I stepped off the porch and was looking around the front of the house when Ernie drove up, followed by a black Honda Civic. Ernie got out and was joined by a dark-haired man. They walked up the sidewalk, and Ernie introduced me to Cherry Rubio's brother, Chris. He was tall, with an acne-scarred face, and the weight of his sister's death made his shoulders sag. He shook my hand, a dazed aura about him, yet his eyes held tense anger.

"Detective Moore wouldn't tell me much," Chris said, his voice hard and level. "He says it's too early to tell what exactly happened to my sister." He gazed at me expectantly, wanting more.

I eyed Ernie. He gave me the slightest of shrugs, as if to say it was my call as to what to tell Chris.

"Detective Moore is correct," I said. "It's very early in our investigation, and at this point we're trying to gather as much information as we can. I assure you that we will tell you everything we know at the appropriate time."

Ernie stepped back and let me run the conversation, but he was listening carefully, and I knew he'd signal me if there were any discrepancies in what Chris had told him earlier.

"You can't say too much or you could jeopardize your case," Chris said. He stared at his sister's house, and his mouth screwed up in a mix of frustration and anger. "I want to go inside and look around."

"We can do that in a minute. We still have some investigators inside. We need to let them finish."

He rolled his eyes. "Fine." The universal word used to convey the exact opposite of its original meaning. Everything was not fine. He crossed his arms, disappointed, and yet seeming to know enough about police work to realize arguing would be futile. He would have to wait.

"I appreciate your understanding." I smiled sympathetically. "Are you okay if I ask you a few questions now? It might be hashing over the same things you told Detective Moore."

"I already told the detective that I don't know what she did last night," Chris said. "We're pretty close, but that doesn't mean I know what she does all the time. Although right now, I wish I did."

I nodded and eased him into the conversation. "Tell me about Cherry. That's an interesting name."

Some of his intensity eased. "What my mom always said was she was thinking of the name Sherry, but I'd say Cherry. So she named her that. I was three," he said in explanation. He looked down the street as he gathered his words. "She is ... was ... really great. She was my little sister, you know? I looked after her." He shook his head sadly, struggled to keep his voice even. "Don't get me wrong, we could fight, especially growing up, but things were tough and I needed to make sure she was okay. We were a little team against the world. She's a bit shy, but if you talk to anyone that really knew Cherry, they'll tell you she was nice, that she genuinely cared for you. She was working hard and going to school, and yet she still took time to volunteer at a women's shelter, and she did charity bike rides."

"I saw a nice bike in her kitchen."

"Yeah, I helped her get that, a Christmas and birthday gift a few years ago. She loved to ride, and she had a piece-of-crap bike. She knew she needed something better, but a good bike can be expensive. I helped pay for it."

"Right." I moved into the crux of my questions. "What did you think of your sister's ex-boyfriend, Manny Guerrero? And am I correct that they had broken up?"

His jaw tightened. "Yeah, they weren't together anymore. I didn't like the guy at all. I told Cherry that, but she didn't listen to me." His hands clenched and unclenched. "If Manny had something to do with this, I swear I'll ..." His voice trailed off.

"What kind of car does he drive?"

"A Charger. Nice car. Not a nice guy," he tacked on.

"Why don't you like Manny?"

He pointed at Ernie. "As I told him, Manny wasn't nice to Cherry. I think he smacked her around some, but when I asked her, she always denied it. I think she knew if she told me the truth that I'd go after Manny." His voice caught and he choked up for a minute, put a hand over his face, and muttered something. "I'm sorry," he finally said as he looked at me again. He wiped his eyes. "I just can't believe this is happening. My mom is crushed."

"I understand," I said. "Is your dad around?"

He shook his head. "Nah, he ran off when we were kids. He wasn't any good anyway. He was abusive to my mom."

"Did Cherry talk to you about her breakup with Manny?"

"Yeah." Chris wipe sweat off his face, then rubbed his palms on his slacks. "She let me know she was going to do it, and she was a little worried what his reaction would be, so I suggested she go to a restaurant and do it there. You know, people around, he would keep his cool. Only that didn't happen. He blew up at her anyway. She said he made quite a scene, and the waiter finally had to get management to ask him to leave. He did, after making a lot of noise, and Cherry called me. I drove over to the restaurant and picked her up. She was pretty shook up about it, wondering if Manny would come by the house and bother her, so she spent the night at my place." He stared at the ground.

"Did Manny do anything to her after that?" I asked.

He thought about that. "I don't think so. She thought he had come around once or twice, but then she said she was seeing someone new, so I don't think she was home that much."

"Was the new man Rex?" I asked.

He frowned. "I don't know how serious she was with the new guy, and she never told me a name."

"The name Rex doesn't mean anything to you?" I pressed.

He looked at me and shrugged. "No."

"You saw her with somebody a week or so ago, correct?" Ernie interjected. "He was getting into his car when you came down the block."

I hadn't heard that. "That's true?"

Chris nodded. "Yeah, he was tall, maybe a bit older, with brown hair. I don't know if that was a date, though. The car was parked a couple of houses down from hers, and she looked like she was talking to the guy. He drove off and she walked back to her house while I was parking in front. When I asked her who it was, she said nobody and then let it go. We went inside, and I didn't think about that again until today."

"What kind of car?" I asked.

"A Corvette."

"Was Cherry interested in buying a new car?" I asked. "I found a brochure for a dealership in the kitchen trash."

"She may have been interested, but she couldn't afford one," he said. "Money was tight for her. She was going to college, wanting to get a better job." He shrugged. "A new car was a dream for the future. For now, she didn't have money."

"Did she have any valuables around the house that you're aware of?" Ernie asked. "Jewelry, money that she might've hidden?"

"I don't think so." He hesitated, thinking. "You know, I hate to say this, but I got the feeling she was going out with some guy that had money. More money than Manny, anyway. She didn't have much, so I think it was kind of nice to have a guy around that would spend on her."

"Do you know of anyone else, a friend or possibly an enemy, that she'd recently talked to? Someone who might've done this to her, or known who would've done this?" I asked.

He shook his head.

"Did Cherry do anything or go anywhere recently that had you concerned?" I pressed.

Another headshake. "Sorry," Chris murmured.

Nancy emerged from the house, carrying a few paper bags. "We're about finished," she said to me. I nodded.

Chris watched her walk toward a van, then he focused on me. "When will you let me look around?"

I glanced behind me. "Let me see what's going on."

He gulped at that and nodded. It was one thing to say he

wanted into his little sister's house, it was another to actually go in after what had happened. I looked at Ernie to signal him to keep Chris calm, then went inside. Todd was still in the bedroom, scanning the floor.

"Find anything in the carpet?" I asked.

"No." His gaze roved around the room. "I think we have everything we need. It's a small house, didn't take us as long as they sometimes do."

Nancy appeared. "I've got everything finished in the basement and kitchen," she said. She had a couple more paper bags in her hands. "I'll take these to the car, and help get everything else gathered up."

Todd helped her gather their equipment, and after a few more minutes, they finished.

"The brother's going to look around the house," I said to Todd. "Hang back with us, okay?" I wanted ample witnesses to attest that the crime scene hadn't been manipulated.

"Sure," he said.

When I returned to the front porch, Chris was just finishing telling Ernie a story.

"... and man, you should've seen Cherry," he was saying, "I thought she was going to puke right there." He laughed, then sadness overwhelmed him again and tears ran down his cheeks. He quickly wiped them away with his shirtsleeve. "Can we go in now?"

I nodded. "Please don't touch anything."

"No problem."

I stepped inside, and he and Ernie followed. The house was almost as hot as outside, the air still stifling. Todd stayed out of the way but watched closely as Chris took in the room. He stiffened when he saw the fingerprint powder on surfaces.

"Oh man," he whispered.

"Is anything out of place?" Ernie asked.

Chris looked around carefully, then shook his head. He gulped again and finally found his voice. "Where was she found?"

"In the bedroom." We led him there, and he stood in the doorway and stared at the bed. "What can you tell me? How did she die?"

"She was strangled," I said quietly.

He put a hand to his face and stood there for a moment. "Was she raped?" He could barely get out the words.

"I don't know," I said. "An autopsy will be performed, and we'll know more then."

"I want to know everything."

"Okay." I wasn't going to argue that, but I knew he wouldn't be prepared to hear all the crime scene details. No one ever was.

Ernie moved passed me. "I'm going to let you look in the closet. Would you mind telling me if you see anything unusual, or if something might be missing?"

"Sure," Chris said. "I don't know everything she owned."

I gestured at him. "We just need you to try."

Chris hesitated before moving slowly into the room, his gaze now averted from the bed. Ernie opened the closet door and stepped aside. Chris was careful not to touch anything as he looked inside.

"I recognize some of her shirts and dresses." He pointed to a red one. "She liked that one, and she looked good in it. I told her that." He stood for a minute, silent. "I don't know if something is missing." He suddenly turned around and stepped away.

Ernie opened dresser drawers next, and we watched Chris. He peered into each drawer, but didn't touch anything. "I don't know about her underwear and stuff," he said as he gnawed his lower lip. "Again, something might be missing, but I couldn't tell you."

Ernie closed the drawers, and I pointed to the jewelry box.

Chris studied the rings, necklaces, and bracelets. "A lot of times she wore a silver bracelet that had little cherries etched on it. Our mom gave it to her. It was her favorite." He used a finger as if to draw a little bunch of cherries on his wrist. "I don't see that."

I glanced at Todd. He gave me an imperceptible shake of the head. "It might be missing," I said.

"That was her favorite piece of jewelry," Chris repeated. "I find it hard to believe it's not around."

"We'll make sure we didn't overlook it somewhere," I said.

Chris stared at the jewelry box for a long time, and I let him have his moment.

"I don't think there's anything else gone," he said. "You might ask some of her friends."

"Who?"

He held up a finger. "Lisa and Karen. I don't have a clue about their numbers, but I think Lisa lives in Lakewood, and Karen lives somewhere downtown."

"Do you have last names?"

He shook his head and reached into his pocket for his phone. "Let me look on Cherry's Facebook page." He tapped the phone screen several times, then said, "Lisa Fernandez and Karen Flynn. I don't know where they live though." He emitted a bitter laugh. "Geez, I should tell them about Cherry. I guess I need to message them and tell them to call me." He swore again. "They'll know something's up when they hear from me." He stared at me, his eyes determined. "I should tell them, not you. That's a crappy way of hearing about your friend's death. No offense."

"None taken," I said. I made note of their names and gestured for everyone to leave the room. We walked through the rest of the house, and he didn't notice anything amiss, although he kept saying there might be things he wasn't aware of. When we reached the kitchen window, he stared at the cut screen and swore.

"I told her she needed to be careful about leaving the windows open at night." He shook his head. "It's been so damn hot lately, though, I can see why she would've left them open." He wiped his brow. "It's hot now, and I'll bet it was hot last night."

"I am sorry for your loss," I said as we led him back to the front door.

He gave me a hard glare. "I just want you to find who did this." His breath came in short, pained gasps.

"We'll do that," I promised him.

We walked back outside. Some kids rode by on their bikes, slowing as they passed the house. Curious. A squirrel chattered in a tree, then it was quiet.

"When will we be able to get into the house?" Chris asked.

"As soon as we can," I said. I wasn't going to release the house to him until I was sure we'd collected all the evidence we could. Once we left, there was no coming back for us.

He didn't say anything else, but whirled around and hurried down the sidewalk. One of the neighbors came up to him, a woman with long black hair. She hugged him and they stood by Chris's car and talked, both periodically gesturing at the house.

Todd materialized behind me. "That's it for us," He held a large plastic toolbox in his hand. "I'll be in touch."

"Thanks."

I watched him join Nancy at the van. He put the toolbox in the back, got in, and the van drove away.

"What do you think?" Ernie asked as we stood on the front porch.

I waited until a noisy truck passed by. "We need to find this mystery man Rex," I said. "And the neighbor Blaine Sinclair had an interest in Cherry. I want to check his alibi, make sure he wasn't the jealous type, didn't like the rejection, so he murdered her." I pointed back toward the house. "I'm going through the house one last time. Then I can follow up with her friends."

"Who were they again?" he asked. I gave him the names and he wrote them down. "I'll see if I can find out where they live and work. I'll flip you for one of them."

"Spats is getting warrants for the electronics, and we'll have to go through all that, see what calls she made and received."

"I'll take Karen Flynn."

"I thought you would flip me for one of them."

"I was kidding." Ernie lumbered off the porch and to his car. "I'll get back to you."

I watched him for a moment, then went back in the house for one final look around. I inspected each room, pictured them in my head. I made sure we hadn't missed anything, and then I went back to the front porch.

"We're finished here," I said to the officer standing guard.

He nodded and gave me the paper with the log of entries and exits from the house. I thanked him and watched as he walked to his squad car. He'd had a long, hot, and extremely tedious morning. Once he was gone, I closed and locked the door, then headed down the sidewalk. Chris had finished talking to the neighbor. I motioned to him, and he came over.

"We're done in the house," I said.

"Okay." He stayed rooted in place.

"Again, I'm sorry for your loss." I hated saying that, but I never knew what else to say that could capture what I felt. And hearing condolences from a cop never quite hit the mark.

"Yeah, sure."

"If you notice that anything is missing, will you let us know?"

"Uh-huh."

He was still staring at the house when I got into my car.

CHAPTER EIGHT

I cranked the air conditioner and checked my phone. Spats had texted me Elaine Nowicki's work address that Blaine Sinclair had provided. Elaine worked at Stratton Energies in the Republic Plaza, and Spats texted the address that Sinclair had given him. I was there in twenty minutes. However, I had to drive around another five before I found a metered space two blocks away. It would've been easier to call Elaine, especially on a hot day, but it's better to talk to a person face-to-face. I want to see reactions, expressions, gauge a person's mood. Also, when I take someone by surprise, it doesn't allow them to lie as easily.

Republic Plaza is the tallest skyscraper in Denver, but probably my least favorite in terms of design. It's made of concrete, an absolutely plain rectangle with square black windows, although it tries to make up for its bland exterior with a dramatic, three-story marble lobby displaying interesting works of art by local artists. I rode the elevator up to the twentieth floor. The offices for Stratton Energies was to the right of the elevators. I strode through a glass door with the company logo on it and up to the front desk. I showed an earnest-looking receptionist my badge and asked to speak to Elaine's supervisor.

The woman hesitated, suddenly nervous. Then she picked up the phone and dialed a number. She kept glancing at me as she spoke quietly, then cradled the receiver and said to me, "She'll be up here momentarily."

I thanked her and stepped aside. I scrutinized a framed poster of an oil well. Not particularly riveting. The front-desk woman looked around nervously, unable to work with me there. Seconds later, a woman in a gray business suit rescued the receptionist from her discomfort.

"You're a detective?" She introduced herself as Kay Grafton.

"Thanks for your time," I said. "I'm in the middle of an investigation, and one of your employees, Elaine Nowicki, might have some pertinent information. She's not in any trouble, however it's important I speak to her as soon as possible."

Kay had edged us away from the front desk. "Of course," she said. "Let me get Elaine for you." She turned and asked the receptionist to call for Elaine. Then to me, "I hope this is nothing serious."

"Just routine," I said.

Moments later, Elaine Nowicki entered the reception area. The look on her face was not surprise or concern. She introduced herself. "Blaine said you might want to talk to me. I was sorry to hear about his neighbor." She turned to her supervisor. "It's okay, Kay. Blaine's neighbor was murdered last night, and he said someone might come by to talk to me."

"Oh," Kay murmured. "Someone was murdered? That's terrible." Now she eyed us curiously.

"May I have a moment of your time?" I asked Elaine.

"Of course." She led me down a short hallway to a conference room with a long oval table. Kay followed us, then continued down the hall. Elaine sat down in a black swivel chair and gestured for me to take another. The chair was much too comfortable. If I had to sit in it during meetings, I'd likely fall asleep.

"I hope I'm not in any trouble?" she asked, the tone inquisitive but not threatened.

I shook my head. "I'm working the murder investigation, and I was wondering when you last saw Blaine." I tend to use that phrasing rather than asking her to confirm what Blaine had told me. If suspects work out a fake alibi with somebody else, it often falls apart when they're asked about the last time they'd seen each other.

Her smile was full of relief. "Oh, that's easy. He came over to my place about ten o'clock or so. We watched the news and Jimmy Fallon, and then we went to bed. He left my house about eight this morning, and I assume he went home to work. When he called me to tell me about Cherry, I'm sure he was at home because I heard his cat meowing in the background. She's a sweet cat, but a pest. She talks up a storm."

"He was with you all night?"

She nodded. "Yes, he was. We usually spend the night at one another's houses." A hand went to her mouth. "Is he in some kind of trouble? You have to know Blaine, he's a sweet guy. He wouldn't hurt anyone."

"It's just routine." She seemed relaxed, and for the moment I didn't have any reason to doubt her. "I really appreciate your time."

She let out a small sigh and glanced at the door. "Boy, I'm really going to have some explaining to do. Everyone will wonder why a cop wanted to talk to me."

"I'm sorry about that," I said as we got up and I followed her out of the conference room.

Her smile was warm. "Don't worry about it. I don't think I've broken the law in my entire life, and neither has Blaine."

"How long have you been together?"

"Two years now. I think he might pop the question soon."

"Won't that be nice," I murmured.

By now we'd reached the lobby, and I thanked her again and left. I'm sure she was already explaining to her coworkers why I had visited.

As I rode down the elevator, I thought about what information I had so far. It wasn't much. Manny Guerrero certainly looked as if he could've murdered Cherry. But what about this mystery man Rex? How could I find him, or had Manny made him up just to get us focused elsewhere?

I walked outside and cursed the summer heat. I was sweating before I made it to the corner. Then my stomach growled, reminding me it was lunch time. There was a good restaurant nearby that served a variety of healthy salads, and I knew I had time left on my meter, so I strolled there. Harry worked nearby in a high-rise on Arapahoe Street. I thought about calling him for lunch, but then remembered that he had important clients visiting the office all day and was having lunch with them. I went inside the restaurant with a tiny feeling of disappointment. I would've liked to see Harry. I thought about Elaine Nowicki and her comment about having been with Blaine Sinclair for two years. And it seemed she was anticipating a marriage proposal soon. I'd been with Harry for over ten years, but we hadn't gotten married. My fault, not his. I love him and can't imagine myself with anyone else. But forever? I wasn't sure whether I could keep that commitment. And if I couldn't, I admit, I worried about what my perfect sister Diane would say. I didn't want to think about the endless judgment and snarky disapproval she'd dole out.

The restaurant was crowded, the air conditioning blasting. I waited in line, and ordered a Cobb salad and a glass of water. I paid and took my tray to a small table by the window, sat down, and as I ate I watched people passing by. Downtown Denver is a busy place, with people coming and going seemingly at all times of the day and night. I took a bite of my salad and stared out the window. Near an expensive hotel, a Mercedes and a dark-colored Corvette were parked on the other side of the street. No sooner had I noticed them than I heard a voice I had hoped not to hear for a long time.

"Sarah Spillman, how nice to see you."

I looked up into Darren Barnes's cold eyes. He had that same fake smile mortared on his face as he'd worn the night before, but now he was dressed more casually in khakis and a blue shirt.

"How are you doing, Darren?" I tried to be as nice as I could. Inside, I was fuming. My peaceful lunch had just been ruined.

He held a tray with a salad bowl and a soda on it. He nodded at the table. "May I join you?"

My mind raced. On the one hand, I could turn him down. But how would that look, and what might that do to Harry and his business association with Darren? Or I could stay. But how long could I endure conversation with Darren before I could make excuses and go? Before I could come up with an escape, Darren answered for himself and sat down.

"It's a hot day," I said blandly. I began eating more quickly.

"Yes, it is." He took a bite of his salad. "That was quite a ceremony last night, wasn't it?"

I nodded, took a few more bites, swallowed them quickly, and washed them down with some water.

"It's so good to see you," he said.

"If I didn't know better, I'd think you were stalking me."

He held a hand to his chest. "Moi?" His laugh was oily. "I hated that you left right after the ceremony."

"I was tired."

He smirked. "I was just getting started."

"That's nice," I said. I pulled out my phone to check the time. "I am in a bit of a hurry."

"Another investigation?" He sipped some soda, sat back, and contemplated me. "You know, I could find a position for a smart woman like you at my company."

"I'm fine doing what I'm doing."

"I suppose you are." He took a few more bites of his salad. "I just don't see why a pretty woman like yourself would want to be a cop."

"Pretty women can't be cops?"

"My, aren't we defensive? That's not what I mean. I was paying you a compliment."

One I didn't want. I chose not to go down that road with him. I looked out the window and noticed the Corvette again. "Is that your car?"

He glanced over his shoulder and shook his head. "No. It's similar to mine, but not quite the same."

I took another bite of salad. "I'll bet a Corvette is expensive."

"They are. I looked at a few dealerships, Corvettes Only of Denver and Colorado Corvettes before I found the one I really wanted."

I thought about the brochure in Cherry's trash. "Are there a lot of places that sell them?"

"There's a few dealerships that specialize in Corvettes. Other places will get used ones in that they need to sell, so if you want to shop around town for a used Corvette, you might find one. I wasn't."

"Wasn't what?"

"Willing to shop around." He eyed me. "I didn't think I was unclear."

"Oh. How much would a new one cost?" I asked.

"More than you could afford on your salary."

I own a '65 Mustang that I would never replace, not even for a Corvette. I love the car, even though I don't drive it much anymore. I wanted to wipe the smirk off his face. Instead, I shoved my half-eaten salad away from me and stood up. “I need to get back to work.”

He sat back, an amused smile on his face. “I can’t see you driving a fancy car.”

“I can.” I said as I took my tray and walked away.

“I’ll call you sometime,” he called after me.

I ignored that, threw out my trash, and when I left the restaurant, I could feel his smarmy eyes on me.

CHAPTER NINE

As I stepped outside, I again felt as if I needed to shower after my conversation with Darren Barnes. I stalked to my car and refocused my mind on Cherry Rubio and her death. Ernie was trying to connect with Karen Flynn; now it was time for me to talk to Lisa Fernandez. I hoped she could give me more information on Cherry, flesh out the picture that I had of this woman.

The station was nearby, so I dropped by there. When I walked upstairs to my desk, Spats and Ernie were not there, but my supervisor, Chief Inspector Calvin Rizzo was. He saw me and came over.

"What's going on with the Rubio investigation?" he asked. Captain Rizzo is a well-built man, with broad shoulders and a commanding presence. He's the kind of boss I like, not one to dictate what I should do. He'd gone to the coffee machine, and now held a steaming cup in his hand.

I filled him in on our short-lived investigation and what we had so far. He nodded his head thoughtfully, and when I finished, he said, "It doesn't sound like you have much to go on so far." It wasn't a criticism, just a statement of fact.

"No, but it's early." I leaned back in my chair. "It sounds like Cherry had been dating someone. We don't know who that is. Manny Guerrero–Cherry's ex–mentioned someone named Rex. Manny didn't know his last name. I don't know if Manny threw out a name to us, to keep us from looking at himself, or if this is the guy Cherry was seeing. Anyway, we're trying to track Rex down, along with some of her close friends. I'll be paying a visit to Lisa Fernandez, one of Cherry's friends. I also have officers continuing to talk to Cherry's neighbors. Maybe somebody saw or heard something that will give us some direction. We'll see about any surveillance footage as well. The killer likely showed up in a car, and maybe we'll be able to trace a strange car in the neighborhood back to our killer."

Rizzo sipped coffee. "Keep on it." Then he tapped my desk and walked away. He's a man of few words, which I appreciate. He's no-nonsense, like me, and even though I've run afoul of him a time or two, he backs me up.

I turned to my laptop and spent a few minutes getting information on Lisa Fernandez. After a little digging on LinkedIn, I found that she works at Milton Industries, an oil and gas company located in the Granite Tower in downtown Denver. I called her office and confirmed she was there, then hung up. I wanted to talk to her in person, just like I had with Elaine Nowicki. I wondered if Chris had contacted her about Cherry's death yet. That would certainly change the tone of the conversation. I googled the exact location of her office, shut down my laptop, and left.

In minutes I was again looking for a parking place among the Denver high-rises. I finally found a spot near the Granite Tower. I squeezed in between two large trucks and paid the meter. When I walked into the glass-façade building, I got on the elevator and rode to the tenth floor, then emerged into the lobby for Milton Industries, which took up the entire floor. I crossed to a desk opposite the elevator, where a woman was typing on a computer. Soft music played from a nearby phone that she quickly shut off. She looked up at me without a smile, as if I were bothering her.

I introduced myself. "I'd like to speak to Lisa Fernandez's supervisor, please," I said.

The woman hesitated and gave me a once-over. She blinked a few times as she worked overtime trying to figure out what I wanted. She didn't ask for identification, but I showed her my badge. She finally nodded, picked up a phone, then paused. She surveyed me with fake disinterest and spoke into the phone. A moment later, she hung up and gestured. "Megan will be up in a moment."

I thanked her and waited. It truly was just a moment, as Megan appeared in the lobby, her expression somewhere between concern and confusion.

"Hi, I'm Megan Deaver," she said hurriedly. "What can I help you with?"

"Thanks for your time," I said. I pulled her aside, showed her my badge, and got right to it. "We're working an investigation, and I'd like to talk to Lisa Fernandez. We think she might be able to help us, and I need to talk to her right away." Her expression quickly went to fear, as if she thought Lisa might be guilty of something. I held up a reassuring hand. "We don't think she's involved, but she may have information for us." She stared at me, so I tacked on, "It's really important that I talk to her. Time is precious."

She found her words. "Yes, of course. If you need to talk to her, that's fine with me. I'm happy to help any way I can."

"Thank you."

"Let me get Lisa. Take as much time as you need."

Before I could say more, she spun around and rushed out of the lobby. The front desk woman caught herself staring at me, and she quickly looked away. She busied herself on the computer as she watched me out of the corner of her eye. Muted conversations and keyboard clattering from other rooms drifted to me. I crossed my arms and waited. Finally, Lisa came around the corner. She was a tall woman with long black hair and light makeup that was a bit smeared. Her eyes were red-rimmed, her mouth sagging. I wonder how long ago she'd heard about Cherry.

Before I could say anything, she held up a hand. "Chris messaged me to call him, and he told me what happened to Cherry." The glance behind her was subtle. "Let's not talk about this here," she said. She waved for me to follow her and said to the woman at the desk, "I'm going downstairs."

The woman nodded at her, not sure what to say.

Lisa went to the elevator and pushed a button. It wasn't until the doors slid shut that she let out a long breath and said, "What happened to Cherry? Chris didn't say much."

She punched the "L" on the bank of buttons next to the elevator door. I told her briefly what we knew, giving no more details than we'd given to Chris Rubio. She listened, her jaw open.

"I'm stunned," she said as she stared at the ceiling. "I don't even know what to say." Tears welled in her eyes, and she delicately brushed them away. "Chris told me everything he knew, and I ran into the bathroom and just cried. I ..." She couldn't say more.

The elevator didn't stop until we reached the lobby. The doors opened and she walked out, sidestepping a man waiting to get on. She had long legs, and a fast gait. We started toward the building entrance, then she cleared her throat.

"I need some water," she said, her voice hoarse. "My mouth is so dry."

I gestured toward a Russell's convenience store, one of many located in the downtown high-rises. We went in and she purchased a bottle of water and paid for it, never saying a word. We walked back through the lobby and outside. She hurried to a concrete ledge away from the heavy glass doors. We sat down and she took a long gulp from the bottle before looking at me.

"I just don't understand. I saw Cherry the other night. How could this happen?"

I didn't answer that. "How was Cherry when you saw her?" I asked. "Was she happy, anything unusual going on with her?"

She shrugged and stared at the huge columns on either side of the building entrance. She smoothed her pant leg. "She seemed fine. I mean, things have been a little stressful for her lately, with her summer classes. She really wanted to take a break from her schooling, but she also wanted to get her degree finished up, so she took a few classes. She worked really hard, and she only has ... had ... a year left before she'd get her degree. That was so important to her." She hung her head and sniffled. Then she looked up. "I'm sorry."

"Don't be. Hearing news like this is the worst thing."

She nodded and stared at the street. "It's weird thinking about her in the past tense."

"Tell me more about her."

She took a long time to answer. "I'm going to miss her smile. She could be shy, but she was a lot of fun. I've known her for about eight years. We met when we worked at another job together. She was smart and funny, and she was working really hard. That impressed me. I think her childhood was a little rough. Her parents got divorced, and her dad was abusive. She barely graduated high school, and she didn't know what to do, so she got an office job. Then she decided that she wanted to go to school, to get a business degree." She ran out of things to say. Her eyebrows pinched. "Do you have any idea who might've done this to her?"

I sat back and crossed my legs. "I was hoping you might be able to help us with that."

"Me?" She shook her head. "I don't know of anyone who'd want to hurt her."

"She'd broken up with her boyfriend, Manny Guerrero, about a month ago."

"That's true." She sighed. "Manny was an okay guy, I guess, although I always told her she could do better."

"Her brother wasn't fond of Manny."

She watched some women emerge from the building, don sunglasses, and head to the corner. Lisa then tipped her head, thoughtfully. "Manny tried hard, if you know what I mean. He could be a nice guy, when he wanted to be, but she told me he struggled with his anger sometimes." She was holding something back.

"Did he hurt her in any way?"

"He hit her once. Not hard, but still." She shook her head again, then fanned herself with a hand. "It's hot out. I don't think he ever did anything else to her. You know he had a domestic violence charge in the past?" I nodded. "Cherry said he'd actually learned something from all the counseling he'd done. However, she also talked about him having moments of anger, times when he would explode, then quickly catch himself. She never said he hit her after that one time, but I think she got tired of not knowing what might set him off. From what I could tell, the relationship got to be where it was convenient, somebody to hang out with, and well, you know, sleep with. Then I think she met someone else, and she decided to play the field again, so she broke up with Manny."

I felt sweat on my back, wishing we'd stayed inside. "What did she tell you about the actual breakup?"

She took another drink. "Her brother Chris had told her to take Manny to a restaurant and tell him there, so Cherry did. Manny got upset anyway. I guess he left her there, and Chris had to come pick her up. She was a little concerned about what

Manny might do, but in the end, I think it turned out okay." Then her jaw dropped. "You think Manny did this?"

I kept my face even. "I don't know yet. We have to look at everything." My phone vibrated, and I glanced at the screen. Ernie texted, saying he had talked to Karen Flynn and he was heading back to the office. I looked back at Lisa.

Her brow furrowed. "I'm just not sure Manny would do that. But I guess you never know."

"Was she seeing someone else?"

"I think she dated a couple of guys, one that she seemed to be getting into."

"Did Cherry mention Rex?"

Lisa nodded. "Yeah, that's one of them. I think she was more serious with him."

My nerves tingled. "Did she tell you his last name?"

"No, she didn't."

"What do you know about him?"

"Not a lot. I've never met him. He works at Littleton Chevrolet, and Cherry met him through somebody at one of her classes. He showed up there a time or two, and he and Cherry got to talking."

I wanted to do a fist pump, but resisted. I finally had a little something on Rex, maybe enough to find him. "Was Cherry interested in a new car?"

"If she was, she didn't tell me."

"What else did she say about Rex?"

"That he was more mature than Manny, and maybe a lot of the guys that she'd gone out with. He had money, too. She liked that."

"Was he older?"

She thought about that. "I guess it depends on what 'older' is. I think he's maybe late thirties or early forties, and that would be a lot older than a lot of the guys Cherry dated in the past."

She had me there. I was in my late thirties. I guess to a lot of people that was "older."

"Did she have any concerns about Rex?" I asked. "Any red flags about him?"

She fiddled with the half-empty bottle, the plastic crackling. "No. She thought he was sexy, and they were having a good time. I don't think she was thinking about it too seriously just yet."

"So you saw her not too long ago," I said, prompting for more information about that.

She nodded. "Yeah, we went out after work for happy-hour food. Cherry was on a tight budget, so we go where they have a happy-hour buffet. You can eat a lot without paying too much. And then I needed to run some errands."

"Did Cherry tell you what she was going to do after she left you? Was she going to meet Rex?"

"She told me she was going home, but it's possible she was meeting Rex." Her lip trembled. "Geez, I can't believe all this ..." She couldn't finish the sentence.

"Was there anybody else that Cherry mentioned, someone she didn't get along with, someone that might have wanted to hurt her?"

She thought about that as she took another drink. "No. Most people liked Cherry. I know people say that about their family and friends, but in this case it was true. Cherry was quiet and sweet, and I don't think anyone would've wanted to hurt her." She glanced at her phone, took a deep breath. "I should probably get back inside."

"I noticed Cherry had a nice bike in her house. Did you ride with her?"

She shook her head. "She was a dedicated cyclist, but I'm not."

"Do you remember her wearing a bracelet with cherries etched on it?"

"Sure, all the time."

"It wasn't at her house."

She shrugged. "She probably had it on. If not, I don't know where it is. Is that important?"

"Maybe." I pulled a business card from my pocket and handed it to her. "If you think of anything else that might help our investigation, anything you think of that we haven't discussed, please give me a call. That card has all my contact info on it."

"Sure." She took the card and stared at it. "This isn't normal at all. It's stuff you see in the movies, not something that happens to *you*." We stood up. She finished the water and threw the bottle in a recycle can near the building entrance. "I mean, you'd think you'd be able to leave your windows open." She rubbed her arms and shivered. "I'm scared to death now."

I thanked her for her time and watched as she strode toward the entrance. Her head was down, and when she reached the glass doors, it seemed to take her great effort to push through them. I wondered how long it would take her to feel normal again.

CHAPTER TEN

I left the Granite Building with a feeling that we had a small lead. I knew where the mystery man Rex worked; now I assumed I could get his last name. As I navigated the one-way streets of downtown toward the office, Spats called me.

"I've got the warrant for Cherry's electronics. Now I'm working with the phone company on those records, and I'm pushing to get them as soon as possible. I'll also get Tara working on Cherry's laptop," he said, all business.

"Perfect." I caught him up on what Ernie and I were doing. "I'm headed back to the office now to call the dealership that Lisa mentioned. If she's correct that Rex works there, and I can get a last name, I'll do a little research on him before he and I have a chat."

"I thought maybe Guerrero was just making up the name to get us focused somewhere besides on him," Spats said.

"Me too. It still may not lead anywhere."

"Stay positive." I laughed, and he continued. "When I get the phone records, I'll work through them, see if I find anything interesting."

"I may be running around," I said, "so keep me posted."

"You got it."

I ended the call and zipped through traffic back to the station. When I went upstairs, Ernie was just sitting down at his desk, his chair squeaking with his bulk. He looked up at me as he clamped an unlit cigar stub in the corner of his mouth. "What have you got for me?"

"When are you going to quit smoking those filthy things all together?" I said.

"Don't bust my chops right now," he groused.

I sensed something in his tone and backed off. "I know where Rex works." I sat down at my desk and looked at him triumphantly.

He took the cigar out and pointed with it. "You might not think that was such a revelation if I had found it out from Karen," he said wryly. He dumped the butt in an ashtray and gulped some Coke.

"Way to steal my thunder."

Normally, that might've elicited some laughter from him. Instead, he stared at me for a long moment. "Tell me about Rex."

"Well," I said, "that's about as exciting as it gets. I only have that he works at Littleton Chevrolet. I'm going to call there now, see if I can get a last name. And I found out a bit more about Cherry."

"Yeah, I learned a lot about her myself."

"You go first."

He leaned forward and rested his elbows on his desk. "Man, this case is really getting to me." He scowled. "Karen hadn't heard about Cherry yet, and she was brokenhearted. She cried so much. I don't blame her a bit, and it was hard to see her hurting. Cherry sounds like she was just a sweetheart." Ernie's married, and he has two teenage daughters. This one was hitting particularly close to home with him. "Karen and Cherry have known each other for several years," he went on, the scowl growing darker. "Karen is getting married in the fall, and Cherry was going to be a bridesmaid." He picked up the cigar, considered it, then threw it in a trash can in disgust. "Karen knew Manny, and like everyone else, she didn't like him. She said he could be nice when he wanted to be, but she felt like Cherry wanted different things in life than Manny did. They were just going in different directions. She was focusing on her career, and that was taking a lot of her time. Cherry liked school, and Karen said that other than struggling a bit with math, she was doing well. She seemed smart, and she was going places. Oh, and both Karen and Cherry liked to ride their bikes, so they did that in the summer, and they've participated in some charity rides. Cherry liked to go dancing, or just hang out at the bars. Manny didn't like that too much, but he didn't say a lot when Cherry wanted to go out with her friends. Apparently she'd been doing more of that lately, right before they broke up."

I opened up my laptop and logged on. "What did Karen say specifically about Cherry breaking up with Manny?"

"Not a lot," he said. "Mostly glad that Cherry had moved on."

I nodded. "Lisa said that too. From what I've heard so far, everybody thinks it's better that Cherry broke up with him. Did Karen remember Cherry wearing that bracelet with the cherries on it?"

"Yes, she does. Said Cherry wore it a lot."

"And apparently it's gone." I thought for a moment. "Did anyone dislike her?"

"I found one employee who didn't. He thought she was a pain in the ass."

"He?"

He grunted. "Yep. I'm following up on him."

"Good. Did Cherry talk to Karen about buying a new car?"

Ernie thought about that, shook his head. "No she didn't mention that."

"Cherry had that car brochure in her kitchen trash, and then Lisa said that Cherry had met this guy Rex and he works at Littleton Chevrolet." I pointed at the screen, where I had pulled up the dealership's website, then filled him in on the conversation I'd had with Lisa.

"Did Cherry talk to Rex solely because she was interested in buying a car?" Ernie asked.

"Or was she seeing Rex?" I'd found the dealership's number. "Let me see if I can figure out his last name." I picked up the phone and dialed. After a few rings, a woman's silky voice answered. I pictured a sultry movie actress, not someone at a car dealership. Once she had rattled off the dealership name and how they had great bargains on cars, I asked, "Does someone named Rex work there?"

"Rex Land?"

I raised my eyebrows at Ernie. "Yes, Rex Land." He gave me a thumbs up.

"Yes, Rex does work here, but today is his day off. Were you working with him to buy a car, or would you like to speak with another salesman?"

"I'll wait to talk to him. When will he be in again?"

"Let me check." She put me on hold for a moment, then came back on the line. "He should be in tomorrow. Would you like me to take a message?"

"No, thank you." I ended the call before she could ask me more questions. I looked over at Ernie. "Rex Land."

"So I heard."

I googled his name. "Let's see what I can find on Rex."

"I'll look up his criminal history," Ernie said.

Someone raised their voice in another room, and Ernie and I

turned in that direction. Then there was laughter. Ernie shrugged.

I turned back to my laptop. "I've got a people-search site, says he's forty-two years old, and the addresses listed are for Denver and Albuquerque, New Mexico. He's got some relatives listed, same last name. If I need to, I can figure out who they are." I pursed my lips. "I'd like to know if he's married." I navigated to other internet pages and checked some other sites. "Based on the people associated with him, and no corresponding last names, it doesn't look like it, or that he has kids. It would've made things more interesting if Cherry had been seeing a married man."

He typed on his laptop using his index fingers. "Yeah. A motive for Rex. Doesn't want the wife to find out about the affair. Alas, that's not the case."

"Alas?"

Ernie grinned, some of his humor returning. "My poetic side's coming out. Can't help it if I'm so erudite."

"What's with the big words?"

"Just trying to change my mood. Besides, it's only three syllables. E-ru-dite." He kept typing, then said, "He doesn't have a criminal history."

"Let's see if I can find a LinkedIn profile." After a bit of searching I had some decent information. I glanced at Ernie. "It looks like Rex has worked at several auto dealerships over the years, both here and in New Mexico. I wonder if it's normal to bounce around to several, versus staying at one."

"Dunno."

I went on. "He's been living in Denver for about ten years, at two different locations. He went to high school in New Mexico, but I don't see any college information."

"I've got his driver's license photo." Ernie used his legs to propel his chair around to look at my monitor. "Not bad looking, maybe a little old."

"Sheesh, you're the second person who thinks that late thirties or early forties is old. He's not *that* old."

"Eh, I'm older than both of you," he said. He tapped the screen. "It's the gray in his hair. It makes him look older than forty." He was being careful in his clarification, trying not to set me off again.

I tapped the screen. "Did Karen know whether Cherry was dating an older man?"

"Nope." Ernie rolled back to his desk. "She did say that Cherry mentioned Rex, but that she seemed a bit sly about it, not giving a lot of details. Karen said that's the way Cherry sometimes was, she could be a little aloof in discussing a new guy, that she'd been that way with Manny until after she'd been dating him for a while. So Karen wasn't totally surprised that Cherry wasn't saying too much about Rex."

"I think I found his Facebook page," I said. "He's not on the site much, or he has his privacy settings where I can't see his posts. I saw a few pictures of himself standing by an SUV, and a Corvette. There's a few of him with an older woman with curly blond hair. She kind of looks like him. His mom? She *does* look older."

Before he could retort, his desk phone rang. I went back to my laptop, but was listening to him.

"Moore. Yeah, uh-huh." He grabbed a pen and jotted notes. "Okay, got it." He hung up and looked at me, his eyes dancing. "One of the officers who's been canvassing Cherry's neighborhood says a man across the street from her has surveillance cameras set up."

"What's his name?"

"Jeff Conway. After he heard about Cherry, he watched the video from Tuesday night. He thinks he might have seen someone in her yard during the night. And a lone car drove down the street during the night."

"That could be interesting. We need to watch the footage ourselves."

He nodded. "Yeah. Could be something, could be nothing. I'll give him a call."

I listened while he phoned the neighbor. He held the phone up to his ear, then sighed. "He's not answering," he murmured to me, then, "I'll leave a message." He left Conway his number and hung up. "Let's hope we hear from him soon."

"I'm not finding much more on Rex Land." I thought for a moment as I worked a pen through my fingers. When I'm mulling things, I get fidgety. Somehow, the pen helps.

Ernie pecked at his keyboard. "You want Conway's home address? I just emailed it to you."

"Thanks. Let me know when you hear from him. In the meantime, I think it's time to pay Rex a visit."

Ernie popped his knuckles and stood up. "I've got a few of Cherry's neighbors to follow up with, then I'm heading home. You have a good night."

"I'll see you later." I was typing up a few notes when the phone interrupted me.

"Spillman."

"Hey, it's Chris Rubio, Cherry's brother."

"Yes. What can I do for you?"

"I wanted to let you know, I went through Cherry's house, and so did my mom." He'd had time to digest the news of her death, and he was in more control now. "I don't think anything's missing, other than the bracelet with the cherries on it."

"You're sure?"

"Yes. I hope that's helpful."

"It is."

I thanked him for his time and hung up. Theft did not appear to be a motive. Interesting. I stared at the monitor for a second, then grabbed my car keys and headed for the door.

CHAPTER ELEVEN

Rex Land lived in a two-story house in the Highlands Ranch neighborhood south of downtown. It was a little before three as I drove south on Santa Fe, and because traffic was already building in anticipation of rush hour, it took me quite a while to get to Highlands Ranch. The area was once just fields, but over the last thirty years Highlands Ranch has grown into one of the country's largest suburbs. I finally passed C-470 and soon turned east into a development with houses all built with the same three or four floor plans.

When I pulled up to Rex Land's house, a teenage boy was mowing the lawn next door. I strode up the walk and knocked on Rex's front door. With the lawnmower engine droning, I couldn't hear whether anyone was inside the house. After no answer, I rang again, then knocked loudly on the door. The teenager paid me no mind, and I peeked in a front window. It seemed that Rex was not at home. The lawnmower engine stopped as I walked down the sidewalk. The young man bent over to empty the grass bag.

"Hey," I called out to him. "Have you seen Rex around?"

He stood up and stretched his back. "No, I haven't. I've only been out here a little while. You sure he's not at work?"

I shielded my eyes as I talked. "No, I called there."

He wiped his face with his shirtsleeve, then bent down again and dumped the grass catcher in a black trash bag. "He's got a pretty cool Corvette, and he likes to take it out driving. Maybe he's doing that. Or he's camping." He finished emptying the grass and put the catcher back on the mower. "Sorry, I have to get back to work." He put the trash bag on the mower and rolled it across the driveway.

"Thanks," I said.

He didn't reply as he made his way around the side of the house and disappeared. I looked around and didn't see anyone else. The lawnmower started again, its low hum a surprisingly comforting sound for me. It reminded me of summer evenings when I was a kid. We'd play outside while my dad mowed the lawn, then we'd play hide-and-seek as it grew dark. The smell of cut grass reminded me of something fruity, like watermelon. I glanced at Rex's house one more time and walked slowly to my car. I got in, turned on the A/C, then got on my phone.

"Spats," I said when he answered. "I need a surveillance camera on a suspect's house. Do you have time to chase that down?" I explained the situation. "I don't want to sit out here all night. At least one of the neighbor kids has seen me already and might say something. Plus, we know how neighborhood watch folks will sometimes see a strange car and call the cops. I don't want Rex slipping through the cracks, so we need to know when he shows up."

"I'll get on it, and we'll get someone out there ASAP. We can get a camera set up across the street from his house, and an on-duty person can monitor it."

"Perfect."

Camera surveillance is so much easier to do than it was a few years back. With a warrant, our surveillance teams can install a surveillance camera into a fake utility box that then can be placed almost anywhere. It looks just like something utility companies use. The boxes even have stickers with warnings not to tamper with them. Very sneaky. The cameras can be monitored remotely and can be zoomed in and out. All this meant I could move on to something else, and I'd be alerted if the cameras spotted Rex Land.

"I'll make sure to give out Land's description," Spats said, "and we'll be notified if he shows up at his house."

"I'll hang out here until they get the equipment in place. Unless one of the neighbors makes a fuss about a suspicious person in the area."

I thought that might get a laugh out of Spats, but nothing. Before I could say more, Spats ended the call. I stared at the phone for a moment, then put the car in gear and drove around the block. I parked at the corner and waited. I was tempted to talk to some of Rex's neighbors, but I didn't want to alert him that we were looking for him, so I decided to just cool my jets, which is hard for me to do. I spent a little bit of time on my phone, researching him more. Besides the pictures of him with his Corvette, I found one where he was outside a bar in Castle Rock. In another he and a group were hiking. A car passed by and I looked up, hoping it would be him. Instead, the car pulled into a driveway a few houses down from his. A woman got out and walked into her garage. She didn't even notice me. I continued to watch his house. By the time I saw what looked like a technician with Xcel Energy, but who I knew to be a detective, I was fidgety and itching to move. He spent a few minutes setting up the surveillance box and walked away. Now that I knew the house was being monitored, I could go. When Rex came home, we'd know it, and I'd get a call.

I drove back toward downtown, this trip taking even longer

because rush-hour was in full swing. I crawled back up Santa Fe and noticed lots of cars in the HOV lane without a passenger. That really chaps me. As I sat in traffic at a standstill, I was tempted to pull rank and stop one of them. Then, I guess because I was already angry, I thought about how Harry had said I should deal with my feelings about Diane. That made me even crankier, and when I finally got back to the station, I stomped upstairs. Ernie was not there, but Spats was, his forehead resting on his hands. That wasn't usually the case with him. He looked up when I walked in.

"You look like you've been through the ringer, yourself," he said.

"That's what summer rush hour traffic will do to you." I slumped in my chair and studied him. "You don't look too hot yourself. You okay?"

He waved a dismissive hand and pulled some papers closer. "I'm fine."

I watched him for a few seconds longer, and he gave me a small shrug, as if to say let it go. I groaned and stretched. "I hate stop-and-go traffic."

"I'm not sure anybody likes it." He seemed to pull out of whatever mood he was in. "Can you imagine someone's dating profile? 'Loves long walks on the beach and sitting in rush-hour traffic.' "

I laughed at that. Spats has a good sense of humor. "Rex Land never showed up at his house. I waited until the surveillance camera was in place, and then I left. Thanks for getting that warrant so quickly."

"Sure." He tapped his desk. "So what are you thinking? Did Rex kill Cherry and then split town?"

"I don't know. The neighbor kid thought he might be driving around town in his Corvette, or that he's off camping."

"Unfortunately we won't know until we find him."

I nodded. "Tell me you have Cherry's phone records."

"I do." He held up some papers. "I've been following up on them. I was hoping we'd have calls from strangers that her family or friends don't know about, but so far the numbers are only her friends, her brother, and her mom, along with some businesses." He held up a finger. "And a few to Rex Land. I had a long talk with her mom and compared notes with Ernie. She didn't have any more information than what we got from Chris."

"How many times did Cherry call Rex?"

He glanced at the paper. "Three times." He told me the dates and times. "Nothing seems out of the ordinary with that."

"What's his number? I want to call him."

He gave me the number, and I wrote it down and dialed it. It went to voicemail, a standard electronic voice telling me the person at this number was not available. I swiped in frustration at the phone to end the call. Spats looked amused.

"Whenever we talk to Rex Land, we need to make sure he says he made the same number of calls. It better be close, at least." I threw up my hands. "I've been so focused on Rex, I didn't think about Manny Guerrero. What's the update with the surveillance on him?"

"He was at the shop all day," Spats said. "Except for lunch. He went to a nearby Mexican restaurant, was there for an hour, and then went back to the shop. At six, he left work and drove to a bar. Nothing suspicious so far."

I sat back and rubbed my neck. "I need to talk to Tara to see when she'll be able to examine Cherry's laptop. Right now, though, we don't have much."

"Are we dealing with a pro? Nobody's seen or heard a thing, nothing seems suspicious."

"Except for the dead body."

Spats snorted. "Yep." He yawned and stretched, then looked at his watch. "Crap, I need to get home. Trissa and I are having dinner with her parents." Spats and his girlfriend, Trissa, have a newborn baby. Spats also has an eleven-year-old daughter from a previous marriage. I'd met Trissa a few times, and although she was pleasant, I hadn't gotten a real sense of her.

I matched his yawn with one of my own. "Yeah, I don't want to make it a late night, although if Rex makes an appearance, I'll have to talk to him. I might stay here for a while, see what more I can dig up on him." I looked at the time on my laptop. "But if I don't find something compelling soon, I'm going to head home."

"Sounds good." Spats shoved away from his desk and stood up. He adjusted his tie, tipped an imaginary hat to me, and walked out of the room.

The office was quiet, and I relished the silence. I spent a while on the internet, poking around to see what more I could find on Rex. I didn't come up with much. He had been salesman of the month at a dealership two years before, but other than that, I found nothing notable about his sales career. I couldn't find if or where he went to college, and I didn't find any indication that he'd been in any financial trouble. Lorraine Freeman, another detective on the force, stopped to say hello. She's a tall black woman with a great sense of humor, and I'd worked with her on an undercover case. We chatted for a few minutes, and she left. It was quiet again. I stared at the laptop until the words on the page began to meld together, and I finally gave up. I got up to stretch, and my desk phone rang.

"It's Jack. I'll be doing the autopsy on Cherry Rubio tomorrow morning at ten. I thought you'd want to know."

"I want to be there," I said. "I'm coming up with nothing so far."

"Don't expect me to make any conclusions. You know I don't do that."

"I know."

Jack wasn't one for chit-chat. "I won't hold up the autopsy, either, so make sure you're on time."

"I will."

With that, I heard the dial tone. I had no sooner put down the receiver than my cell phone rang.

"Hey, Harry," I said.

"It's a late night at the office for me, and I'm just leaving," he said. "Are you in the middle of something or do you have time to grab a bite to eat?"

It was almost eight. "I was hoping to hear from a surveillance team. Other than that, I'm starved. How about Tres Hermanos?"

"I can be there in about half an hour," he said.

"I'll meet you there. If I do get a call, I'll have to leave, though."

"No problem."

I ended the call, made a couple of notes for myself, texted Ernie what I was doing, and left.

CHAPTER TWELVE

Tres Hermanos is a new Mexican restaurant off Sixth Avenue, not too far from Harry's and my house. The restaurant is known for its burritos, so big they make two or three leftover meals, and margaritas to die for. But I like their fajitas best. The service is great as well, although it's a little on the pricey side, but still reasonable. When I arrived, Harry was casually pacing outside the door. His face lit up when he saw me. I approached and tipped my head up to give him a kiss.

"I called ahead and put our name on the list," he said. "They should have a table ready."

Tres Hermanos is popular. It doesn't matter what night of the week it is, it's always crowded.

"How was your day?" he asked as he took my hand. "You have a new case?"

"Yes." We walked into the restaurant, and I began telling him the details. I had to stop while we asked the hostess for a table outside. When we were seated quietly in a corner, away from the door, I told Harry about my case in muted tones.

"That poor woman," he said at one point. "That kind of

violence ..." He paused as the waiter came to our table. He had the beginnings of a dark beard, the look reminiscent of George Michael. He served us some chips and salsa, gave us menus, and asked what we'd like to drink. "I'll have a margarita on the rocks." Harry arched an eyebrow at me. "You?"

"A glass of water with lemon," I said.

The waiter nodded, then politely asked Harry for his license.

"I haven't been carded in a while," Harry said as he pulled out his wallet. "I feel younger already."

The waiter laughed nervously and glanced at me. "We have to card everyone."

"It's no problem," Harry said to put the waiter at ease. When he left, Harry studied his license. "Dang, I looked so much younger then."

I smiled. "It's funny you say that. I talked to a woman today who thought that maybe our age was 'old.' "

Harry suppressed a yawn. "After a long day like today, I do feel old."

I nodded. "That bad?"

"Just one issue after another." We perused the menu and Harry settled on a burrito with beef and green sauce, while I chose the fajitas. When the waiter returned, we ordered, and we munched on chips and salsa. "That's really good." Through a mouthful he said, "I've really had to be on my game lately, and I may have to go to New York."

"When?"

"Next week. I'll have to leave Sunday night so I'm there for some early meetings on Monday." He sighed. "Only for a few nights."

The waiter came with our drinks. Harry took a big gulp. "That hits the spot."

I sipped some water and finished telling him about the case, then about being near his office at lunch. "I almost called you," I said. "But I knew you were with clients."

"Yes, I wouldn't have been able to pull away."

"It's okay. Oh–you're not going to believe who I saw at lunch today."

He waited and finally said, "Who?"

"Darren Barnes."

"Really? I wonder what he was doing in the area." He crunched on some more chips. "He must've had some business downtown."

"I swear, I feel like he's stalking me."

He laughed at that. "The guy's too busy telling everybody about his award. Don't give him a second thought."

I frowned. "I suppose so."

We sat in companionable silence for a few minutes. I glanced at my phone a time or two in the hopes I would hear news that Rex Land had come home, but no messages. The waiter returned with our meals, the huge plates balanced with ease on one muscular arm. He asked if we needed anything else, then quietly retreated. Harry and I were in a corner, tucked away from some of the louder conversations. Mariachi music played in the background, enough to be pleasant, not loud enough to be distracting. I ate a bite and stared past Harry.

"What's going on?" he asked. "You thinking about your case?"

I shook my head. "I was thinking about Diane and what you said to me last night, about not letting her overshadow me."

"Oh?" His tone was curious.

My neck tensed and I rolled it around. "Lately, I get so angry every time I think about Diane."

He rested his fork on his plate, wiped his hands, and waited. When I didn't say anything, he spoke. "What is it with that anger? I mean, I know Diane is a bit self-centered, that she thinks mostly about herself, but you have so many good qualities that you downplay. You can stand on your own two feet, and you don't need her endorsement. Or anyone else's for that matter."

I picked at my food and thought about that. "All I ever wanted was Diane's approval. I know you've heard me say that a lot over the years."

He nodded. "Yes, and I'm saying you don't need it."

"Yeah, but when I was growing up, I did need it. I thought that if she liked me, things between us would be better. Especially after losing Uncle Brad." When I was little, my Uncle Brad was my favorite, and I always thought I was his, too. We seemed to have a special connection. He'd known that Diane and I didn't get along, and he understood me. He had a heart attack and died when I was eight years old, and it affected me as few other things have in my life. After he died, I didn't have anyone to talk to about Diane. My parents had favored her, at least it seemed so in my eyes, and I'd never been able to tell them how that felt. I suddenly didn't feel nearly as hungry as before, and I put down my fork.

"What?" Harry said.

I drew in a heavy breath. "I'm ashamed to admit it, even to you, but when I was about nineteen or twenty, I did something I shouldn't have, I mean, really shouldn't have, all because I wanted Diane to like me, to think I was cool. As a matter of fact ..." I lost my voice for a second, thinking about that fateful night. "She even said that if I would help her, we'd be like best friends, that it would be the coolest thing that I could do." I laughed derisively. "Of course, that was the farthest thing from the truth. She was half-drunk that night, and she didn't remember things clearly anyway. And when it was all over, when I'd done what she needed, it didn't matter. She still couldn't have cared less about me. I took a huge risk for her. Harry, I broke the law, and it didn't even matter. She got away scot-free, went on to have a great career and perfect family. For me, I spent years wondering if what I'd done would jeopardize my career. When I applied to the police force, would they find out, and would it derail my career before it even started? As time went on, and I moved up in the force, I realized what I'd done probably wouldn't ruin my career, but someone could still blow the whistle on me. And even more, the guilt I feel over what I did ..." I couldn't finish the sentence. "I'm still so angry at her. I risked so much, and she didn't even care. She acts as if it never happened. She's just oblivious."

Harry reached across the table and took my hand. "You can't let your anger consume you, Sarah. Diane doesn't think about the past, and she probably has no idea that you're upset with her. Your carrying around that anger only hurts you."

"It's not that simple." I let go of his hand.

He sat back. "Like I said last night, your anger is really starting to overshadow things, how you deal with other people, how you hear things. Like Darren Barnes. He says something rude and you think about Diane. Your feelings are all tangled up. Not everybody is Diane, and Diane isn't everybody else. I'll admit that Darren is kind of an asshole, but he's not Diane."

That made me laugh. We stared at each other for a moment.

"Would you do me a favor?" Harry finally said.

"Sure." I took a bite of fajitas and waited.

"While I'm gone, why don't you go out to dinner with Diane, talk about all of this? Maybe you'll find that even if she doesn't change or even really hear you, you'll feel better."

"What good will that do?" I snapped. "She denies doing anything wrong, and she doesn't see that what I did was any big deal."

He shook his head, somewhat exasperated. "It's not about her, it's about *you*. You need to do this for you, you need to clean the slate for you. I don't care what Diane does in all this, I care that you move on and let it go."

I stared into his dark eyes for a long moment. "You know how hard that will be for me? You know how stubborn I can be."

"I sure do. I also know that this is becoming bigger than it should be, and it's going to destroy you."

"It bothers you that much?"

He glanced away and didn't answer. When he looked back at me, I saw something in his eyes I hadn't seen before. A look of uncertainty, maybe about us. It scared me.

"If you really want me to, I will," I said.

He took a bite and chewed slowly. It was a delay tactic that gave him time to think. "I want you to do this," he said. "I want you to move on, for us."

I reached for my glass, and my hand shook. I quickly set down the glass. "Okay, I will."

We ate the rest of our meal in an uncomfortable silence, not the same way the meal had started. I had never felt on unsteady ground with Harry, but for the first time, I wondered if that was the case. I didn't want to lose him. I also didn't want to deal with the albatross that was Diane. I frowned. I had a choice to make.

Harry pushed his plate away and signaled for the check. I wished my phone would vibrate with a text that would call me back to work. I gulped and suddenly realized the many times I'd used my work as a way to avoid things with Harry. For the first time, I saw some of his frustration in our relationship through his eyes.

"I'm sorry."

"For what?" he asked.

"You put up with a lot."

He shrugged and smiled. "Yeah, I do. But you're worth it. I love you."

"I love you too."

After he'd paid the check, we drove home. We spent a bit of time in the living room in a silence midway between companionable and uncomfortable, and then went to bed. He wasn't sleeping, and neither was I. We were quiet, though, and it was a while before I heard his breathing even out. I stared at the ceiling and went over our conversation. I never realized how much Diane played a part in how I treated him, and how it was taking a toll. He understood that my work sometimes got in the way of us. But I hadn't realized that Diane was getting in the way, too. I swore silently. I had a lot to do with this case in order to find Cherry's killer. I also *had* to carve out some time to talk to Diane. Right before I fell asleep, I thought about Rex Land. No one had called to report that he'd shown up.

Where was he?

CHAPTER THIRTEEN

He stared at the wall and thought about the woman. Her eyes had held such terror as he laid on her, pumping. That look had been almost as satisfying as his release. Once he had finished, he'd put his hands around her throat. She had struggled, but he was too strong. When she finally lay still, he set to work.

He was careful to remove all evidence of his crime, to clean her and place her neatly on the bed. He didn't like seeing her naked body. Ironic, given what he'd done, but true. Then he put all evidence of his presence into a bag he had in his pocket. Once he assured himself no one was about, he slipped out the back door and was gone.

He held up the bracelet with the cherries etched on a little band. The moonlight glinted off it. She'd been wearing it when he took her. It must have had special meaning for her, for her to wear it to bed. And it would have exceptional meaning for him, too, so he'd taken it off her limp wrist. She wouldn't need it anymore. He twisted it between his thumb and fingers, again thinking through last night. No one had seen him, he was certain.

He was sure he was safe. It was just like before. He'd get away with it.

The urge was returning faster, though. He was already feeling that edge again, the nervousness he tried to control until it ruled over him and he had to act. He dropped the bracelet and got up and paced the room, going from the dresser in one corner to the bed against a wall in the opposite corner. Back and forth, back and forth. He focused on nothing but his footsteps. Outside, a cat meowed, its screech piercing. He paid no attention to it.

After a long time, he realized he was sweaty and his legs were tired. He snatched up the bracelet and went into the living room. He turned on the TV, the silvery glow lighting the walls and ceiling. He fiddled with the bracelet again, rolling it between his fingers. Then, when his eyes began to droop, he stood up and plodded to the kitchen. From the freezer, he pulled out a Ziploc bag and opened it. Inside was another brown paper bag. He opened it and put the bracelet in with the rest. Then he closed the paper bag, placed it back inside the Ziploc bag, and put that back in the freezer.

Then he went to bed.

CHAPTER FOURTEEN

Spats called me as I was driving to the station the next morning.

"I just talked to the detective doing surveillance on Manny Guerrero, and I got a report about the surveillance camera near Rex Land's house." His voice dragged. "Guerrero went home after he spent a while at the bar, and he didn't leave again. Land never returned to his house."

"Land never came home?" I repeated.

"Yeah. A desk cop named Neville is monitoring the surveillance camera now. He'll call one of us if he spots Land."

I checked the dashboard clock. "It's too early to call his work to see if he'll show up there."

"If he does go to the dealership today, we should be there."

"I agree with that," I said. "Turns out, one of Cherry's neighbors has some surveillance video, and he called Ernie back this morning. We're going over to look at it now. Can you get a detective to watch Littleton Chevrolet and let us know if Land comes in for work?"

"I need to be down that direction anyway to follow up on one of Cherry's friends, a woman on Cherry's phone list. I'll stop by the dealership then and watch for Land. If he doesn't show up when they open, I'll discreetly find out when he's due."

"Perfect," I said and ended the call.

Spats seemed a little down, and I attributed it to his being tired. I made a mental note to ask him, then the thought was out of my mind as the heavy traffic took my attention. I made my way to Alcott Street and passed by Cherry Rubio's house. You'd never know by looking at the little house that such a vile thing had occurred inside just the other night. I saw Ernie's dark sedan parked across the street from the house and I pulled up behind him. He got out, the usual cigar stub firmly held at the corner of his mouth.

"You feeling any better today?" I asked, knowing how close to home Cherry Rubio's death had seemed to hit him.

"Yeah, it helped to see my kids last night." Then, before he let anymore of his sensitive side show, he cleared his throat and gave the slightest nod toward the house. "The neighbor's name is Jeff Conway. He's newly retired, and he's been worried about some break-ins in the neighborhood, so he recently installed some surveillance cameras." Ernie started toward the house, then grabbed the cigar from his mouth. He studied it for a second, as if realizing it might not be the best look for him when we talked to Conway. He shook his head in disgust and almost threw it on the ground, but saw the look on my face. Instead, he reached into the car and dropped the stub into a soda bottle. "They don't even have ashtrays in cars anymore," he groused.

"That's because they figure it might encourage people to quit."

"Chewing on it helps me think. Sort of like when you fiddle with that pen of yours and tap, tap, tap on the desk when you think."

"Well ..." I didn't have a response to that.

He stood up and stretched, then tucked his shirt in. "Let's see what this guy has for us."

We strode up the walk and rang the front doorbell. A minute later, a stocky man with a shaved head and a thin mustache opened the door.

"Oh, you're the detectives? Come on in." He opened the door wider. We stepped into a small living room, similar in size to Cherry Rubio's, but made to feel even smaller by a humongous television that dominated the wall opposite the door. Two lounge chairs were positioned in front of it, with a small coffee table between. The room couldn't hold anything else. The smell of bacon wafted in from the kitchen.

"Thank you for meeting us," Ernie said. He introduced me, and Conway shook my hand.

"It's terrifying what happened to Cherry," Conway said. He blinked hard a few times, a tic of some sort. He had the look of a feral cat, alert and edgy. "I wouldn't have thought something like that would ever happen around here."

I pointed toward the street. "Did you see or hear anything Tuesday night?"

"I wish I had, but I'm afraid not. I slept through the night." Blinking again. "I have some issues with my nerves, so I take a sleeping pill at night."

"I see," I murmured. "Did you know Cherry well?"

He thought about that, blinked a few times rapidly. "Not really. She kind of kept to herself. I saw her outside, sometimes with her boyfriend, but that's about it."

"Are you aware that she had broken up with her boyfriend?"

His eyes widened. "I didn't know that, but I don't talk to her."

"She had been seeing someone else, possibly an older man. He's tall, with darker hair. Have you seen him around?"

Conway thought about that for a moment as he rocked on his

feet. "I don't recall him." He crossed his arms. "I hate to say it, but the only way I might be helpful is with the surveillance video."

"You told an officer you watched all the video from Tuesday night?" Ernie asked.

"That's right." Conway took a remote from the table and directed it toward the TV. "I've got this all queued up. I figured you folks don't have a lot of time to waste."

"We appreciate that," I said.

Conway pressed a button and the TV lit up, the images in black and white. "I'll let it run for a moment." We all watched the screen. "Earlier in the evening it was just like it always is, cars and people coming and going. I didn't think you'd want to see that. It got quiet about eleven, no more cars at all. Until about two. First we have a dark SUV going by. A little bit later, we have some motion near Cherry's house." We watched the car, then saw what appeared to be a shadow at the upper part of the screen. Unfortunately, the camera angle was bad and hadn't captured any more. "See, it's right here!" He stepped up closer toward the TV and pressed the pause button.

I stared at the screen, where the image was. "Does that look like a person?"

Ernie's face contorted. "Too hard to tell. It could be a coyote, something like that."

Conway looked at us, disappointed. "I thought you'd want to see it."

"Definitely," Ernie said.

"I watched the video after the officer interviewed me about what had happened to Cherry."

"Have you seen any strangers around the neighborhood lately?" I asked.

He shook his head, blinking. "No. I keep an eye out because there had been some break-ins a few months back, but I haven't seen anything suspicious. I saw Cherry with her boyfriend a few times. One time a few weeks ago, they got into a fight. Other than that, I pretty much know the people I've seen."

Ernie pointed to the TV. "You've got this whole security stuff set up to run through the TV?"

Conway nodded. "Yeah, it's pretty slick. I've got a camera installed out front, mainly to pick up any activity around the front porch, and I've got one set up over the back door so I can see if anyone tries to approach my back door. You can see here," he touched the screen with a finger, "how I can see the street and part of Cherry's house, and part of the side of the house." He backed up the video and showed us again. "And right here, that's part of her back yard."

I looked at the time on the video. "Two a.m."

"Yes, that's correct. So first, we have this car driving by slow." He ran the video again, and we all watched as the SUV drove by.

"Stop it there." I stared at the screen. "Can anyone make out that license plate?"

Ernie and Conway stared at the screen. "Looks like a B, or maybe at P," Ernie said. I nodded agreement. "If you let us have this video, Mr. Conway," Ernie smooth-talked him, "we might be able to get a technician to enhance it."

"Sure, that's no big deal," Conway said. "Anything to help you find Cherry's killer." He turned back to the screen. "Let me keep running this."

We all stared at the black-and-white images of the empty street. Nothing moved, so it seemed as if it the video had been paused, but it hadn't. Then Conway said, "There!" He pointed at the screen again.

Ernie and I simultaneously took a step forward and looked at the screen. Conway had his finger pressed on the corner of the screen where Cherry's back yard was visible.

"You see that?" he asked. "I was wondering if that looked like some movement."

"Back it up," I said.

He complied, and we watched again, this time in slow motion. Conway was right. It did appear that something moved in Cherry's back yard.

Ernie bent down and put his nose close to the television. "I still can't tell what that is. Is that someone's legs? Or like I said, a coyote."

Conway scrunched up his mouth. "I've watched this a few times, and I'm not sure. If I had to guess, I think it's somebody's legs."

I frowned. "It's so far away, I don't know if we could identify anyone."

"Maybe enhancement will help." But Ernie sounded doubtful. He smiled at Conway. "You said we could have a copy of this?"

Conway was ahead of us. He slipped a hand into his pocket and grabbed a USB drive. "I've got it right here for you." He handed it to Ernie. "You can keep that."

Ernie held it up. "Thank you."

Conway looked between us. Blink, blink. "It's such a shame. A break-in is one thing, but to murder someone." He ran his hands over his arms. "You think it'll be in some other neighborhood, not yours. I have a daughter about Cherry's age. I can't imagine what I'd do if that happened to her."

I glanced at Ernie. He gave me a look and cleared his throat. Conway stared at us. I knew he wouldn't sleep well for a while. We asked him if he could think of anything else that might be helpful to our investigation, and we gave him our cards. We thanked him for his time and left.

CHAPTER FIFTEEN

"Don't you need to get to Cherry's autopsy?" Ernie asked as he and I stood on the street.

I watched a car go by, then checked my watch. "I have a little bit of time."

"What do you think?" Ernie kicked at the rear tire of his car. The murder was still hitting close to home for him.

"Did you notice his blinking all the time?"

"Uh-huh. A nervous tic. I didn't get the sense he was covering anything, though, did you? He rapes and murders her, then tries to throw us off?"

"We don't know she was raped."

"Come on," he snarled.

I shrugged. "I get it, she probably was. Let's see if the autopsy confirms it."

He opened his mouth to protest, thought better of it, and put his hands on his hips. "I'll look into Conway, run a background check, but I don't think he's our guy."

I thought for a moment as I pictured the surveillance video in my mind. "I'm glad Conway showed us the video, but it's not a lot to go on. I couldn't tell if that shadow near Cherry's house means anything or not. And the car could've been anyone, although I'd like to know if we could get anything from that license plate."

"If we can get the full plate, I'll follow up on it. Like you said, it might not be anything." Ernie sucked in a breath, then let out a little laugh. "We're being watched."

I glanced toward Conway's house. He was standing at his window, watching us. "Too bad he's seeing more with us here than the night Cherry died."

"You got that right." Ernie held up the USB drive. "I'm going to get this to Tara right away. We'll see if she can enhance any of the images so we can get the full plate number, and if we can figure out what that was near Cherry's house. I've also tracked down a few more of her friends. I'll be talking to them today."

I checked my phone. "I should head over to the ME office for Cherry's autopsy."

"Let me know what you find out."

"Will do."

I went back to my car and got in. As I started it and pulled into the street, I saw Ernie jamming a new unlit cigar into the corner of his mouth. It was like his pacifier. If it made him feel better and helped him think, I didn't care.

As I headed east, I called Diane. It went to voice mail. I felt my stomach knot up, and I took in a calming breath. I tried to sound cheery as I left her a message to call me back.

"I'm trying, Harry," I said to no one. "I'm trying."

The Medical Examiner's Office is off Sixth Avenue, not far from Cherry's house. And yet, because the location is so hard to get to, I barely made it on time. Like the other industrial buildings surrounding it, the office is drab, with gray walls that feel like death. When I entered the building, the wall of cold air slammed into me, almost taking my breath away. I checked in and hurried down a hallway to Jack Jamison's office.

Jack was sitting at his desk, his nose in a file. He had pictures of his family on his desk, almost out of place among professional books and manuals, and autopsy files that were a constant reminder of mayhem and destruction. Maybe images of his family gave him hope, a sense of life. I suspected the picture of fall aspens that hung on one wall did the same thing. He looked up as I leaned against the door jamb.

"Glad to see you're on time. I don't have time to wait, always backed up."

"I wouldn't disappoint you," I said.

He got up and moved gracefully around the desk. "Let's get this going."

I followed him down the hallway and into a foyer that led to an examination room. He went straight through double doors while I took stairs to an observation room above. I looked down onto a metal table with a body covered in a sheet. Jamison was joined by an assistant, an Asian woman with long black hair pulled into a ponytail. She glanced up at me, then turned to Jack, who had donned a headset and was putting on latex gloves.

The smell of an autopsy is difficult to describe, and even though I was observing from above, the odors drifted up to me. I've been to a number of these over the years, and I've never quite gotten used to it. To get through it, I tell myself that it's just a body on the table.

"All right, I'll get started." Jack touched a button on a nearby laptop and began dictating. "This is Dr. Jack Jamison, performing an autopsy on Cherry Rubio, a female who may have died from strangulation." He continued with the hospital case number, then cleared his throat. "The female is thirty-two years old, she has dark brown hair and brown eyes." He removed the sheet. Cherry's body now lay exposed, rigid and pale.

I stared at her for a moment, seized by an ache so sudden it stunned me. There is something about a seeing a person so vulnerable, so laid bare. I still see the human being that once had life. I wanted to shout at Jamison to leave the poor woman alone. Instead, I drew in a quick breath and remained stoic.

"We performed X-rays before this examination, and the hyoid bone in the neck was broken, along with a laryngeal fracture, possibly consistent with strangulation. An examination of the neck shows a significant amount of bruising, not necessarily consistent with a rope or other ligature." He bent down and studied Cherry's neck closely. Then he looked up at me. "It would appear to me that the bruises are more significant on the right side, and the bruises show a possible hand pattern." Jack next examined the entire body. "I see no other external signs of trauma, no needle or puncture wounds. The X-rays show a break of the left ankle, a prior injury."

With his assistant's help, Jack used a scope and performed a rape analysis. "There is significant tearing and bruising of the vagina, but no signs of semen. It is possible the victim was raped."

My jaw clenched. Jack was careful to draw no conclusions, but he didn't have to. It was clear Cherry had been raped and murdered. I jotted a few notes in a small notepad as I listened.

That part of the examination complete, Jack started the autopsy. "I will remove the skin from the face." The assistant helped, and once that was finished, he picked up a small round saw and cut off the top of the cranium. "I am weighing the brain, and further inspection shows no damage to it." Once he finished with that, he made a Y-incision from each shoulder to the sternum, then straight down the center of the body, then a horizontal line at the pubic area. Once that was complete, he peeled back the skin and weighed and examined the organs. He noted no damage to her internal organs, and he moved on.

"There are no contents in her stomach, nothing to conclude what she had last eaten."

My cell phone vibrated in my pocket, and I ignored it. Jack next drew blood and his assistant packaged the vials so they could be sent to a lab for analysis. He scraped underneath her nails, and I had to tamp down a pain when I saw her painted toe nails. A simple act for Cherry to do to make herself pretty. An act robbed from her. I shut away the thought and continued to watch the autopsy.

"There appears to be some matter under the index finger of the right hand," Jack went on. "Possibly skin. We'll send this out for analysis." He put the contents from his scrape into a container and continued his work.

The entire autopsy took a little over an hour, and Jack concluded with a quick summary. Then he shut off the recorder, gave a few instructions to his assistant, and signaled me to meet him outside the examination room.

"What do you think?" I asked in the hallway as I took a few deep, satisfying breaths that weren't tainted by the autopsy odors. My cell phone vibrated again, and I again ignored it.

"We won't have the toxicology report for several weeks," he said. "If she had any drugs in her system, we'll find it."

"The bruising on her neck. You think the guy was left-handed." He hesitated and I pressed him. "Come on, what did you see?"

He frowned, showing his distaste for my question. "There was more bruising on the right side of the neck, so it's possible, if this person were facing her when she was strangled, that the attacker is left-handed. But I would not use that for evidence." Now he wagged a finger at me. "A good defense attorney would be all over that, and it would go nowhere in court."

"I know," I said. "I'll see where that goes *outside* of a courtroom."

"You'll need a lot more than that to convict anyone."

I glanced toward the door. "Raped and murdered." My blood boiled. I leaned against the wall. "She was such a small thing. It wouldn't take that big a man to do that to her."

Jack shrugged. "I'll have a full report for you in a day or so." He scratched his head. "It never ends, does it?"

"What?"

"The death, the destruction." He blinked sadly. "The horrible ways human beings treat each other."

"It doesn't make any sense."

He shook his head, then gestured back at the autopsy room. "Unfortunately, I've got another one in a little while, so I need to go. It never ends," he repeated.

I walked him back to his office. His last words hung in the air like a premonition as I left the building.

CHAPTER SIXTEEN

As I walked back to my car, I checked my phone, thinking the messages would be from Diane. Instead it was the on-duty officer named Neville who was monitoring the surveillance camera at Rex Land's house. I punched buttons on my phone to get to his messages. I hoped it was good news.

"Hey, Spillman, it's Neville," the first message said. "You wanted to know the minute we saw Land. Well, he showed up at his house. It's nine o'clock. He's inside now. I'll also call Spats."

The second message was just as brief. "It's Neville. Land was inside for about thirty minutes, and he just headed out. I'll let Spats know as well."

I sat in the car for a moment and called Spats. He answered after three rings with a curt, "Hey."

"It's me. Neville called me about Rex."

"Right. I didn't want to call while you were at the autopsy. Our man is on the move." Sounds of static came through the phone. He was driving. "Land showed up at the dealership, was there for a few minutes, then left. I'm following him now. Oh, he's going to a Starbucks."

"Near the dealership?"

"Yeah. I guess the coffee at the office isn't good enough? Probably means he'll head right back to work."

"I'll head to the dealership now." I put the key in the ignition and started the car. "Let me know if he goes somewhere else, and I'll meet you. I want to talk to him."

"Me too."

He ended the call, and I raced through the meandering side streets from the Medical Examiner's Office back to Sixth Avenue. Traffic on Sixth is always busy, and it was slow going until Broadway. I went south, hitting several red lights, and my impatience grew. My phone rang again. This time it was Diane.

"Sarah, I got your message. I've got just a few minutes. What do you need?"

I sensed an underlying tone, one that said I was bothering her. I was in a mood myself, and almost snapped at her. Then I thought about what Harry had said, and the tension that seemed to be hanging over us, so I quickly put my emotions in check. I avoided chit chat with her, knowing neither of us wanted that at the moment.

"I was wondering if you might have time to go out to eat," I said.

"When?"

"Harry is going to be out of town next week. I thought maybe we could get together sometime while he's gone."

There was a long pause. "Okay. This week isn't good for me anyway. Aaron and the boys will be camping next week, so that would be fine." Diane has two sons who are ten and eight. My nephews are sweet, but boisterous.

"How about Tres Hermanos, on Monday?" She likes Mexican food as much as I do–one of the few things we agreed on–and since I'd just been there, it was the first place that popped into my head.

"That'll work." We agreed on a time, then she quickly said, "I need to go, I'll see you then."

"Sounds good."

I ended the call, satisfied that I had made the effort, leery about the dinner itself. By now, I was passing Hampden, and Littleton Chevrolet appeared on the right. I turned in and parked a distance away from the entrance. Then I called Spats.

"I just got here," I said. "Is Land back at work?"

"Yeah, I'd have called you if he'd left."

Of course he would've, I thought wryly but didn't say. I still had Diane on my mind. I gave my head a little shake to clear thoughts of her and of our relationship from my mind.

"Meet me at the entrance," I said. I ended the call and got out. By the time I crossed the parking lot, Spats was by the door.

When we entered the showroom, a young man with an eager smile approached. "How are you two doing today?"

"We're fine," I said, maybe a bit too curt. I cut him off before he could start into his salesman shtick. "We're not looking for a car. Is a supervisor available?"

The smile faded as he realized he wouldn't have an opportunity to make a sale. "Of course, let me get him." He was still exceedingly polite. "You can have a seat." He gestured at some chairs lined against a glass wall that looked out to shiny new cars in the lot.

Spats and I declined, and we checked out a new sedan as he walked away. Soft music was piped in through speakers, but otherwise it was quiet. We waited longer than I felt necessary before a well-built man in a blue suit approached.

"I'm Bob Mosley, the manager. What can I help with?" His voice was deep and polished. "Is there a problem?"

I showed him my badge. "We're in the middle of an investigation and we think one of your employees, Rex Land, might have information that would be helpful. Would he have a few minutes to talk to us?"

His eyes narrowed slightly, not in a threatening manner, more inquisitive. "Uh, yes, let me go get him." Before we could say more, he spun around and crossed between cars where a few small offices faced the showroom. He stood in a doorway for a moment. Through the upper glass wall, we saw a man sitting at a desk. He craned his neck to look at us, then stood up and walked around the desk. Mosley stepped back, and I got a better look at Land. He was tall, with brown hair that was smoothed back. He said something to Mosley and walked over to us.

"I'm Rex Land," he said. I recognized him from his Facebook pictures. He was slender with a slight paunch, well-dressed in a dark suit, a gold watch on his right wrist. His face and hands were tanned, the sign of someone who was outdoors a lot. He raised eyebrows at us. "My manager says you'd like to talk to me. What can I help you with?"

I glanced around the showroom. "Would you like to talk here?"

He shrugged. "Yeah, better come into my office."

He led Spats and me to his small office. He stared past us into the showroom to see who was watching, then closed the door. He indicated we could sit in two small chairs in front of a desk with a phone on the right, a monitor on the left. Through the blinds behind him, I saw rows of brand-new Chevy cars in a variety of makes and models. Land took a seat, put his hands on the desk, and laced his fingers. Then he looked at me expectantly. I gazed at Spats, who raised his eyebrows to give me the go-ahead.

"Thank you for your time," I began. Land waited. "You know a woman named Cherry Rubio?"

He nodded, curious, as his manager had been. "Yes, I know her. Well, I've gone on a few dates with her, so I'd say we're acquaintances. I don't know her very well."

"When was the last time you saw her?"

He thought for a second. "It was about a week ago. We had dinner and a movie. What's this about?"

"We heard she was enjoying being with someone who had money to spend on her."

"We went to some nice restaurants. I wasn't trying to wine and dine her, then take her to bed, if that's what you're implying."

I studied him carefully. He didn't seem nervous, and yet he was careful. "You haven't heard about Cherry?" I asked.

He shook his head. "You have me a little worried, though."

"Cherry was murdered the other night," Spats said.

He sat back in his chair, speechless. "What night?"

"Tuesday."

Rex rubbed his hands over his face, starting at his brow and going slowly over his open mouth. "I can't believe it. I just saw her last Friday night. How did it happen?"

"Someone broke into her home," I said vaguely. "When you saw her last, how did she seem to you?"

He stared past us. "She was fine, I guess." Now a little hesitation. "We had a nice time. I dropped her off at her house, and that was it."

"Did you go inside?"

He shook his head. "To be honest, I didn't think it was going anywhere."

"It?"

"A relationship." He paused, searched for words. "She was really nice, and I enjoyed her company, but she was super busy with her school and work, and I don't think she had a lot of time for anything serious. And for me, I'm the opposite. I'd like to settle down with someone."

"And you last saw her last Friday night, correct?" I asked. "Not since then."

"That's right," he said.

"When was the last time you talked to her?"

"That night."

"Before that, how often did you talk?"

He thought about that. "A few times, you know, calling to set up a date, or following up. It wasn't a lot."

"And you never went into her house?"

He shook his head. "How did the killer get in?"

I didn't answer that, but with a glance volleyed to Spats the question I wanted him to ask. "Would you mind coming down to the station to get fingerprinted?" Spats smiled. "It's just routine. We need to track down the prints we found in her house, eliminate suspects."

Rex gazed between us. "Uh, sure, I can do that. I work until closing tonight, and I have to be here at ten tomorrow morning. What if I went down to the station before that?"

"That'll work," Spats said.

"I wasn't in her house," Rex reiterated.

Spats and I continued good-cop/bad-cop. "We have to check," Spats said firmly.

Now it was back to me. "Did Cherry give any indication she might be scared of anyone? Another man?"

He thought quickly. "No, not at all. I know she had a difficult relationship with her former boyfriend, but that's the extent of what she told me, just that it was difficult. I don't even know his name."

"She had a brochure for a Corvette in the trash."

His phone rang. He glanced at it, then back to me. "Yeah," he said. He let the phone keep ringing. "I gave that to her. I met her at Arapahoe Community College. She was there when I was with a friend of mine. We talked a few times, and she found out I sell cars. She said she really loved Corvettes, but she also said she couldn't afford one. I told her that I could help get her into a Corvette cheap, someday, whenever she thought she could buy one. I had a brochure in my car and I gave it to her." He shrugged. "I sound like a stereotypical car salesman, don't I? Maybe at first I was, but after I'd seen her a couple of times, I did tell her I'd help her get a good used car and get the best deal I could. I meant it, too." The phone stopped ringing. He looked at his hands. "I guess that won't happen now."

Spats and I exchanged a glance. I knew what he was thinking. Was Land sincere or a really good actor?

The youthful salesman tapped on the door, then poked his head in. "Hey Rex, you have a call on line three."

Land shook his head. "Not now."

"It's important, that lady who says she–"

Land threw up a hand, then said, "Okay, I'll get it."

"Thanks." The salesman looked at Spats and me and quietly closed the door.

"Excuse me, I guess I have to take this." Land picked up the phone and talked for a moment, then cradled the receiver on his shoulder, grabbed a pen near the monitor and wrote down a few notes. Finally, he hung up and apologized again.

"Where were you on Tuesday night?" Spats asked.

"I was at home, alone." His jaw went slack as he realized the intent of the question. "You don't think I did this to Cherry? No way."

It was just enough indignation to seem plausible. If he was guilty, he was good at not showing it.

"What about last night?" I asked casually.

"I went camping. I sometimes like to go toward Fairplay, just get away, even if it's overnight. This job, believe it or not, can be stressful. You know, nobody likes a car salesman." He gave me a small smile, knowing how his answer sounded.

"I appreciate your time," I said. Spats and I stood up "We may need to ask you some more questions."

"We'll let you know," Spats said casually.

Land kept his face neutral, not revealing anything as he led us out of the office. Mosley was nearby, waiting to hear what we'd wanted. Land didn't acknowledge him. "Whatever you need," Land said. "I'm here to help. I hope you find whoever did that to Cherry."

He walked us to the entrance, likely not wanting us to talk to anyone else. Spats held the glass door for me, and as I walked through, an older couple entered. Land cleared his throat and gave them a big smile as he welcomed them into the showroom. I heard him complementing the woman's blouse as the door closed.

"He doesn't have an alibi for the night Cherry died," Spats said as we walked to my car.

"No." I got in and rolled down the window as I thought about our conversation with Land. "Nothing stands out that would make me absolutely think he was Cherry's killer. On the other hand, nothing made me want to dismiss him, either."

"I'm not ready to take him off my list."

"Me neither. Spats, I want a warrant for his phone records to see if he was calling Cherry more than he admitted to us."

"You got it."

"I'm going to follow up with his neighbors to see whether anyone remembers seeing him the night Cherry died."

"Time to start eliminating suspects."

"Right."

CHAPTER SEVENTEEN

As I drove to Rex Land's neighborhood, I mulled over the conversation with him. He had been very calm and collected. He seemed upset about Cherry Rubio's death, but not overly so. On the one hand, he didn't have a big connection with her, so not being terribly distraught made sense. On the other hand, that didn't mean he couldn't have killed her. And he didn't have an alibi for the night of her murder.

I parked at the end of the block and wished for clouds as I walked up and down the block and knocked on doors. Only a few of Land's neighbors were home, and they didn't know anything about where Rex had been the night of Cherry's murder. Having accomplished nothing with my time, I headed back to the station. When I got there, I stopped by Tara Dahl's office. As usual, she had earbuds in, with a pounding beat blaring from them.

I gestured at the laptop in front of her. "Is that Cherry Rubio's?"

She jumped when she saw me and took out the earbuds. "How many times have I told you not to sneak up on me?"

"It's hard not to do when you have the music blasting. You're ruining your hearing."

"Yes, Mom," she joked.

Tara and I have a friendly ongoing difference of opinion about her taste in loud music, and I don't hesitate to chide her about it regularly. And, like just now, she sometimes refers to me as "Mom," even though I'm no more than about ten years older than she is.

I pointed at the laptop again. "Cherry's?"

She shook her head. "No, Sarah, I've got another one that I'm finishing. Then I'll get to this woman's. She was murdered?"

"Yes, and raped. I was at her autopsy earlier today."

"Any suspects yet?"

"The field is wide open. Right now my suspects are an ex-boyfriend and a guy she'd been recently dating. But it could be anybody."

She grimaced as she lifted her coffee mug. "Well, hopefully you'll narrow things down soon."

I drew in a breath. "I don't have a lot to go on. This guy was pretty good."

"You think you have a pro?"

I leaned against the doorjamb. "Or somebody who's watched plenty of television and knows how to cover his tracks. They all slip up, though. It's just a matter of time before we find out which mistake this particular killer made." My voice held more confidence than I felt.

Her scowl deepened. "How much time?"

I didn't answer.

When I got back to my desk, I had a report from Todd. He'd run a DNA check on the hair fibers found in Cherry's bed. Some had been hers, one hair had not matched anything in our databases. He'd also run a check on the fingerprints he'd found at Cherry Rubio's house, and he had a report for me. Cherry's prints were all over the house, naturally, and he'd also identified prints for Manny Guerrero because he'd been printed when he was arrested for that domestic violence charge. Other than that, Todd had come up empty. Unless somebody had been arrested, or fingerprinted for something like a background check, there wouldn't be a record in our systems. I went over the report again, then picked up my phone and called Todd. He answered after two rings.

"You caught me before I left for lunch. I suppose you have questions about the report I sent you."

"You gave me slim pickings," I said. "There's nothing else for me to go on?"

"Unless you can find the owner of those hair fibers, no."

"This guy was good."

"You can say that again."

I thanked him for his time and hung up. I sat back and stared at the report on my monitor, disappointed. The few leads I had were going nowhere. My phone rang, and I glanced at the screen.

"Ernie, tell me you have something."

The phone sounds were scratchy; his signal not good. "I talked to another friend of Cherry's, but it didn't lead to much. She knew Cherry was dating someone who was a bit older than she was, but she didn't know more than that. Apparently, Cherry wasn't saying much. All the friend knew was that Cherry went out to eat the night she was murdered."

"Where?"

"The friend didn't know."

"Did she see this other guy that night?"

"Again, the friend didn't know."

"Give me something," I groused.

Ernie gave a wry laugh. "I wish I could. I'm just not coming up with anything."

"Neither am I."

"I'm going to chase down a few more of her friends and talk to some of her coworkers," Ernie said. "I'll let you know if I find out anything."

"I'll do the same." I ended the call, got on the computer again and wrote some notes on Cherry, Manny Guerrero, and Rex Land. I got lunch, came back, and touched base with Spats. He had gotten the warrant for Land's phone, and he was working with the phone company to get a list of calls Land had made in the last several weeks. The afternoon wore on, and I had nothing more than I did before. I still didn't have a clue to who might've killed Cherry. At the end of the day, Ernie and Spats both showed up. We were pow-wowing about the case and how little we had when Rizzo came in. Ernie and Spats both nodded at him.

"Do you have any update on the Rubio murder?" He eyed me carefully.

I shook my head. "Not so far. We're still digging up everything we can, but so far ..."

"We got squat," Ernie interjected. "Our leads go nowhere."

Rizzo nodded thoughtfully. "Any good evidence from the crime scene?"

"Some hair fibers, and some prints," Spats said, picking up with information I'd given him when he'd returned. "None of it points to anyone in particular."

Rizzo stared at each one of us, then tapped my desk. "Keep on it." With that he turned and left.

Spats looked at his watch. "Crap, I gotta go."

Ernie gazed at him across the desk. "What's the big rush?"

"I need to meet Trissa. Let me know if anything important comes up." Spats smoothed his hair and adjusted his tie, actions he routinely did without being aware of them. He barely gave us a nod as he dashed out the door.

Ernie glanced at me. "Everything okay with him?"

I looked toward the door, where Spats had gone. "I'm not sure. Is it me, or is he not quite as cheerful as normal?"

Ernie thought for a moment, then shrugged. "I don't know."

My eyes went to my monitor. "I feel like we're missing something," I said. I stared at the screen, but nothing came to mind.

Ernie and I both worked at our laptops, filling out reports on other cases. Time crept by. Now and then the sounds of conversations and phone calls drifted in from other rooms. Someone typed, the clicking of the keyboard loud. I finally checked the computer clock and decided it was time to call it a night. Harry was working later, but would probably be home by now. I wasn't making any headway, and I wanted a little time with him before he went out of town. I looked over at Ernie. He yawned and stretched, the buttons in his shirt threatening to burst.

"We're not doing much good here now," I said.

He growled. "I wish we were. The more time passes, the more likely Cherry's killer gets away."

I know," I murmured.

Neither of us wanted to leave, but reluctantly we finally did. I went home and had a quiet dinner with Harry. I asked about his work, and he was unusually vague, just that he was super busy.

"Everything okay?" I asked.

He nodded. "Sure. The usual stuff."

A long silence ensued.

"I talked to Diane today," I finally said as we sipped wine.

"Oh?" His dark eyes were not as inquisitive as I might've expected, more cautious.

"Well, 'talked' is a relative term." No laugh from him. I went on. "We're going out to eat on Monday at Tres Hermanos." I figured he might pretend to act jealous that I was going there with her instead of him, but he didn't say a word. "I thought it would be a good time to meet her, when you're out of town. And she was busy until then anyway."

"I hope you have a good visit and clear the air."

"Me too."

I looked at him over my glass. On the surface, he seemed fine. Something was there, though. I almost said something more about Diane, but in my head I sounded defensive, so I kept quiet. I would have dinner with her on Monday, and I hoped that would help resolve some of the issues between her and me, and maybe clear the air with Harry, too.

We finished dinner and cleared the dishes. He watched a little TV, and I tried to read a book, but the words weren't sinking in. We watched the news and went to bed, companionable, but not close. My worries finally drained me, and I fell asleep.

In the meantime, a killer was out there, lurking.

CHAPTER EIGHTEEN

The window was open. That was good.

He crouched at the edge of the yard and studied the house. A cricket chirped, but then even it went silent. This was truly the dead of night. He finally slipped toward the house, his eyes searching for surveillance cameras at the front. He swore to himself. People with their cursed security cameras. The cameras, with their improved technology, had made things a lot more difficult for him. He had to spend a lot of time researching security systems and cameras to figure out how they worked, how far they could see, how good the video quality was. Even so, as popular as the cameras were, most people still didn't use them.

He studied the area high above the front door and windows, where people usually installed security cameras, but also where intruders couldn't reach them. Nothing. He looked at the corners of the house, and in a tree on the side near a window, in case any were installed there. At the last house, he'd spotted a camera near the front door, and one camera most likely meant there were others. He knew then that he couldn't go into that house, and that had infuriated him. The urge was growing more intense. He couldn't ignore it; he had to act. He shook his head now. People and their damn cameras.

He crept to the side of the house and checked the eaves as well, assuring himself no surveillance equipment had been installed. Finally, he sneaked around to the back of the house. Nothing there either.

He crouched and listened for a moment longer. The house remained dark. He adjusted his mask, the heavy material almost suffocating in the heat. But it was necessary to keep his face obscured.

A half moon disappeared behind some clouds, and he slinked up to the side of the house. He quickly reassured himself that he hadn't missed any cameras. He stood up and stepped to the window. He listened and heard nothing inside. With one final look around, he raised the knife and slashed the window screen. He eased the window up, pausing when it creaked. No lights went on. He glanced around. Only stillness.

Once assured that he hadn't waked anyone inside, he quietly hoisted himself through the window.

CHAPTER NINETEEN

When I walked into the office the next morning, Spats was at his desk, his head cradled in his hands just like last night. He didn't move, didn't seem to notice me.

"What's up with you?" I asked as I sat down at my desk. Voices came from the other room, an argument of some sort. I tuned it out and focused on Spats. "Hangover?"

He looked up. His eyes were tortured, his tie slightly askew. For Spats, that was unheard of. Something was going on.

"What's wrong?"

He sat back and rubbed his temples. "Nothing. It was a long night. And no," he said in answer to my raised eyebrows, "it's not a hangover."

Spats and I had been partners for a long time, and although I wouldn't say I'm as close to him as I am to Ernie, I know him pretty well, and I care deeply about him. "I don't want to push, but ..." I hesitated, treading carefully, knowing I *was* pushing. "Is it something with our case? Something doesn't seem right? I know it doesn't seem like we've made any progress." Then I stopped.

It took him a long time to answer. "Things aren't going so well with Trissa and me."

I wasn't expecting that. "What do you mean? You've got the baby and you just met her parents. I thought things were all right."

He regarded me, his jaw slack. He finally spoke. "I guess I did, too. But it's the job." He threw up his hands. "Isn't it always the job? 'It takes so much time, you're focused on your work, you're not here for me.' " He put the balls of his fists to his eyes. "You know that's how my first marriage ended. She couldn't stand the long hours, the fact that I would be thinking about the case even when I was home." He gazed at me long and hard as if searching for answers. I didn't have any to give. "Does that happen to you?"

I gave that some thought. "Yes, it does."

"How does Harry handle it?"

I leaned forward and rested my elbows on the desk. The question seemed particularly apropos at the moment. It took me a minute to answer. "Harry puts up with a lot." I shot him a sheepish look. "I know this may come as a shock, but I'm not the easiest person to get along with."

That drew a tiny smile from him, as I hoped it would. I chose my words carefully, not one for too much vulnerability. "Harry knew a little bit about me when we met. It was a blind date, but he'd done some research on me."

"He's a detective, too," he said with good-natured sarcasm.

"Something like that." I thought about Harry. As with most people, the person that he'd fallen in love with wasn't the same one ten years later. "I had just been promoted to detective when I met Harry. So he knew about the job, and he said he understood about the hours and how I could be pulled away from him. But even he hadn't anticipated just how intense I can be."

Spats growled, a low bass sound. "Yeah, they say they understand, but it's different when it actually happens."

I couldn't argue with that. "Yes it is. Harry's had to make adjustments, that's for sure." And then, once again, I thought about Diane, how I hadn't realized that lately my relationship with her was coming between him and me, too. "For me, it's not so much the job–or just the job–it's other things." He looked at me, waiting for more. I didn't know how much else to say. He was searching for answers, ones I didn't know if I had. "You know I don't get along really well with my sister."

"Yeah."

I was careful again. "It's stuff I should've addressed a long time ago, and I haven't. And I've become aware that it's affecting my relationship with Harry in a negative way. I want to blame any problems we have on the job. Only I can't." His brow furrowed as he listened. He was taking it all in. I scowled. I didn't like to think about all this, but I needed to. "I'm having dinner with Diane on Monday, and I'm going to talk about some things, clear the air. I don't want to get into all of it. Let's just say I don't like looking in the mirror, but sometimes I have to. And it's not fun." I shifted my gaze to look at a map of Denver on the wall nearby. "I need to, for Harry and me."

He took a pocketknife from his desk drawer and cleaned under a nail as he mulled that over, his way of not having to look at me. "I know what you mean. I thought things with Trissa were going along okay. I guess that tells you how much I know."

"Maybe go out to dinner, just the two of you, not the baby. And you can really pay attention to her."

"Yeah." He put the knife down. "I hardly get to see my daughter; I want to make sure I get to spend more time with my son. I want to do it right this time."

"You will. Make it important, and you will."

Spats let out a laden breath and straightened his tie. "Yeah, that about sums it up." He cleared his throat. And with that, we were back to work talk. "I talked to the guys who're watching Manny Guerrero. He's been quiet, only went to work and then home last night. He worked on a car in his driveway for a while, then was in his house, alone."

"Think he knows he's being watched?"

He shook his head. "I doubt it. The surveillance team is good."

"Let's keep them on him another day."

"Sounds good." He then pointed to his monitor. "I finally got Cherry's phone records. I'm going through them now."

That led me down a side trail. "Did Rex Land show up to get fingerprinted?" I looked around, as if he might materialize in the room.

Spats glanced around, too. "Nope. I checked, but he didn't show."

I shook my head in disgust. "I'll call him when he gets in to work and ask him about it. Maybe he forgot," I said, more in jest to myself.

"You're joking, right?"

I snickered. "Yes. Why not come down here unless he's hiding the fact he was actually inside Cherry's house?"

Spats shrugged and got back on his computer, and I spent some time on paperwork, my mind wandering to Harry and to Diane. Then I caught Spats staring at me.

"What?"

"Cherry received several calls from Rex Land," he said.

"What'd you find?" I knew I sounded way too eager, but at this point, I was grasping at straws. So far we hadn't found anything that would lead us to a killer.

He stared at his screen. "Didn't Rex Land say he hadn't talked to Cherry at all since last Friday night? And that he hadn't talked to her very much in general?"

I nodded. "That's right." I walked over to his desk, rested my palms on his desk, and leaned in toward the monitor.

Spats pointed at the screen. "Look right there. That's the night Cherry died."

He was right. Rex had called Cherry at about ten the night she died. The call had lasted only a few seconds.

"Look at the call duration. He called, she didn't answer, and he didn't leave a message," I concluded.

Spats nodded "And check this. His number comes up several times over the last few weeks. He downplayed how much he'd talked to her."

I turned and leaned against the desk. "It looks that way to me." Then I turned around. "What's the number? Let me call him and see why he didn't show up to get fingerprinted."

"Here it is."

I dialed the number and waited. It went to voice mail. "Mr. Land, it's Detective Spillman from the Denver Police Department." I said, in my best authoritative-yet-polite tone. "I believe you were going to come to the station for fingerprinting, but that didn't happen. Could you please call me at your earliest convenience? We'd really like you to do this." I gave him both my desk and cell numbers, thanked him, and ended the call.

"I'll bet he doesn't get back to us," Spats said.

"Me too."

We were staring at each other when Ernie walked into the room.

"What's with you two?" he asked. He talked around his unlit cigar stub. "Did you get some good news?"

I arched my eyebrows and smiled. "Rex Land hasn't exactly been truthful with us." I told him about Cherry's phone records.

Ernie began talking so fast, the cigar popped out of his mouth. He was quick to snatch it before it hit the ground. "You're going to love this then. I've been looking at that car that you and

I," he glanced at me, "saw on Conway's surveillance camera the night Cherry died. It took me a little while, but I figured out the license plate number, and I just ran the plate. Let's play Jeopardy! Guess who it belongs to?"

Spats and I exchanged a glance.

"I don't want to play," Spats groaned.

"Too bad." Ernie grinned. "Take a guess."

"Rex?" I asked.

"Ding, ding!" A smile spread across Ernie's face. "He was in Cherry's neighborhood the night she was murdered."

I digested the information. "It seems Rex wasn't at all truthful with us. You know how that makes me feel?"

"I don't want to guess," Spats moaned.

"I'd say a tad angry," Ernie said.

"I'll second that," Spats said.

They knew me well. "That's right." I checked the time. Almost ten. I stared at my phone for a moment, as if that might make Land call. "Rex should be at work now," I pronounced. I locked eyes with each of them. "It's time to pay him another visit. And this time I won't be so cordial."

Spats stood up and blinked hard, as if he were trying to focus himself. "Since I went with you before, I should go again. Once we grill him, I want to press him about his fingerprints again. He shouldn't have any problem letting us get prints."

"I can't wait to hear how this interview goes," Ernie said. "In the meantime, I'm working with the techs to see if we can figure out any more from Conway's surveillance video."

My stomach knotted with excitement. I grabbed my keys, and Spats followed me out the door.

~

When we walked into Littleton Chevrolet, Bob Mosley headed us off before we got too far into the showroom.

"Hello there," he said, careful not to identify us as detectives. "What can I do for you two?" He seemed to realize what we'd likely be there for, and followed up with a quick, "Um, Rex isn't here at the moment."

"Do you expect him in?" Spats asked, not quite as friendly as he'd been yesterday. He exaggerated looking at his watch. "I thought he said he'd be here early today."

Mosley nodded. "He went with a customer on a test drive. He should be back shortly. Would you like to wait?"

"That would be great," I said. Mosley led us toward some chairs on the other side of the showroom, away from any inquisitive customers. "What is Rex like as an employee?" I asked as Mosley started to walk away.

He stopped and turned around, forcing a smile. He glanced over his shoulder to see whether anyone else was listening. "He's a good salesman, very friendly with the customers, and I haven't had any problems with him." He shifted from foot to foot. "Is something wrong?"

"This is just routine."

He clasped his hands together and smiled at us. "Can I get you anything to drink? We have coffee, tea, and sodas, and water. Or maybe you'd like to look around outside?" His nervous words tumbled over each other.

Spats and I shook our heads in unison.

"We're fine," Spats said. He sat down and casually crossed one leg over the other.

"Well ... okay." Mosley edged away and went into his office. We could see him watching us through the doorway while we waited.

"You think he'll call Rex and tell him we're here?" Spats whispered. He continued to look into Mosley's office.

"I doubt it," I said. "You're making him nervous enough as it is."

I watched Mosley as well. He busied himself at his computer, and he didn't pick up his phone. A few minutes later, Rex strolled into the showroom with a man with perfectly tended black hair and a gold watch so big that I spotted it across the room. Rex noticed us, and his eyes flickered with unwanted recognition. He talked to the man for a few minutes longer, Rex wore an edgy smile. Finally, the man shook Rex's hand and left. Rex walked over to us.

"I see you're back." His tone was neutral, and he was careful to look directly at me.

"Do you have a few minutes?" I asked.

"I'm really kind of busy."

"Really?" Spats looked around the empty showroom.

Land's shoulders sagged just a bit. "Okay, come with me." He led us back to his tiny office and shut the door. We all took the same seats as we had the other day, and he put his hands in his lap. I wasn't sure, but I thought I detected a slight shake in them before he hid them. I waited long enough to make him uncomfortable.

"What's this about?" he asked.

This time, I let Spats take the lead. "We did some checking into Cherry's phone records," he began. "What we found was very interesting."

"Oh?" Rex was trying hard to remain calm. He wasn't quite succeeding, betrayed by a tiny warble in his voice.

"You called Cherry several times, the last time the night she died." Spats stared at Rex, almost daring him to deny it.

Rex was too smart for that. "Um, yes that's correct."

"Do you mind telling us why you didn't share that before?" Spats asked.

"I thought I did." Rex smoothed a hand over a large desk calendar.

Spats made a show of looking at me, and I shook my head, confirming Rex hadn't shared that. Spats turned back to Rex.

"No, you didn't tell us that," Spats went on. "You told us both that you hadn't talked to Cherry very much, and you hadn't talked to her the night she died."

Land stared past us, then answered carefully. "It's not what you think."

"What is it then?"

Land looked as if he was being led to the gallows. He looked everywhere but at us and did not find an escape. "I guess I have to tell you, don't I?"

"It's probably a good idea," Spats said.

"I know this looks bad, but it's not what you think. I actually did call Cherry several times. A lot more than I told you. And I called her the night she died, that's true. But it was because ..." He hesitated, and his face turned red. "I really liked her, okay? Only she didn't like me, and I had trouble with that rejection." He let out a pained sigh. "When my marriage broke up, I was devastated, and lonely. It was really hard. I hadn't been interested in anybody since my wife divorced me, and when I met Cherry, she was so nice ..." He paused. "I guess I came on to her a little too strong. When she told me she didn't want to see me anymore, I didn't take it well. I still wanted to see her, so I called her again and tried to get her to go out with me again. She wouldn't, and I bugged her."

Spats rubbed his chin. "There was a car in her neighborhood around the time she was murdered."

Rex looked at me, as if I might rescue him. Instead, I said, "A neighbor has surveillance video. It shows an SUV driving down Alcott Street at around two a.m. It took us a little time, but we were able to figure out the license plate for that vehicle. It was your car."

He bit his lip, seemed to ponder whether he should lie, then thought better of it. "Yeah, I drove by about that time. I guess you could say I didn't want to let things go, and I went by Cherry's house to see if she was with someone else." Now he almost whined. "I didn't kill her. You have to believe me. Maybe I was being stupid to drive by there, but that's all I did. I looked at her house, and then I went home."

"Can anybody verify your drive-by, or when you came home?" Spats asked.

Rex went white. "No, they can't."

"Were you in the neighborhood earlier in the evening?" I asked, thinking about how Cherry's neighbor Blaine Sinclair had seen her with someone.

"No, it was later. All I did was drive by her house." He glanced behind us, and I turned around. Mosley was standing in the showroom, watching us. "I'm going to get in real trouble over all this," he said. "Please, you need to believe me. And don't let my boss know what's going on. I need this job."

Spats gave me a barely perceptible flick of his hand. I leaned forward and stared hard at Rex. "Did you do anything to Cherry?"

He shook his head vehemently. "No, I did not. If you want me to take a lie detector test, or anything like that, I will."

"We don't have your fingerprints yet," I said. "You never showed this morning."

His eyes widened. "If you need me to do that, I'll do it right now."

"That would be good." I continued to stare hard at him. "Is there anything else you want to tell us?"

He shook his head. "I'm telling you the truth." Then he stood up. "I'll talk to my boss now, and I'll go right down to the station. He won't be happy that I have to leave, but I don't care."

Spats and I stood up, and we walked into the showroom with him. Land went straight to Mosley. We heard him explaining in low tones that he needed to leave for a while. His voice grew quieter, and I couldn't hear more. Mosley stared at us, then nodded. Land returned, his face grim.

"He says I can go. He wants to know what this is about, but I didn't tell him much, just that I had to help with an investigation." He made himself sound more important than he was.

"You can ride with us," I said.

Land's jaw dropped. He searched for an excuse, then stopped himself. "Uh, sure."

"We'll go over everything again in the car," Spats said.

"Okay." Rex nodded. "I'm telling you the truth."

He was eager for us to believe him. I wasn't sure I did. We walked to my car, Land looked nervous. He clearly wanted to be anywhere but with us.

CHAPTER TWENTY

Nothing came of our chat with Rex Land, nor did his fingerprints match ones found at Cherry's house. If he was guilty, he knew to keep a low profile. He likely suspected we were watching him, which couldn't be helped.

We stayed on the case that day and Saturday, but our investigation went nowhere. Tara finished an examination of Cherry Rubio's laptop. It held no discernible clue to her killer. Ernie had followed up with the coworker at the construction company who didn't like Cherry. That man had an airtight alibi because he was out of town the night Cherry was murdered. The piece of skin that had been removed from under Cherry's nail at the autopsy hadn't led to a DNA match. Land and Manny Guerrero were kept under surveillance, and neither did anything suspicious. Harry, as he'd said he was going to do, went out of town on Sunday night. I missed him, but I also enjoyed some of the peace and quiet of the house when he was gone.

Monday morning, I got to the station early. It was quiet, and I took time to catch up on some paperwork. I was deep into a report when Ernie lumbered in with a cup of coffee in one hand.

"Did you get a little rest?" he asked.

I stared at him, thinking something was missing. "The cigar." I was a little slow this morning. "Where is it?"

"Trying to quit," he said. "Filthy habit."

"Uh-huh." I wasn't sure I bought it.

"Okay, the wife has been bugging me." He leaned forward, logged onto his computer. "We'll see how long it lasts."

I laughed and went back to my paperwork. Spats rolled in, looking more rested than I'd seen him in days.

"How're you?" I asked.

He sat down and smiled. "Not too bad. I had a good talk with Trissa last night."

I nodded. "And?"

Ernie glanced at Spats, then at me.

"It's a start," Spats said. "I'm doing what I can."

Ernie's gaze kept moving, to Spats, then to me. "Anyone want to tell me what's going on?"

"Just ... some stuff with Trissa," Spats said.

"Ah." Ernie pursed his lips. "Gotcha."

I didn't know if he did get it, but he wasn't asking. He worked the computer mouse and stared at his monitor.

Spats shrugged, then looked at me. "Did Harry get out of town okay?"

I nodded. "Last night."

"A little time to yourself," he said.

"Uh-huh." I yawned. "Unfortunately, I didn't sleep well."

"Thinking about this case?" Ernie asked.

I nodded. "Yeah. I sat outside in back for a while. It was weird, at one point, I had a strange feeling I was being watched."

Ernie eyed me. "Were you?"

"I'm sure it was just me being tired." I pointed at my monitor. "I'm finishing with some paperwork, then I'm going to go through everything we have, see if I missed something. Spats, anything happen with our surveillance on Rex and Manny?"

He shook his head. "Not so far."

I thought about that. "If either one killed Cherry, I'll bet they slip up soon."

"Could be," Spats said.

"Hey," Ernie interrupted. "We got a mention in the paper."

Spats angled in his chair to look at Ernie. "You're not working?"

"Pfft." Ernie took a sip of coffee. "I'm checking the paper first. Anyway, the *Post* did a write-up on Cherry Rubio. They mention the detectives–us–and they included your picture, Sarah."

"Was it the one from a few years ago?" Spats asked. "The department photo where she's trying to look serious?"

"Trying?" I said.

Ernie grinned. "Yeah, that one."

"It's not flattering at all," I groaned.

"The article has a little bit on Cherry," Ernie went on. He tossed up a hand. "Nothing we didn't know. It gives a little more about you, Sarah. Oh, you're a 'respected homicide detective.' That's nice." He hummed as he continued to read, then sat back. "Nothing more, really. Whoever wrote it didn't have a lot of crime-scene details, so he embellished the article with crime stats in the neighborhood, nothing even close to rape or murder."

"How did you get to be respected?" Spats joked.

I grinned. "You don't want to know."

Ernie burst out laughing. "Don't go there." He checked the article again. "Spats and I are barely mentioned, but I'll have to let the wife know about this anyway. She's got a scrapbook with articles about me."

"You sure you want an article where you barely get a mention?" Spats asked.

"I'll take what I can get."

The ribbing died down, and the room grew quiet. We kept working, and the floor filled with more noise as other detectives arrived.

"Hey," Ernie said again, this time his tone serious. "A woman was assaulted and killed in her home the night before last. The killer came through an open window."

I sat up. Spats stared at Ernie.

"What about the screen?" Spats asked. "Was it cut?"

Ernie was staring at his monitor. "Doesn't say."

I leaned over. "Where was she killed?"

"Brighton," Ernie said. He grimaced. "This article is short on details. Doesn't say how she was killed."

We didn't breathe for a second.

"Is it the same guy?" Spats murmured.

We glanced at each other, wondering if our case had just grown hot again.

I quickly looked on the internet and didn't find any more information on the murder. "We need to let Rizzo know." I called him and asked if he had a minute. He must've sensed the urgency in my voice, and he came into our little office area right away. He perched on the edge of Ernie's desk, crossed his arms, and looked at us. "What's going on?"

"Our man might have acted again," Ernie said. He gestured at his monitor. "There's an article in the news about a woman in Brighton who was raped and murdered last Thursday night. The killer came through a window."

"Did they release the victim's name?" Spats asked.

"Yes," Ernie said. He scooted his chair up to his desk. "Let me see. Oh, it's right here. Jane Lasley. She's forty, divorced, and she worked at CenturyLink."

Rizzo's lips formed a hard line. "That's similar to your case. Cherry Rubio, correct?"

I nodded. "On the face of it, it looks the same. We don't have details on the second murder."

Rizzo stared at the floor as he thought. Then he announced, "Let me make a phone call to the Brighton Police Department. I'll find out who's the lead on that case, and we'll see if you can talk to them." A man of few words, he stood up and marched out of the room.

"The victims aren't the same age," Spats said.

I shook my head, got on my computer, and googled Jane Lasley. I found a picture of her. "She had blond hair and blue eyes."

"That's not similar to Cherry Rubio," Spats said.

"No, it isn't."

We lapsed into an uneasy silence, all of us waiting to see what Rizzo would say. Ten minutes ticked by, and I was about to tear my hair out while I waited. Then he entered the room and looked at me.

"Sarah, run up to the Brighton station. You'll meet with a detective named Jim Olsen. He's expecting you."

"I've got to finish up on that shooting from last week," Spats said. "I'll do that while you're gone."

Ernie nodded. "I'll be catching up on a couple of things myself, but I want to know what you find out."

"As soon as I know it," I said.

I grabbed my keys and gave them a wave. Both had a look in their eyes, a buzz of excitement, knowing we might have something that would move our case forward. So many times we had pieces that would lead us to a killer, but we didn't know how to put it all together. I hoped we might find something soon that would get us closer.

"You think we might have the same man committing both murders?" Olsen asked me.

He was a big man, at least 6-4, with big hands that could palm a basketball, thick curly red hair, and a scar over his left eye that gave him a slightly sleepy look.

"It could be." I was sitting across from him in a small interview room at the Brighton Police Station. He'd gotten coffee for us, then led me into the room where we could talk in private. He handed me a paper cup of coffee. He had a manila file tucked under one arm, and he set it on the table. "It's actually better than you think," he said of the coffee. "Not the stereotypical police station crap you hear about in the movies."

I laughed. "This is just fine." I took a sip, then looked around. The walls were gray, the room cool, no noises filtering in. I looked at him over the cup. "Tell me about the murder. The paper said the killer got through an open bedroom window. Did he cut the screen?"

Olsen nodded. "That's right. Jane Lasley had left a window open in her family room at the back of the house. You know how hot it's been, and she didn't have air conditioning." He shrugged. "So you leave windows open. Anyway, the killer sliced an X in the screen and climbed in. This happened sometime after eleven p.m. because a neighbor thinks he saw a light still on in Jane's house around that time. She was raped and strangled. We're not sure how she was strangled. The killer may have used his hands." He gulped some coffee, set the cup down, and laced his fingers. "Jane was forty years old, and she worked as a computer systems analyst at CenturyLink. She went to a small college in Kansas, and from what her coworkers and friends say, she was pretty bright. Have you seen a picture of her?"

I nodded. "I found something online."

He gave an appalled wag of his head. "People put so much online. They have no idea how easy they make it for criminals."

"True," I said, then diverted away from a general discussion of social media. "Are you suspicious of something in her online activity?"

He shook his head. "Not so far, but we're checking on all that." He sipped more coffee. "Anyway, you saw what Jane looked like. Does she look like your victim?"

"Like we have a perp going after the same body type?" I shook my head. "No, Cherry Rubio was thirty-two, with dark hair and eyes." I described her in a little more detail.

"No, they don't sound alike at all."

"Did anyone see or hear anything the night of the murder?"

"Not a thing. Jane didn't have surveillance cameras, and neither did anyone around her. She went out to eat and on her way home, she talked to a friend for a while. That's the last anyone talked to her, that we know of."

"Who discovered her?"

He scratched his head, sending his curls askew. "The next-door neighbor. Jane had Friday off, and they were supposed to go out to lunch. When Jane didn't show, the neighbor came over. She has a key, and she let herself in. And she found Jane."

"That had to be grim."

He nodded. "Yeah, from what I hear, the neighbor is still really shook up."

I shifted on the uncomfortable seat. "Where was the body found? The paper didn't say."

"That's the interesting thing. She was on the bed, and it's like he posed her."

My gut tightened. "Let me guess. She was lying face up, covered by a sheet, but her arms were outside the sheet, lying at her sides."

He arched an eyebrow. "That's right. We found no physical evidence on or around her. It's the same as your case?"

"Yes," I said.

We stared at each other.

"It sounds like the same guy," Olsen said in a low voice. He swore under his breath.

I pushed back from my chair, feeling my muscles tighten. "Do you have any suspects?"

"Not so far. According to everyone who knew her, Jane wasn't dating anybody. She'd been with a guy for about a year, but that ended about six months ago. We tracked him down, and he's living in California. We had several people verify he was there the night of Jane's murder."

I grimaced. "So he's not a suspect."

"Not unless he can teleport back and forth. His alibi is rock-solid."

I thought for a moment. "Her family and friends can't think of anybody that would've wanted to hurt her?" I asked the question, but I was pretty sure I knew the answer.

He shook his head. "No one is aware of her having any issues with anybody, and it doesn't appear she was seeing somebody new. The autopsy was done the other day." He opened the file and showed me some pictures.

I scooted back up to the table and looked at an autopsy photo of Jane. Even in death, she was pretty, her face soft, her blonde hair cascading around her shoulders. I picked up one of the photos and studied the bruising on her neck.

"Whoever strangled her was pretty strong," he said. "A couple of bones in her neck were broken."

I stared at the picture some more, and he and I discussed the similarities in the crimes.

"No semen, correct?"

"No," he said. "It appears that the killer knew to wear a

condom, and we suspect he wiped down the body. He was thorough. We didn't find any hairs or clothing fibers that might lead us to him. Nothing."

"Did the ME say anything about whether the killer was right or left-handed?"

"He didn't say. It doesn't appear that she was drugged, but we'll have to wait for the toxicology report."

I looked at photos of Jane's bedroom. "And no fingerprints?"

"Only ones that made sense, like the victim's and her family."

"How did he leave?"

"Our best guess is through the back door. It was unlocked."

"That's what I think my guy did," I said. "You've already committed the crime, why bother going back out the window?"

"And why lock the door?"

"Exactly." I shuffled through more photos. "Was anything missing from the house?"

"Theft doesn't appear to be a motive. However, a ring that she wore a lot is unaccounted for. Her parents are trying to track it down."

"Tell me about the family."

"Both parents live here. They're devastated, of course. She's got two brothers, both live out of town. We've talked to several of her friends, and no one has been able to give us any clues so far."

"Has anyone mentioned Manny Guerrero or Rex Land?" I told him about both suspects.

He shook his head. "I haven't heard of either, but now that we have those names, we can circle back with her family and friends." He jotted the names on a piece of paper in the file.

"Did Jane have an interest in a new car? Did she like Corvettes?"

"Oh, Rex–the car salesman." He pursed his lips. "I don't think so, but again, we'll follow up on that."

I thought for a second. "I'd like to talk to her parents. I might pick up something that would help in my investigation, now that we may have the same guy doing both killings."

"Sure, I can give them a call. They're retired, so they'll probably be home. Especially after what's happened."

"How do you want to handle it? Do you want to go with me, or do you think if you show up a second time, the parents might get spooked?" Sometimes when a person is questioned again, a new detective will handle the interview, in case the person might feel threatened by a second interview and change their story.

"I trust the parents," Olsen said. "I don't think they're hiding anything from us."

"Good. Then why don't we go together?"

"Let me call them. Her father's not been handling this well. He was like a statue when I was at his house. Hardly said a word, and let the mother do all the talking." His chair scraped loudly against the tile floor as he stood up. I waited as he left the room, finished my lukewarm coffee, which wasn't bad, and then got up and paced. I stared at the walls, wondering, not for the first time, what a suspect being questioned might think about these tiny interview rooms. Olsen returned ten minutes later.

"I talked to Jane's mother. She'll talk to us now."

I nodded and followed him out the door.

CHAPTER TWENTY-ONE

"Jane could be a pain in the ass."

Olsen and I were sitting in the kitchen of a sprawling house in a sparsely populated area of Brighton. Across from us sat Francie Coulter, Jane's mother. She was plump, with short silver hair that framed her face well. Her eyes were a piercing green, her face weathered from years in the sun. She wore cowboy boots, Levi's, and a plaid shirt. A cowgirl at heart. She twisted her wedding ring with her right hand as she talked. She let out a small laugh at her comment.

"I know you're not supposed to say that about your own flesh and blood, but it was true." Her lips formed a thin line. "Don't get me wrong, I loved my daughter, but she and I could certainly clash." Whether she realized it or not, she was coming across as harsh.

Olsen glanced at me, and I took the lead talking to Francie.

"When was the last time you saw your daughter?" I asked.

She twisted the ring and mulled that over as she stared at an antique china hutch full of dishes and vases. "It must've been about a week ago, I guess. We aren't like some mothers and daughters who talk every day; it's probably about once a week." She looked out an open window to a large yard and garden. A bird was chirping loudly. The Rocky Mountains could be seen in the distance. "We just don't share that much. That last conversation was more of a fight." She choked up for a moment, thinking about it, then cleared her throat. "We were fighting about something that happened when she was in high school. She said I grounded her and didn't let her go to one of the school dances. It's a silly thing, isn't it?"

Sympathy for her washed over me. I wanted to reach out and take her hand, but resisted. "No, it's not. Sometimes things from the past can be very hard to let go."

She stared at me perceptively. "You've had some experience with that."

I was slow to answer, feeling vulnerable. "More than you know."

My openness seemed to soften her. "It's one of those things," she said, trying to dismiss the argument she'd had with Jane. "I kept telling her that's not the way it happened, and she kept insisting that I'd ruined her chances for dating a boy she was really interested in." She stopped with the ring and started tapping the table. "The silly thing is, she didn't end up with him anyway. She married a man named Wayne, but it didn't last long. She got divorced, and that was that." She put her hands on an oak table. "Now that I think about it, I don't even remember why we had started arguing about it, but we did, and I finally said I wasn't going to talk about it anymore, and that I'd see her Sunday for dinner. She always comes over for dinner on Sundays." Her mouth parted, but no words came.

"How is your husband doing?"

"Not good." She glanced toward a hallway behind her. When we had come in, she told us that her husband was sleeping, and she wasn't going to bother him. "We were at the funeral home this morning, and that totally took it out of him. Jane was his baby girl, and now she's gone."

"He had a hard time talking to us before," Olsen murmured.

"That's right," Francie agreed. "I don't know if he said two words. He's a wreck. The funeral is tomorrow."

"Do you know what your daughter did on Thursday night?" I asked.

"I didn't talk to her much, remember? We had to piece that together, with his help." She pointed at Olsen and didn't say more.

He stepped in. "From what we've been able to gather from one of Jane's friends, she went out to dinner that night. We're not sure where."

Francie nodded. "Yeah, I'm afraid I can't help you with that."

I raised an eyebrow at Olsen. "She ate alone?"

"Alone, or with someone we haven't talked to yet."

"Right." I turned back to Francie, kept my voice soft. "I heard she wasn't dating anyone at the moment."

"Right."

"You're sure she wasn't seeing someone?"

"Someone who could've done ... that ... to her? No." She closed her eyes, as if to blot out what had happened to her daughter.

"Was Jane interested in cars, specifically Corvettes?"

Deep, troubled lines furrowed her brow. "Not that I know of. She had a new Honda that she seemed to like. But Corvettes? I highly doubt that."

"Did she mention a man named Rex?" I described him.

She thought about that. "That name isn't one you hear every day. No, that doesn't sound familiar."

"What about Manny?" Another description from me.

"No, I hadn't heard her mention that name, either."

"It may not have been either of those men, but she was interested in somebody," a new voice said.

We turned in surprise to see a man I guessed to be in his early seventies approach. He was medium height and lean, all his weight going to a paunch. His arms were as tan as his face. He limped over to the table and sat down next to Francie.

"I thought you were resting," Francie said to him.

"I'm up." He reached across the table to shake my hand. "I'm Chuck."

Before I could say anything, Francie gave him a disapproving look. "How do you know who Jane might've been interested in?"

"She told me."

"When did she tell you this?"

"A week or so ago. She was going to go on a blind date."

Francie crossed her arms. "What else do you know?"

"More than you think," Chuck said. "Jane had a hard time talking to you." It was delivered matter-of-fact, with no malice.

Francie didn't take offense, just said, "I told them that."

"What do you know about this blind date?" I asked.

He adjusted a baseball cap and looked at me with eyes the color of pewter. "I don't know if she actually went on the date, but she was interested in some businessman. She said she'd met him on some online site, and they'd chatted online. She wanted to meet him in person. I told her she needed to be careful, that she should meet him in a public place and let me or her friends know where she was. You can't take chances."

"No, you can't," Francie said.

He frowned darkly. "Jane said I shouldn't worry, that the guy was nice, and that she knew to be careful." He stared past me, obviously knowing that hadn't been case.

"Did she describe him at all?" I asked.

"It's funny you ask that. She didn't want to say much about him, but I pushed her a little, so she described him, going overboard on the details for her 'nosy' dad. If I remember right, she said something about him being tall, with brown hair and eyes. A beautiful smile with white teeth. She teased me about him being devastatingly handsome." The last statement brought a little beam to his face. "She seemed happy." His voice faded.

"What else did she say about him?"

"Just that he drove an expensive car. She made some joke about him liking fast cars, that he talked about them a lot, and she said that if the date went well, she'd ask him for a ride."

I glanced at Olsen. His eyes were wide.

"What kind of car? A Corvette?"

"She didn't say."

I waited a moment. "Do you think this was the man last Thursday night?"

"If she did, she didn't tell me," he said. "Her style was to joke with me some, then tell me what happened after the fact. She knew I could be protective."

"You don't know of anyone who might've wanted to harm your daughter?"

Chuck shook his head. "No one. This whole thing isn't supposed to happen, you know?"

I nodded, but kept on with my train of thought. "Jane never mentioned that someone might be stalking her, or that she saw anyone around her house?"

"No."

I asked him if he'd heard of Rex or Manny, and he said no. I couldn't think of anything else to ask at the moment, so I looked at Olsen.

"We certainly thank you for taking the time to talk to us again," he said.

He and I stood up, and so did Francie. Chuck stayed seated, his hands resting on the table, shoulders sagged in defeat. Francie touched his arm, then led us to the door.

"If you need anything else, call," she said.

We thanked her and went outside. The air was dry and still, and heat waves danced off the asphalt drive.

Olsen donned sunglasses and looked at me. "What do you think?"

"She didn't know my two suspects by name, but that doesn't mean a lot," I said.

"What about that description the father gave about the man Jane was interested in?"

"It could fit Rex. It could also fit a lot of other men."

"That's the first I heard about the blind date," Olsen said as we got into his brown sedan. "Chuck hardly said a word when we first talked to them."

"He's had some time to adjust."

"I guess."

As we drove back to the station, he said, "We went through Jane's phone records, and I can't find any calls from someone we haven't been able to identify."

"Would you mind sending the list of numbers to me, and I'll see if any of them look familiar? And I'll send Cherry's to you, so we can cross-check to see if any are the same."

"Sure."

"Let's compare fingerprints as well."

"I'll share everything I have. I want to find this guy. And I may want to talk to the family and friends of your victim, too."

"Absolutely, just let me know, and I'll set something up."

As we drove back to the Brighton station, clouds thickened above us, dark and moody, and then a thunderstorm broke. Heavy rain poured down, then just as quickly stopped. By the time we got out of his car, the air smelled fresh. We stood in the parking lot for a minute.

"I'm going to be looking into this more," I said. "These two crimes fit the same M.O."

He nodded. "Yeah, I'll run some checks myself." He scratched his head. "I'm glad you gave me a call. I'd like to find this perp."

"Keep me posted, will you?" I asked.

He nodded. "I'll email you shortly. And you do the same."

I thanked him for his time and left.

CHAPTER TWENTY-TWO

I emailed Olsen my case notes when I returned to the station and hoped I'd hear from him soon. Ernie and Spats were both gone. Someone was fixing coffee in the break room, then it was quiet. I decided to hold off on talking to Rizzo until I did a little more research. It sure looked as if the two cases could be connected. But I wanted to see if I could find other similar crimes. I rubbed my eyes and stared at my monitor. I didn't want to think we had a serial killer on the loose.

I logged onto the computer and first went to the *Denver Post* site and began searching articles. I tried the word 'rape,' going back the last month. I first had so many hits that had nothing to do with rape, I wasn't sure what to do. I narrowed my search. No results. I expanded the search, going back two months. The results were still too vague and the articles didn't match my searches.

"What's the point of a search that doesn't work?" I said to no one.

I gave up on the newspaper site and searched the internet. In bypassing the *Post* site directly, I finally found an article in the paper about a woman who had reported being sexually assaulted in an alley outside a bar in downtown Littleton. That didn't fit the pattern of our killer. I continued, trying various words and phrases, and finally I was rewarded. Two months ago, a woman named Chelsea Baird had been assaulted and murdered in her home in Southwest Denver. The article was scant on details, and the police hadn't found her killer. A boyfriend had been suspected, but they'd eliminated him from the list.

A little more internet research gave me more information, but now it was conflicting. One local nightly news channel said Baird was twenty-four. Another channel reported her as late thirties. She was possibly a manager at a call center, or she was an analyst. She was discovered either by a friend or by a relative. I finally found that the killer had entered the house through an open window. I did a little fist pump. Maybe I was onto something.

I googled Baird to find her address, then got sidetracked on her social media sites. I found a picture of her. She had a round face, long chocolate-brown hair, and stark blue eyes. Her smile seemed warm and genuine. She had a lot of friends on Facebook, a lot of followers on Instagram. She tended to post pictures of her dogs and her hikes in the mountains. Realizing I had work to do, I turned back to her address and found that it was in Jefferson County. After several phone calls, I finally figured out the right department and the right homicide detective–Brady Thompson–that had worked the case. I called the department, but he wasn't there, so I left a message for him to call me.

I hadn't dealt with serial killers in my career, but I had learned about them in college. That was longer ago than I cared to admit, so while I waited for Thompson to call me back, I spent some time reading about serial killers. More than eighty percent are male, and they tend to be Caucasian and under forty years old. They're intelligent, and they can be social or non-social. It was all stuff I'd heard before. I thought about killing patterns.

Two women that had been murdered in the same way, their bodies left positioned in the same way. The killer had entered the houses in the same way, and cut the window screens in exactly the same way. It could have been coincidence, but I wasn't buying it.

I got a cup of coffee and searched the internet for a while longer, but I couldn't find any evidence of another rape and murder similar to Cherry's and Jane's. I closed my eyes and let my mind wander, hoping for some revelation. Someone was typing in another room, and I heard a soda can drop from a vending machine down the hall. No revelations, however. After a while, my desk phone rang.

"This is Detective Thompson." His voice was low and gruff. I introduce myself, and he said, "You mentioned some questions about Chelsea Baird. What would you like to know?"

"I understand you're the lead detective on that case?"

He growled. "Yeah, that's true. Chaps my hide that whoever did that to her got away. She was only twenty-two, barely out of college."

I finally had Baird's age. I wondered what else the news sites had gotten wrong. "What exactly happened?"

"She came home from work that night–a neighbor saw her getting her mail–and that same neighbor saw her leave again. From what we've gathered, she went out to eat, then came home. She was apparently sleeping in her bed, although I don't know that for sure because as far as we can tell, she was home alone. The killer came through an open window. He raped her, strangled her, and left her on the bed."

"Did he position the body a certain way?"

He hesitated. "As a matter of fact, yes. Baird was lying face-up, covered with a sheet, her arms outside the covers."

"At her sides."

"Yes. He positioned her that way."

My nerves tingled. "You said he came through a window?"

"He cut the screen in an X pattern, probably with a knife. He slipped in, did his business, and left."

I swore under my breath.

"What's this about? Is it this guy operating again?"

I nodded as if he could see me. "It looks like it. This is now the third one." I told him about Cherry and Jane. Then it was his turn to swear.

"That sure fits a pattern," he said.

"Did you find any DNA evidence, anything that might point to who did it?" I asked.

"No. This man was good. I didn't find anything at all at the crime scene. The only suspect we considered was her ex-boyfriend. However, we checked him out thoroughly. He was seen at a bar late the night she was killed, and we have surveillance footage showing him coming home around two a.m. He couldn't have gone over to her house, raped and murdered her, and got back to his apartment within that timeframe. I looked at him really carefully, and I'm confident it wasn't him."

"She lived in a house?"

"Her older brother owns the place, and she rented a room. He was out of town, so she was alone."

"Was anything taken from the house?"

"No. That wasn't a burglary. You want to know if something personal of hers was taken, a memento for the killer. There was, but right at the moment I can't remember what. Hold on a second." The phone clattered down, then papers rustled. He came back on the line. "Yes. Her parents and brother said she had a little anklet thing that she wore a lot. It had a tiny garnet in it, her birthstone. That's missing. They thought that was strange, as she tended to wear it a lot."

"Did you find any fingerprints at the scene that you couldn't explain?"

"No, we didn't. I would love to say I had more to give you, but I don't." He exhaled loudly. "Tell me about your case."

I filled him in about Cherry Rubio's death, and then how Ernie had discovered Jane Lasley's murder from the news.

"I hadn't heard about that one," he said. "But I'm working on an investigation now that has me going twenty-four-seven. I'm sure I would've heard about it eventually, but if we've got a serial killer on the loose, we need to get on it now."

I thought for a second. "It's summertime, and the nights have been hot. He's going into houses where they're leaving the windows open. I wonder if he operates in the winter."

"That'd be interesting."

"I'm going to do some research on that," I said. "One final thing. Did anyone you interviewed mention the names Rex Land or Manny Guerrero?"

"Not that I recall. I'll go back through my notes, though, and if I see those names, I'll let you know."

"Thanks."

Thompson and I agreed to exchange information on our cases, and share anything new when we had it, and I hung up. Ernie strolled in with a paper bag from Wendy's.

"How'd it go?" he asked as he sat down and dived into his hamburger.

I filled him in on my talk with Olsen and our interview with the Coulters as I checked my email. "Olsen just sent some case notes on Jane Lasley's murder, and her phone records. I need to go through them."

"I can help," he said as he wiped ketchup from the corner of his mouth.

I then told him about my conversation with Thompson. "Three murders done in the same way. Does that make sense?" I asked. "Is this coincidence?"

"Do you believe in coincidences?"

Before I could answer, Spats came in with a sandwich from a deli across the street.

"Did no one think to ask me if I wanted lunch?" I asked.

They exchanged a glance, then laughed.

"Didn't know where you were," Ernie said through a bite of hamburger.

"Sorry," Spats mumbled, then, "Are you going to tell me how it went with that detective in Brighton?"

I repeated what I'd learned. "There's more." They both stared at me expectantly, and I told them about my conversation with Detective Thompson.

"Three murders with the same MO?" Spats asked.

"Yes," I said. "Over the course of a few months."

Ernie wiped his hands with a napkin, his face grim. "We need to tell Rizzo."

I nodded. Spats put down his sandwich, and we went to Rizzo's office. He was reading a file when I tapped on his door. He motioned for us to come in. His office was what you'd expect, with awards and pictures of him with local dignitaries. One wall was a window, so he could look out to the corps of detectives, but with blinds in case he wanted privacy.

"How did your visit to Brighton go?" he asked.

Ernie and I took seats across from his desk, and Spats stood nearby. I laid out all I had learned for a third time. It was sounding less crazy.

"A serial killer?" Rizzo looked understandably concerned.

"It could be," I said, not quite sure I wanted to commit to that.

Rizzo glanced at Ernie and Spats for their input.

"It's looking that way," Spats said. "We need to put in more legwork to know for sure."

Ernie nodded agreement. "Go back over everything, see if we missed something."

Rizzo picked up a white stone paperweight as he mulled over what we'd discovered. The room had a faint pine smell from an air freshener in the corner. "You'll contact other departments in the state to see if they have any murders that fit this pattern?" He framed the request as a question, giving me leeway in the investigation.

"I thought we'd start there," I said.

"Let me know what you find," he said. "If we have an active killer on the loose, we may need more help."

He held up a hand, his way of dismissing us. He'd give us latitude to reach out to other departments, but I also knew that he was concerned. As we all were. If we didn't find this man, how many more women would die?

CHAPTER TWENTY-THREE

He stared at the picture. The detective was pretty, he thought. Not stunning. Her shoulder-length blond hair framed her face well. He couldn't tell for sure what color her eyes were, but he imagined them brown. The picture wasn't terribly flattering, what with the detective being in her uniform, but she was still attractive. "Lead Homicide Detective Sarah Spillman ..." he read from an article in the paper.

"Sarah Spillman," he said to himself. The name had a nice ring to it. He wondered what she was like in person.

He read the article again, savored the scant details. It talked about the rape and murder of Cherry Rubio, a thirty-two year old woman who had been home alone. He hadn't known her name until he read it. It made sense though, he thought, as he fiddled with the bracelet with the cherries on it. He looked at the picture of the detective again. She would be nice to have. He thought about that. Could he afford that risk?

The urge ran through him, a burning sensation. It was coming way too fast. He wasn't able to control it as he once could. Usually he could work in the summer months, when it was warm. He'd get a few women, and it satiated him through a long cold winter when it was much harder to break into homes. Then this last winter he'd assaulted a woman in an alley and gotten away with it. It was dangerous, though. He couldn't help it. He couldn't control himself. Now that it was summer, he could act more freely again. But the impulse was starting to take over.

He stared at the article again and focused on the detective, her years of service, how she was well-respected. The police were saying they would catch the killer for sure. He smiled, amused, and then he grew angry. Did they actually think they were smarter than he was? How did they think they would catch him?

He stared at the picture of the detective. Spillman. She would regret the day that she thought she was better at this than he was.

CHAPTER TWENTY-FOUR

When we got back to our desks, we first started with contacting other departments, each of us tackling a different part of the state. I took the counties in the Denver metro area, and in Colorado Springs, a sprawling city of half a million people sixty miles south of Denver. Ernie tackled northern counties that included Fort Collins and Boulder, both college towns, both good areas for a serial rapist and murderer to operate. Spats took Pueblo, a much smaller city in the southern part of the state, and counties surrounding it. I drafted an email that detailed the specifics of our case, that we had encountered two other murders with similar crime patterns, and we suspected there was a serial rapist and killer operating in the area. I detailed the MO of the assailant's entrance through an open window by cutting the screen in an X pattern, the victims being positioned on their bed, and the absence of any semen, indicating that the assailant may have used a condom. While I did that, Spats and Ernie got the contact information for the departments they would be emailing.

"Take a look at this," I said when I finished the email.

Ernie rolled his chair over and looked at my monitor. His eyes scanned the screen, and then he said, "That sounds good."

"I'll send it to both of you, then let's see what we get."

"I hope it leads to something," Spats said. "If this guy is still out there, when will he strike again?"

Ernie and I didn't want to answer that. Time was slipping away.

Ernie grunted as he rolled himself back to his desk. Each of us has a lot of contacts in the different departments throughout the metro area and even across the state. We put our network to work and sent out emails to all the respective chiefs in the departments we were contacting. Once we did that, it was a waiting game, one we hoped wouldn't result in more victims.

"I'm going to revisit some of Cherry's friends," Ernie said. "Maybe some of them might know Jane. There could be a connection between the two victims that we're missing." He reached for his cigar butt, realized it wasn't there, and swore. I grinned, but suppressed a laugh. I knew this was hard on him to be without his cigar. He pushed away from his chair. "Well, if I'm flatfooting around town, I won't be thinking about my damn cigars."

Without saying anything more, he stalked out the door.

"I'm going over the file from Olsen on Jane Lasley's murder, including her phone records," I said to Spats.

"I need to do a little paperwork, and then I'll compare them to Cherry's," he offered.

I didn't argue. "Sending them to you now." I emailed him the records, reviewed Olsen's case notes, then got on the internet and tried more searches on rapes and murders, using the MO we had for Cherry. This time I didn't limit it to the Denver metro area. I wasn't very long into it when my cell phone rang. I had hoped it would be Harry, but then I realized he wouldn't be calling in the middle of the day. I didn't recognize the number, but I answered anyway, thinking it might be a detective from one of the counties we'd emailed. Spats glanced at me.

"Spillman," I said.

"Well, that's quite the greeting."

I couldn't quite place the voice. It was vaguely familiar. "Yes?" I said.

"I said I'd give you a call."

It dawned on me who was on the other end of the line. "Darren?"

"That's right. How are you doing today?"

I felt heat at my temples as anger rose in me. "Why are you calling me?"

"I told you, I said I would call," he repeated. "I hear Harry's out of town. How'd you like to have dinner with me?"

"How did you get my number?"

"Trade secret," he said evasively. "I've been thinking about you. I'll bet you've been thinking about me."

"Darren, this is not a good time. I told you–"

"Wouldn't dinner be nice?" he interrupted.

I gritted my teeth. "Darren, I do not want to go out with you, and I do not want you to call me again. You understand?"

"Just a friendly dinner. I know you think there isn't anything between us, but I don't buy it. What do you say?"

I swore under my breath, not worrying that he was a business associate of Harry's. I needed Darren off my back. "Don't call me again." I ended the call and looked up.

Spats stared at me, humor in his eyes. "What was that all about?"

I rolled my eyes. "I have somebody who just won't leave me alone." His mouth twitched, holding back an amused smile. "I feel like I'm in high school again," I muttered.

He chuckled, and we continued to work. I went through the information Olsen had shared about Jane's death. The MO matched what I had on Cherry Rubio. After a while, I realized I was hungry so I got some lunch. Later, Ernie called to say that so far, he hadn't found a connection between Cherry Rubio and Jane Lasley. Spats didn't find any common phone numbers between the two victims, either. My mind wandered to my upcoming dinner with Diane. I needed to talk to her about our past, which wasn't going to be fun. Not only that, she and I didn't have a lot in common. I got along much better with my younger brother, Hunter. He thinks Diane can be a pain too, which elevates his status in my book. I felt myself growing edgy. I was working on my computer when my desk phone rang.

"Spillman."

"This is Detective Walker from the Colorado Springs Police Department." His voice was high, a bit nasal, but friendly as well. "I got your email about a possible serial rapist and killer."

My heart skipped with dread and excitement. "Yes, thanks for getting back to me."

"I've got an interesting case for you," he said.

I signaled Spats to come over to my desk, and I put the phone on speaker. "I've got you on speaker with my partner. You have something similar?"

"Unfortunately I do." Spats and I grimaced at each other. "I had a murder last summer that fits your pattern. The killer entered through an open window, and he cut the screen in an X pattern. Everything you say about your victim matches mine."

"The way she was positioned on the bed, covered in a sheet? No semen found?"

"Yep, the exact same thing."

"Tell me about the victim."

"Tracy Henle. She was murdered July fourteenth, in the middle of the night, near as we could tell. She was twenty-nine, worked at a government office, and was renting a small house on the west side of town. She seemed well-liked by her coworkers and had several friends who said she could party a bit, but she was careful in who she dated, and careful with her online activity. We didn't find any indication of anyone stalking her online or in person."

I was jotting down notes as fast as he talked. "What did she look like?"

Spats reached past me and typed on my laptop. He googled the name, then nudged me to look at the screen.

"She had short reddish brown hair, with blue eyes," Walker said. "She was a tad chubby. Cute."

As he said it, I looked at a picture Spats had found. I agreed, Tracy was cute, with wide eyes, a small nose, and an engaging smile. "Fun" seemed to fit her.

"Did you have any leads?" I asked.

"No, we didn't. At first we thought it might have been a neighbor down the street. This man was very interested in her, he'd even kind of stalked her. He didn't have an alibi, and he was pretty evasive when we questioned him. In the long run, we couldn't pin anything on him, and then he moved out of town."

My ears piqued at that. "Where did he move to?"

He gave a little laugh. "I know what you're thinking, did he come up to Denver? No, he actually moved to Santa Fe, and he was killed a few months later in a car crash. So he can't be your guy."

I went from elation to disappointment in a split second. Spats frowned. I thought for a moment. "What did the victim do the night she was killed?"

"She went to dinner with some friends, then they went to a nightclub. She came home alone, and the next day she was supposed to go to her parents' house for dinner. When she didn't show, they went over to her house and found her."

"Ugh," Spats whispered. "Finding your kid like that ..."

I nodded, then continued with Walker. "Did the friends

notice anyone that evening who might've taken an interest in Tracy and then followed her home?"

"No, they didn't. They said it was a night out just like any other."

"With your victim, was anything stolen from the home?"

"She had a gold necklace that she liked to wear. Her friends said she almost always had it on. That's missing." He sneezed, then excused himself. "So what made you contact us? Have you found more victims other than the one you're were investigating?"

"Yes, we have." I explained about my investigation and how it had expanded.

He swore. "I wonder how many victims are out there."

"No kidding. Any physical evidence at this crime scene?" I asked.

"We found some cloth fibers on the sheets, turns out they came from a popular blue jean brand. We haven't been able to trace it back to anybody. There were some skin particles under one of her nails, but a DNA check didn't bring up anything." He swore. "DNA is great, if you have a match. But if your killer hasn't committed a crime before, if there's no reason he's in the system, we won't find him."

I nodded as if he could see me. "Yes, that's so true. I've run into that before. We found some skin under one of our victim's fingernails, but it didn't lead anywhere."

"If you find this guy, that'll help convict him. But until then ..." His voice trailed off.

I thanked him for his time, told him I would probably be calling with more questions, and that I would keep him in the loop. He agreed and said he would send me the autopsy results and photos, and his crime scene and interview notes. I agreed to do the same. I ended the call and set down my pen.

"Not good," Spats said. "We've got a killer on the loose, and no way to find him."

I nodded slowly. "What if it's Rex or Manny?" I emailed Thompson the information I promised, then studied my notes. "I'd love to find out what they were doing the nights of these other murders."

"Right, but how are they going to remember a date last summer?" He peered at my notes. "Do you know what you were doing July fourteenth last year?"

"No, but if I were the killer I might. It'd be interesting to ask them, and see how they respond."

"Land might talk to me, but I doubt Guerrero will."

"Try him anyway." My desk phone rang again and I picked it up with my usual greeting. "Spillman."

"Hey, this is Jim Olsen."

I sat up straighter. "How are you?" Spats looked at me.

I could hear in Olsen's voice, that he hadn't found anything. "I've been going through the notes you sent me, and I don't see any personal connection between our two victims, just the same M.O. of the crime itself."

"I'm afraid I've come up with nothing, either. And I've got more to tell you." I launched into everything that I had discovered since talking to him about Jane Lasley, and by the time I finished, he swore quietly.

"This is bad. We're at a dead end, but it still seems like the same guy, the same M.O."

"Yes," I said. "I'm waiting to hear more from other departments in the state. I'll let you know if we find more victims."

"Thanks," he said. "I'll do the same."

I put down the receiver and said to Spats, "Olsen doesn't have any leads at this point."

"I gathered as much."

I craned my neck to look toward Rizzo's office. "He's not there. We need to update him on all this."

Before Spats could reply, his phone rang and he hurried to his desk to answer. He listened for a second, then said, "Oh yeah? Hold on." He put his hand over the receiver. "Manny Guerrero left work and went by Cherry Rubio's house. He walked around back and watched the house from the alley for about ten minutes, and then he went back to work."

CHAPTER TWENTY-FIVE

I stood up and put my hands on my hips. "What was he doing at Cherry's house?"

"Good question. The move of an innocent man?"

I tapped my hand on the desk and mulled over what to do. "Let's go talk to him. We present a united front again, and maybe we can keep him from lawyering up."

Spats leaned back in his chair, laced his hands behind his head. "What about your dinner with Diane?"

I glanced at my watch. "If we don't take too long with Manny, I'll still have plenty of time to get to the restaurant." He cocked an eyebrow at me. "I'll make it," I said.

He smiled and stood up. "Let's go."

I drove and fought traffic to get to A-plus Auto Repair. My mind was half on dinner with Diane, and I had to keep focusing on the investigation. Wisps of white clouds were high in the sky when we walked in the repair shop. Manny and another employee were talking behind the counter as they looked at the monitor. The garage was as noisy as ever, the air gun going full blast. Manny looked up and froze.

"We need to talk," I said to him.

He glanced uneasily over the counter at a couple sitting in the corner. They were watching a noisy video on the man's phone, and were oblivious to us. Guerrero stared at his coworker, then without another word, stood up and gestured for us to follow him into the back office where we'd talked before.

He opened the door and stepped aside for us. A vein in his neck throbbed. He followed us in, and the door closed with a bang. Before Spats and I even made eye contact, Guerrero said, "What's this about? This is harassment."

I signaled Spats to take bad cop and start the conversation. "You have some explaining to do," Spats said to him. As he had done before, he leaned against the door casually, this time crossing one foot over the other at the ankle.

"I told you I'd only talk with a lawyer present," Guerrero snapped.

Spats called his bluff by pointing at the phone on the desk. "Call him. We'll go down to the station and we can hash this all out. Should be a piece of cake."

People are always telling us they'll "call their lawyer," but how many people actually have one, especially one that will drop everything when called and come to the rescue? Guerrero seemed to be in that second category. He put his hands on the desk, leaned forward, and locked eyes with Spats. They remained that way for a long, uncomfortable moment. Then Guerrero looked at me. I gazed back, my expression saying the next play was his.

He finally spoke. "You're harassing me." He crossed his arms defiantly.

"All we're trying to do is find out what happened to Cherry Rubio," Spats said.

The vein in Guerrero's neck pulsed. "I told you I don't know."

Spats shot me a look. It was my turn.

"You were at Cherry's house today, right after lunch." I stared at him, daring him to lie.

His lower jaw worked as he tried to form an answer. His lips parted, then closed twice. It seemed anything he settled on was wrong. The insolence waned. "How do you know that?" he asked. "Are you following me?"

"Why were you over there?" I asked.

"That's none of your business," he said.

I nodded slowly, as if I were thinking that over. "The thing is, it is my business when there's a murder victim involved. You say you didn't kill Cherry–"

"I didn't," he interrupted.

"Then help me find who did," I went on. "You're not leveling with us. It sure makes it hard to believe you, when I know you're not telling the truth."

In the time it took him to decide to answer, I could've counted to ten. He bit his lip, looked at the floor, then behind us. His gaze finally rested on Spats.

"I know how this goes. I'm a suspect. I can't talk because I don't want you to think I did anything," he said quietly.

I matched his tone. "You saw Cherry the night she was killed. Right?"

He stared at the floor and after another long moment, nodded. "After we broke up, some of my stuff was still at her house. I didn't care about the shirts, but there was a baseball cap that I got when I was in Florida. I wanted that back and I never got it from her. I think she knew it was my favorite, and she wouldn't return it. I finally went over that night and caught up with her outside. And yeah, we were arguing. It made me furious that she wouldn't give the cap back, okay?" He looked up at me, pleading in his eyes. "And that's where I went today. I figured maybe you guys saw it there, and you might think I was lying about us breaking up."

"You think we'd be worried about your stuff there?" I asked.

He threw up a hand. "I don't know. I just knew from the minute you walked in here the other day, and with my history, that you'd suspect me."

"We knew you'd seen Cherry. A neighbor saw you arguing with her."

"Yeah I saw the guy. And when you came in here, questioning me, I knew you wouldn't believe me, so I shut up."

"You're really not doing anything to make yourself look less guilty."

"What was I supposed to do?" he complained.

I raised an eyebrow at Spats. Time for him to take over.

"So what, you went over to her house today to break in? You think that would make you look less guilty?"

Anger flashed in his eyes, and then Guerrero said, "I don't know. I haven't been thinking too good since Cherry died. I know you don't believe me, but I really did love her."

"I heard that you hit her," Spat said.

"Only once. I didn't mean to." His eyes were sad. "It's true. We were arguing and it got out of hand. It wasn't my fault, and I only did it the once."

Spats glanced at me. I wasn't sure either of us believed Guerrero.

"When you were arguing with Cherry, you said something about 'not this time.' What does that mean?"

"She was trying to go into the house without talking to me, and I said 'not this time.' " It was a quick answer, not as if he was lying.

"Where were you the night she was killed?" Spats asked.

"With someone else."

Spats stepped forward, anger in his tone. "Who? You want us to believe you're innocent, tell me who."

Guerrero backed up, even though the desk was between him and Spats. "I was with a married woman, okay? What happens if I tell you who?"

"We can be discreet in talking to her," Spats said.

Guerrero thought long and hard about that. Muffled voices came from the other room, and he stared at the door. He had to get back to work. "Her name is Yolanda Ortiz," he said. He pulled out his phone and looked up the number, then reached around the desk and jotted down the name and number on a piece of paper. His hand shook slightly. He tore it from the pad and handed it to Spats.

Spats took the paper, folded it in half, and tucked it into his jacket pocket. "We'll check on that."

"I'll even take a lie detector test, if you want me to," Guerrero said.

Spats turned to me with a shrug.

"I'll let you know if we think that's necessary," I said to Guerrero. "You should know though, they aren't that reliable."

Guerrero nodded. "Look, I already gave you the name of the lady I was with. You gotta believe me, I didn't do anything to Cherry. I was mad at her for keeping my cap, but that was it. Check my alibi."

"What else can you tell us about that night?"

"Nothing. After we talked, I went home."

"What do you know about Rex?" I asked.

He thought. "One night after we broke up, I called Cherry about my cap. She said she didn't have time to talk, that she was going out, and I heard her mention the name Rex to somebody in the background. So I knew she'd moved on. I don't know anything about him, just his name."

"You didn't see him around when you were there the night she was murdered?" I pressed.

He shook his head. "I don't know. There was somebody around that night. A car drove away and some guy was in it. I don't know who it was."

"What'd he look like?"

"Dark hair, maybe. I told you, I don't know."

"What else did Cherry tell you that night?" I narrowed my eyes, letting him know that the good-cop act was growing thin for me.

"Nothing, I swear. She said she'd gone out to eat and that she was tired, and she asked me to leave her alone. I got mad, and said she had my cap. She told me to go to hell, and that was it."

"You don't know anything else?"

He shook his head. "I know, I should've told you all this before. What can I say, I was scared."

Spats looked to me. I knew he was thinking the same thing: we'd gotten what we were going to get from Guerrero. It was time to go.

Spats put his hand on the doorknob. "We'll check that alibi."

Guerrero looked at him. "It's good." Then he added, "Don't let her husband know. Please."

Spats opened the door without another word, and I followed him out. We walked in silence to my car. Then he spoke.

"What do you think?"

I sat for a moment, my hand on the steering wheel. "I'll believe him after we check his alibi."

"I'll get on that."

"And see about a warrant for GPS monitoring of his and Rex Land's cars. We can't keep tying up all our resources for surveillance, but I'm still suspicious of both."

He straightened his tie. "I'll get cracking on that, set up the surveillance, and get a detective to monitor their activity from a computer."

I started the Escape and put it into gear. "The pieces aren't falling into place. What are we missing?"

He stared out the window. "I don't know."

CHAPTER TWENTY-SIX

Diane flew into the restaurant with a self-important flourish, as if hoping people would notice her. And they did. Even as I raised a hand in a small wave, she was asking the hostess where I was. And knowing Diane, she was probably somehow letting everyone around her know she was a doctor. She'd once told me that she'd worked hard for that title, and she might as well get all the perks that come with it, which included, apparently, preferential seating and no waiting at restaurants. She didn't need to worry about those things tonight, but I'm sure that didn't stop her.

It was six o'clock on Monday night, and the restaurant was packed. I'd dropped Spats off at the station, and then had plenty of time to get to the restaurant. I'd arrived a little early and sat at the bar while I waited for a table. I'd sipped a soda and tried to focus my mind. The room smelled of spices, the air full of conversation. I was searching for positivity and not finding much. That happened frequently when I was dealing with my sister. When a table was ready, I'd sat down. The change of scenery hadn't helped my mood.

Now the hostess pointed in my direction. Even so, Diane

made a big deal of scanning the dining area before she saw me. I waved again. She swooped in with a smile.

"Sarah," she said as she took a seat across from me. "I'm sorry I'm late, I got tied up at the office." Diane is a family doctor, with a thriving practice that keeps her busy, along with time for golf and travel with her husband and kids.

"Fifteen minutes," I said, unable to resist the not-so-subtle jab.

If she heard it, she ignored it. She put her designer purse on the chair next to her, primped her blond hair, fiddled with a metal earring of a feather, and looked all around. "I desperately need a drink. It's been one of those days. Where's the waiter?"

I suddenly felt the need for a drink as well. "He stopped by a minute ago, and I told him to come back. For the moment, I was just having water."

"Sure, sure," she said with a fluttery wave of the hand. "Where is that waiter?"

I saw our waiter, a wiry man in his mid-twenties, standing near the kitchen. I signaled him quickly so that he would get our drinks before Diane exploded.

He walked over, glanced at each of us, and said pleasantly, "Would you like drinks?" He also handed us menus and told us the specials. "May I suggest our margaritas? They're famous around town and–"

"No. I'd like a gin and tonic," Diane said in a rush. "And don't be chintzy with the gin."

He nodded, a little taken aback by her brusqueness, and looked at me.

"I'll have a martini," I said.

"How about a blueberry martini?" he suggested. "They're on special, and they're fantastic."

"No thanks," I said. "Just a regular martini."

"Of course." He nodded politely. "Could I see your IDs please?"

Diane laughed. "Oh, you're trying for a big tip. Trying to make me feel younger than I am."

"We card everybody," the waiter said with a careful smile, as if he wasn't sure how to take Diane. She handed him her ID, and he looked at it for a moment, then back at Diane. The smile remained as he handed it back. "Thank you." He turned to me, his smile frozen on his face.

I handed him my ID, he scrutinized it for a moment, and gave it back. "Thank you. I'll give you a few minutes to peruse the menu." He tipped his head and walked away.

Diane grabbed her menu and opened it. "What's good here?"

"When Harry and I come here, I like to order the fajitas."

She dismissed that and said, "I think I'll try the chimichanga. I'm really not in the mood for Mexican tonight."

"Good choice," I muttered. I decided on my usual fajitas and closed my menu.

Diane put hers down as well. "So." She looked at me expectantly. "How have you been?" There was a subtle little tone in the question and I wondered if she thought I wasn't keeping in touch enough.

"It's been busy. I'm working on a new case."

"Oh, what's happened now?"

She had asked the question, but it was perfunctory. I pictured Harry sitting across from me. He'd listen while I discussed a case. He didn't have to say anything, it was just nice to have his ear. Harry is a treasure, I thought to myself. I needed to resolve things, both with her and with him.

"A rape and murder."

She threw me a palm. "I don't want the gory details."

"I'll spare you, just promise me you'll keep your windows shut."

"That's how the killer is entering houses?"

I nodded. "Yes, and–"

"Don't worry about me."

I got the hint to move on. "How are Tim and Max?" I asked about my nephews.

The waiter returned with our drinks, and we ordered. He had barely left before Diane took a satisfying gulp of her drink and put down her glass.

"They're both fine," she said. "Can you believe Tim will be in fifth grade, and Max in third? Time flies. He and Max will both be in soccer again this fall. I hope you'll come to some games."

"I'll certainly try."

She looked at a TV screen in the bar. A Rockies game was on. I couldn't see the score. "Max may switch from soccer to baseball. He really likes the Rockies."

"Harry and I could take them to a game."

"They'd enjoy that."

I love my nephews and have a good relationship with them, and Harry loves them as well. He's good with kids, and he likes sports, so he and the boys have a lot in common.

"They left for their camping trip this morning." She sighed. "I'll miss them, but I'm looking forward to some time in the house alone."

"You don't have any plans?"

She shook her head. "Other than dinner with you, I'm staying home. I've got some things to catch up on, and I want to relax in front of the TV with no distractions."

"That sounds nice."

"A week of that will be blissful."

She took another drink and rested her chin on her hands. I got that expectant look again. I could only put things off for so long. It still took me a minute to begin the talk I wanted to have with her. Even though I'd been thinking about how to approach her, now that the time was here, I wasn't exactly sure what to say. I took a drink and launched into the conversation.

"Do you remember when we were back in college? I was a sophomore and you were in med school?"

She sucked in a breath through her teeth. "Not this again. I know exactly what you're going to say."

"What you mean, not again? I barely bring it up."

She gave a small shake of her head. "It's just like with Uncle Brad, you blame me for things that are not my fault."

"Not your fault?" I said it louder than I meant to. "The way you treated me when he died ..."

"Please. I thought this was in the past. It is for me."

I looked around. A couple at another table glanced at me, and our waiter was standing near the kitchen, staring at us. I leaned forward and lowered my voice. "Diane, I helped you with something that was illegal, and it could've cost me my career."

"You hadn't even started a career."

"That's not the point. I might never have been able to become a police officer if what I had done had been discovered." The waiter was still eyeing us, so I spoke in an even quieter tone.

She stared at me, her expression saying this was old territory. I again thought of Harry, and steeled my nerves.

"Will you just listen to me for a minute, please?" I begged her.

She sipped her drink dramatically and put down the glass. "If we can get this resolved, once and for all, fine. I'll listen."

"You needed my help," I began. "If you recall, *you* had broken the law."

"What?" She was oblivious to her previous behavior.

"Why do you act as if you didn't do anything? You stole medication from the hospital where you were interning. You could've gotten in big trouble, remember?"

"It wasn't as bad as that," she said, a note of challenge in her voice. "You make so much of everything, just like you did with Uncle Brad's death. You're always blaming me."

I'd heard that before. I ignored the jab and continued. "I don't blame you. You just didn't understand how I felt about Uncle Brad."

"Not this again." Another drink.

I pictured Harry and moved on from Uncle Brad. That was a talk for another time. I'd come here to address the incident in college. "Nevertheless, I helped you cover up not only stealing the meds, but that whole night, everything you'd done, and you've never realized that in doing that, I could've gotten into a lot of trouble."

"But you didn't," she said pointedly.

"I–" I stopped as the waiter brought us our food.

He put Diane's chimichanga in front of her, and set down my fajitas. Then he smiled with a hint of hesitation. I wondered if he could sense the tension sizzling across the table between Diane and me.

"Is everything okay?" he asked.

Diane held up a palm. "We're just fine, thank you." Her tone was contemptuous.

He tipped his head and said, "I'll be back in a minute to check on things."

Diane dug into her chimichanga, took a bite, and nodded satisfactorily. "Oh, this is delicious."

It was as if everything I'd been saying to her had no meaning. Old territory for her, and it didn't matter.

"How are your fajitas?" She said as she pointed at my plate with her fork. I took a bite to placate her and continued the conversation.

"I broke the law for you," I repeated. She began to protest, and I held up a hand. "Let me finish." She looked at me, slightly irritated, but she ate and listened. At least I hoped she was listening. "If you remember, you came to me for help, so I went to the hiking trail, and ..." I thought about that time and didn't want to put it all into words. I'm still embarrassed by what I did. A wrong choice. So stupid. I could blame it on being young, on desperately wanting my sister's approval. Regardless, I wish I could undo all of it.

"Well, go on," she snapped.

"I covered things for you, and when I went back to my car, another car was at the entrance. They could've seen me, my car, my license plate. I never knew if someone was going to report me."

"Surely you don't think anybody cares about that now?"

I thought about that. "I don't know. Probably not. Anyway, I've carried that fear around for a long time. I've also carried around a lot of anger toward you, for never really comprehending what I did, how serious it was, and for never appreciating it."

She put her fork down with a clink. "Is that what this is about? I didn't appreciate what you did enough?"

I stared at her and nodded.

"Well, if that's what it takes for you to put the past in the past and start being a little kinder, then I'm sorry." She sighed melodramatically. "I appreciate what you did. Even though I probably never would've gotten into trouble in the first place. And, as you should recall, I was a little drunk that night when I was in the park. I was *definitely* drunk by the time you came back to my apartment, and I did thank you. And neither one of us got in trouble, so we should have been able to move on."

Part of me wanted to slap the smug look off her face, but another part realized the futility of it. Diane was Diane, and I couldn't do anything about it. Just like she couldn't change me. I had to look at myself. I contemplated her for a moment and realized something I should have a long time ago. All the anger I harbored against her wasn't hurting her, it was only hurting me.

Harry was right. I felt a tad better, even though my talk with Diane was mostly one-sided. I was still going to need to work on letting the anger go. Diane wasn't going to change. I needed to, and that was going to be hard to do, given my stubborn nature. Maybe in that respect, at least, we're not so different after all.

"What?" she asked.

"What do you mean?" I stared at her.

She took a bite of her chimichanga. "You have a funny look on your face, as if you've just figured out something."

I sipped my martini. "I think I have."

Before I could put my thoughts into words, she said, "Well, good. Can we enjoy the rest of our dinner?"

"Of course." I worked on my fajitas, but my mind was still at war. That anger was still there, but at least it wasn't festering like it had been. I hoped that would continue to be the case.

We finished our dinner, our conversation polite but a bit strained, and she paid the check. Diane left the waiter a nice tip, just as she said she would. "He was sweet, don't you think?" she said.

She put her credit card back in her purse. I thanked her for dinner as we got up and walked out of the restaurant. We stood outside for a moment.

"I hope you're ready to move on," Diane said as she gave me a curt hug. I caught a whiff of her perfume. Lavender. I wasn't fond of it.

I looked at her and nodded, and for the first time I really thought I could.

CHAPTER TWENTY-SEVEN

I was exhausted by the time I drove into my neighborhood, not so much from the case, but from my evening with Diane. It was good to get home.

Harry and I live in a ranch-style house on Grape Street, an older home set back from the road. It had a nice yard, a big tree that offered shade, and was peaceful. When I walked into the kitchen, I fixed another drink and went out to the back porch. The sun was setting, and the western sky was a beautiful combination of orange and purple. The air was hot and still, a typical August evening. I sipped my drink and looked around the yard. There was a section of fence that needed fixing. Neither Harry nor I had time to tackle that right now. Every summer I told myself I'd plant a small garden. This was another year that I didn't. I watched as the sky turned from blue to black. I mulled over the conversation with Diane, then my mind turned to the investigation. I was missing something right in front of me, I was sure. My drink was gone, just melting ice that I continued to sip on. A car drove down the street, and a few minutes later, I looked around. Had I heard something? Then my phone rang.

When Harry was out of town, he tended to call later in the evening. It was best for both of us. He usually took clients to dinner, and then worked late into the evening. And I often worked late as well, since there was no one to come home to.

"Hey, hon, how are you doing?" I asked.

"It was a long day, and it's good to hear your voice." He sounded tired. "How was your dinner with Diane?"

"You get right to the point."

He laughed. "I'm sorry, I just knew you'd be thinking about the dinner. How are you doing?"

"It's been a long day for me, too. We've discovered we may have a serial killer on our hands."

He sucked in a breath. "Oh no. How many victims so far?"

I stared into the darkness. "At least four. We don't know if it's just in Colorado or not. I thought I might spend some time on the internet some more tonight to see what else I can find." I told him about the case. It was nice to have someone listen with genuine interest.

"Maybe you should get a good night's sleep," he said when I'd run out of steam. "I know you, you'll get caught up researching things and half the night will go by. And I'm sure you have a long day tomorrow."

"You're right." He knew me too well. But I had a glimmer of progress in my case, knowing the killer might act again, and I didn't want to let it go.

We chatted for a few more minutes about mundane things. I mentioned the fence, and that led to a discussion of other house chores. Then he circled back to Diane. "Now is it okay for me to ask how dinner went?"

"Ha, I suppose so."

"Are you smiling now?"

He had me there. I *was* smiling. "Yes. And I guess dinner went okay." I told him about Diane's and my conversation. "It's funny, but part of me expected her to be more receptive, and yet I knew she wouldn't be. However, I feel better for having talked through some of it. I think there's more to go, but it's a good start."

"What all did you discuss?"

"That whole situation from years ago."

"Oh?" He was tentative, not wanting to push for more.

"It wasn't just that I had helped her and she didn't appreciate it, it was that I broke the law. And it's not just my career. I never should've done what I did. I feel incredibly guilty about all of it."

"Are you going to tell me what 'it' is?"

I sighed. "I don't know."

It took Harry a long time to answer, and I thought maybe I had said too much. Then he was typical Harry, reassuring as always. "I get that you did something wrong, and I'm not condoning it, whatever it was. However, you were what, eighteen, nineteen years old? Wanting a sibling's approval can be a strong motivator. I think that colored things for you. I know I always wanted my older brother to think I was cool." He paused. "Maybe you're being a little too hard on yourself."

I thought about that for a minute, took a drink. The ice clinked in the glass, loud in the quiet back yard. "I've worried for so long that it could affect my career, that somebody had seen me, and that somehow the whole thing might come out. Stuff like that happens to people sometimes, right? Some old mistake, or scandal, gets resurrected and their whole career is blown up? I just never knew if somehow it might come back to haunt me."

"You really think that would happen? You've built up too much of a career, you've solved some hard cases."

"You're probably right."

"And," he went on, "you really don't need Diane's approval. I know you want it, but you don't need it. Do you hear me?"

"Yes," I said in a soft voice. It was so good to hear that from him, even though he'd said it before. For some reason, I was now ready to accept it.

"You know I love you."

"I love you, too. I don't know what I would do without you, Harry."

"I wish I was there right now. I'd pull you close, put my arms around you, and let you know that everything is going to be okay."

"Thank you. For that, and for not ever giving up on us."

"Why would I do that?"

"I don't know. For a moment there, from the time we left that banquet, I've just felt like maybe you were getting tired ... of us."

"Don't ever think that." His voice was emphatic. "Ever."

"Okay." My mind circled around to something else. "Do you think maybe somehow I've given off a signal that things weren't right between us?"

"I don't think so. That's an odd question, though. Why are you bringing it up now?"

Somewhere a gate hinge creaked. I looked around, but saw only blackness. "You're not going to believe this, but Darren Barnes called me today."

Again, he was slow to reply. "My first thought is why, and my second thought is how did he get your number? He called you at the house?"

"No, he had my cell phone number."

"How did he get that? Maybe on a business card?"

I hadn't thought of that at the time. "That's possible, but *I* certainly never gave him my business card."

"Neither did I. What did he want?" I detected a hint of something there, maybe jealousy.

"He asked me out. He's interested in me, and he said he thought I was interested in him too."

"Are you kidding me?" Harry doesn't often explode, but he did now. "What the hell does he think he's doing?"

"I'd like to know the same."

"I don't know who raised him, but in my neck of the woods, you don't do that. He knows you're with me. He has no right doing that."

He was definitely jealous, and I was secretly pleased.

"I know that he's one of your business contacts, and you need to be cordial or whatever," I said. "But I don't want him bothering me anymore. I actually told him that."

"Business associate or not, this is not okay. I'll call him first thing tomorrow, and I can be polite, but in no uncertain terms he'll know not to bother you again."

"I can take care of myself."

"I know you can, but I can take care of you, too."

That made me relax. We chatted for a few minutes more, and by the time I ended the call, the ice remnants were nothing but water in the bottom of the glass. I went inside and put the glass in the sink. I stared out the kitchen window and thought I saw something in the shadows. I watched for a moment and dismissed it as my just being tired. I went through the house and made sure all the doors and windows were locked, and set the alarm.

I took a long, cool shower, dried myself off, and put on a comfy robe. I watched a little TV, then tried to keep my promise to Harry by going to bed earlier than usual. I stared at the shadows on the ceiling, heard a car on the street, then silence. My emotions were playing leapfrog, and I was irritated again. So much for my feeling peace of mind. Diane was part of it; so was this case. Somewhere out there, was a woman in danger?

Sleep wouldn't come, so I finally went into a bedroom that Harry and I had converted into a dual office. I sat down at my desk and logged onto the computer. I spent some time looking at Cherry Rubio, Jane Lasley, Chelsea Baird, and Tracy Henle. The internet has made it easy to learn about people, especially with social media, and as Olsen had said, with how much people put out there for public consumption. I found out a lot about all four women. They all seemed to have active social lives, and plenty of family and friends. I searched more on some of the news articles, and then, as I was scrolling through results, I noticed another article I hadn't read before. I clicked on it and read about the rape and murder of a woman whose husband had been out of town at the time of the attack. The assailant had come through an open window. Then my palms grew sweaty. This wasn't an article about the women in Colorado, it was about a woman in Ohio.

CHAPTER TWENTY-EIGHT

"There's a fresh pot of coffee," I said when Ernie came into the office the next morning.

He studied me. "You look like you didn't sleep much last night." He crossed to the break room, poured himself a cup, and sat down at his desk.

I stifled a yawn. "I didn't. I'm certain we have a serial killer on the loose. If I'm right, this guy was operating in Ohio two years ago."

"You're kidding." He stared at me, his coffee forgotten.

"I was on the internet last night, looking at the murders here in Colorado, and I stumbled across an article about a woman named Courtney Cannell. She lived in a Cleveland suburb. Two years ago, she was raped and murdered, and guess how the killer got in?"

"Through an open window."

"Yep. I was in early, and I talked to the detective on that case. He confirmed the murder has the same M.O. as what we're seeing here. He wasn't sure about any other cases in the state, and he's going to make some calls to see what he can find. I want to talk to Rizzo about our next move. If the same guy is killing all these women, it crosses state lines."

He nodded thoughtfully. "Our case could get turned over to the feds."

"Yes." I tapped my desk with a pen. "I'd hate to see that happen. I'd like to nail this SOB."

"Me too."

I ran a hand over my face. "The problem is, I'm coming up with nothing to lead me to the killer."

"The Chief doesn't know yet?"

I shook my head. "As soon as Spats comes in, let's go talk to him." I pointed to Rizzo's office. "Besides, he's been on the phone."

"I talked to a bunch of Cherry's friends again yesterday, and I need to go over my notes to see if I missed anything."

We chatted about the case until Spats walked in. Before he sat down, I signaled him.

"Is Rizzo off the phone?"

He glanced in that direction. "Yeah. What's up?"

I gave him the lowdown, and he jammed his hands in his pockets, his lips pursed. "Going to be a fun day."

"You can say that again," I muttered.

We all marched toward Rizzo's office. He saw us approaching and waved us in. "What's the update?"

Spats and Ernie took chairs across from the desk, and I leaned against the doorjamb.

"It's not good," I said. "We have a serial killer out there."

Rizzo leaned forward, put his elbows on the desk, and steepled his fingers. "Give me all of it. How many victims do we have?"

"Five, if we count the murder Sarah discovered in Ohio," Ernie said. He rattled off their names.

"Ohio?" Rizzo asked.

I nodded. Then, between Spats, Ernie, and me, we detailed our findings. When we finished, he leaned back in his chair, grabbed the stone paperweight, and mulled over all the information. "Four victims in Colorado, the last one as far back as last summer?" he asked.

I nodded. "Those are the ones we know about. Here, and one in Ohio."

Rizzo chewed on that for a minute. "If it's across state lines, we need to talk to the feds."

"I've got a contact at the FBI office downtown," I said. "I can give him a call and fill him in."

"Good." Rizzo continued to work on the paperweight. "Keep me in the loop. We'll have to go to the press with this, and I want to be careful. I don't want to tip off our boy with what we know and have him go underground. We'll never catch him then. But I also don't want more victims."

"Right," I said, thinking what a fine needle that was to thread.

Rizzo leaned forward and put down the paperweight, his way of dismissing us. Ernie, Spats, and I went back to our desks.

"I've got to work on the surveillance warrants for Guerrero and Land," Spats said. "And then I have to check Manny Guerrero's alibi. Call me if you need anything." He tipped his head and walked out the door.

Ernie sat down. "I'll start going over everything we have so far, and I'll see if I can find any other murders in Ohio that fit our pattern."

"I'll call my FBI contact," I said as I picked up my desk phone. "If he's available, I'll run downtown to see him. I'd rather talk face to face."

"Good luck."

"We need it," I muttered.

~

Special Agent Theo Ackerman is a big man, built like a linebacker, with a high forehead, a buzz cut, and stark gray eyes. I'd talked to him a few times over the years, and he's a good guy, even though he comes across blunt at times.

"A serial killer?" He stared at me across his desk. I'd laid out all the evidence I had, the killer's M.O., and my suspicions that he had been operating for at least a couple of years. Ackerman took it all in, and now he was thinking it through. "And you have at least one in Ohio?"

His office was stark, nothing on the walls, and on his desk only his computer monitor, a notepad, and a coffee cup. I could focus only on him. And he didn't look happy about what I was bringing him. "That's the way it looks. Courtney Cannell was killed two years ago. I don't know of any other murders in Ohio that fit our pattern. Yet. I'm waiting for a call back from a detective in Ohio."

He jotted down some notes. "I'll search through our databases to see if I can find any murders similar to yours, and I'll ask around. It may take a few days."

"That's fine," I said, even though it wasn't. I couldn't push him, though. His jurisdiction was limited, at least until we determined that a killer was operating outside Colorado. Then the FBI could step in.

His face clouded. "Have you ever handled any cases involving serial killers?"

I shook my head. "No, but I've read about them, how they're profiled, that kind of thing."

He rubbed his chin. "You and I may both get more education on them than we want."

CHAPTER TWENTY-NINE

"Let's look at what we have."

I was standing at a whiteboard across the room from my desk with Ernie, Spats, and some of the other detectives who'd been working the investigation. I had pictures of the victims taped to the board, along with a list of what each killing had in common. I stood in front of a whiteboard with a pen and I looked at everyone expectantly.

"What else do we have? Let's think outside the box; the smallest detail could be important."

Spats gestured at the board with a sly grin. "You forgot to note all the victims were women." That received a few snickers.

"Funny," I said.

"Physical type," Ernie said.

I moved to the right side of the board and wrote down that there was no commonality in the physical type of woman the killer went after. That received a few head nods.

"Did they all make some of the same phone calls?" I asked. "I know we've gone through the records, and there's no commonality in the phone numbers themselves, but did we check to see if they all called the same business?"

"That has different phone lines?" Spats asked.

I nodded. Both of them shook their heads. I looked to the other detectives.

"I didn't see anything like that," one named Daniel Hackman said. He always has a deadpan expression, but he's sharp and misses very little.

"I've been comparing the phone lists over and over," Spats said. "I don't see any commonality."

"All had ex-boyfriends." Ernie pointed at the commonality side of the board.

I wrote that down. "That's true, although Chelsea's boyfriend had a solid alibi."

Spats rocked back and forth on his heels. "None of the other victims' families or friends mentioned Rex Land or Manny Guerrero?"

I stared at the whiteboard. "Not so far."

"All the women had something stolen," Ernie said. "Cherry's bracelet, Jane's ring, Chelsea's anklet, and Tracy Henle's necklace."

"What about the woman in Ohio?" Spats asked.

"The detective didn't know," I said. "He's checking."

"What else?" Ernie went on.

"Our perp most likely used a condom, and when he was finished, he probably cleaned up the bodies," Spats mused to himself.

"I didn't find any unusual social media activity for Cherry Rubio," Tara said. She was leaning against my desk, an earnest look on her face. "She wasn't on any dating sites."

"Neither were the other victims," Ernie said. "That we know of."

"Good point," I said. "We don't know much about the Ohio victim."

"The women were possibly interested in men who had fancy cars," Spats interjected.

I wrote that down. We stared at the board. No one said anything else. I took a different tactic, and wrote Cherry Rubio's name down on the left side of the whiteboard, underneath notes I'd already put on the board. I wrote down what she'd done the evening she was killed. I looked over at Ernie, and he nodded, indicating I had the details correct.

"Okay, now what did Jane Lasley do?" I asked.

Spats glanced at some notes. "She worked that day, and she went to a restaurant in the evening. As far as we know, she came home alone, didn't see anyone the rest of the night."

"Except the killer," someone said.

I ignored that and moved to the right, then wrote down Chelsea Baird's name.

Ernie had a cigar stub back in his mouth, and he talked around it. His quitting hadn't lasted long. "Chelsea came home from work, went back out to eat, and she came home alone. As far as we know."

"And Tracy Henle," I said. "She went out to eat the night she was killed."

Spats stepped back and pointed at the board. "Look at that. They *all* went out to eat the night they were killed."

I stepped back and stared at the lists under each woman's name. "Did we just find something in common, a pattern we've been missing?"

Ernie growled. A couple of the other detectives nodded their heads.

"Or coincidence?" I mused. I tapped the closed marker on my hand, then whirled around. "Who's got the case files on all the victims? What restaurant did they go to?"

Ernie was already shuffling through Cherry's file. He shook his head in frustration. "Nothing."

Another detective looked at what we had from Olsen. "Nothing about where Jane ate," he said after a minute. "Maybe they don't know. All I see is that a friend said that she talked to Jane for about half an hour when Jane was driving home from a restaurant."

Spats was with Daniel, poring over the notes we'd received from Thompson. Spats shrugged after a second. "I don't see anything that says what restaurant Chelsea went to. You think she was up here, eating at the same restaurant as Cherry and Jane?"

I held up my hands. "It's a thought. Right now, I'm not dismissing anything."

Ernie gazed at the board. "That was easy to miss."

"Going out to eat is a pretty common thing to do," Tara said skeptically.

I turned to look at everyone. "True. But what if it was the same restaurant?"

Spats cocked an eyebrow. "What about the woman in Ohio?"

"We can't factor that one in just yet," I replied.

"Did our killer stalk these women, watch them at the restaurant?" Tara asked.

"Or does he work there?" Spats said.

"That doesn't answer our problem," Ernie growled. "With the three murders in the Denver metro area, nobody seems to know if all three victims went to the *same* restaurant."

I put down the marker. "We need to go back to everybody again, talk to all the family and friends of each victim. They're not going to be happy, but we have to find somebody who knows which restaurant each of these women went to."

Ernie pushed himself out of his chair. "I'll call Thompson in the Springs and see what I can find out from him. If I have to, I'll head down to the Springs to re-interview Chelsea's family and friends to see if someone knows what restaurant she went to."

"It's been almost a year," I said, "so I don't know what kind of luck we'll have, but it's worth a shot."

"I'll see if Thompson has found any similarities in other open murder cases in the Springs. Maybe our killer was down there before he came up here," Ernie said.

"I'll check Cherry's email again," Tara said. "She might've told someone about the restaurant."

"Thanks," I said.

I heard people shifting on their feet, antsy to get back to their work. I thanked the other detectives for their time, and the rest of the group dispersed, leaving the three of us.

"I'll also talk to Cherry's family and friends again," Ernie went on. "They're getting used to talking to me."

"I've got the court orders for video surveillance on Land and Guerrero," Spats said, "but I haven't verified Manny's alibi."

"You get on that," I said. "I'd like to know if he was lying about being with that married woman."

"I'll let you know when I know." With that, Spats headed out the door.

I went to my desk and called Olsen.

"Sarah, I didn't think I'd hear from you so soon." Olsen's tone was curious.

I tried to temper my excitement. "It may be nothing," I said. "We were going through all the case files, and we may have a pattern. All of the victims in the metro area went out to eat the night they were killed."

"Hmm." A long pause, as he thought about it. "So what restaurant did they all go to?"

"That's what I'm trying to find out."

"What about the killing in the Springs?"

"I don't know about that one," I said. "I have someone looking into it. We read through the case notes on Jane's murder," I said. "I can't find anyone who mentions the name of the restaurant she went to, just that somebody said she talked to Jane for a while when Jane was driving home."

"It took her a while to drive home," he said slowly, beginning to follow my reasoning. "I didn't think that was important, but maybe it is. Did she go to Denver to eat?"

"That's what I'd like to know."

I heard papers rustling. "I know I have reports on the computer," he said, half to himself, "but I'm old-fashioned and still like to write things down." He muttered to himself. "Let's see here. You're right, I'm not finding anything about which restaurant Jane visited. When I talked specifically to Vicki Ivers, the friend Jane chatted with that night, she didn't say."

"Do you have her number? I'd like to talk to her."

"I'd like to be in on it. Let me see if I can get hold of her and set something up. Will you be at your desk?"

"I won't be moving."

He snorted. "Yeah, I get it. When you're on to something, you don't do anything else until you figure it out, right?"

"That's right."

He hung up, and I stood up and paced the little room. I hoped we were on the right track.

CHAPTER THIRTY

After a few minutes, my desk phone rang. I was across the room, and I hurried over and snatched it up. "Spillman." I was sure it would be Olsen, but it was Harry.

"Hey, hon, how are you? You sound almost giddy."

"We may be on to something," I said. "A small lead."

"Oh, what's that?"

I told him, then he offered encouraging words. "Let's hope that does lead to the killer before anyone else dies."

"Agreed." I sat down. "Why are you calling right now? Is something wrong?"

"Not really. I talked to Darren Barnes."

I braced myself. "How did that go?"

"Overall, I think good. Darren's hard to read over the phone, but I didn't want to wait until I got home to talk to him." His voice had a hard edge to it, rare for Harry. "I called him first thing this morning, like I told you I was going to do, only he just got back to me. Can you believe the guy, he was smooth, acting like talking to you was no big deal."

"What'd you tell him?"

"I said you were my woman and he should back off."

I laughed. "I hope you didn't say it like that."

"No, I didn't. I *did* say that you had informed me that he had talked to you a few times recently, and that he had asked you out. He sort of denied it, sort of made it sound like you were the one coming on to him."

"Oh, please!"

"I know. I told him regardless, that you and I were together, and that he needed to leave you alone. I think he got the message."

I wondered if Harry had been more forceful than he was letting on. I breathed a sigh of relief. "What will this do for your business?"

"Don't worry about that. If I have to work with Darren's company, I can deal with him."

"Good. Thanks for doing that."

"No problem. I'll let you get back to work, and I'll talk to you later tonight."

"If you don't have time, I understand."

"I always have time for you, babe."

"Love you."

"Right back at you."

He ended the call. I sat for a moment with a warm, fuzzy feeling. The phone interrupted.

"Spillman," I said, a little less brusque than normal.

"I caught Vicki Ivers between meetings," Olsen said. "She says she can meet us at a Panera Bread restaurant. It's off I-25 and 120th. She had to get to another meeting nearby, so she wants to grab a quick bite to eat while she talks to us."

"That's up north." I glanced at my computer clock. "What time?"

"She said she could leave work now, and she'd explain to her clients that she might be a few minutes late. She can be at Panera's in half an hour."

"I'll be there."

Panera Bread wasn't very crowded when I got there, but I managed to miss Olsen anyway. I heard him call my name, and found him sitting with a woman at a table near the back. The restaurant smelled of fresh-baked bread, and my mouth watered. The day was quickly speeding by, and it was past noon. I needed to get something to eat. I'd barely sat down when she introduced herself.

"I'm Vicki Ivers." She waved her hand at me.

"Thanks for taking the time to meet us," I said as I introduced myself.

Vicki had strawberry blonde hair, thin glasses on a thin nose, and was dressed casually in black slacks and stretchy print top. Her makeup was heavy to the point of being distracting. I guessed her to be about fifty.

"Traffic not too bad?" Olsen asked.

"It was fine," I said, even though the highway had been thick with cars.

Vicki came right to the point, her glare intense. "Do you have more information on Jane's death?"

Olsen shook his head. "We may be on to something different, and we wanted to talk to you." He turned to me. "Detective Spillman is working on a similar investigation, and we think we might've found something both our victims did the night they were murdered."

Vicki had a sandwich in front of her, and she took a bite and chewed. While she did, she appraised me, and by the change in her expression, I had met her approval. "I'll do anything I can to help find Jane's killer. She was my best friend."

"You must miss her a lot," I said. "I've been going over Detective Olsen's interviews, and something in your conversation with him stuck out, and I'd like to talk to you about that." As he'd done when I'd talked to Jane's parents, Olsen sat back and let me lead the interview.

"Fire away." She took another bite. "Sorry, I have to eat on the run."

"No problem," I said. "You said that on the night Jane died, you had talked to her on her way home, correct?"

She nodded. "That's right. We were probably on the phone for close to half an hour, talking about all kinds of things. She was filling me in on an argument with her mother, and I told her about some difficulties with my son. It was a nice catch-up." At the thought of the conversation, her shoulders sagged. "I never figured that would be the last time I would talk to her."

I leaned in. "Do you know what restaurant she went to?"

Vicki thought about that as she glanced out the window. "I don't think she mentioned it, or I would've told Detective Olsen."

"You're sure?" I asked.

She shrugged. "I wish I knew, but nothing's coming to mind."

"What about the type of food? Did she mention what she ate?"

She tipped her head to the side and thought about that. "I'm trying to go through the conversation in my mind. It's funny how you forget things. I think maybe she told me it was a popular new restaurant that she'd heard about that makes fabulous margaritas, and I was going to ask her which one, but we got to talking about my son, and I never got around to it. I do think she said something about having a fabulous margarita." She looked at us and wiped her hands with a napkin. "Does that help?"

Olsen and I looked at each other. Cherry had eaten Mexican

food and had margaritas the night she was murdered. Did that mean both victims might have gone to the same restaurant?

"It could," I said. "I know you went over all this with Detective Olsen, but is there anything else that you remember about your conversation with Jane?"

She took a long sip from a soda. "Not really. I've been trying to think if she mentioned anyone she saw, or if anything happened at the restaurant." She shook her head. "I'm afraid I'm not helping much."

"Did Jane talk about any men she'd been dating, or who she saw that night?"

Vicki laughed. "I think maybe she'd been with a guy. If so, she wasn't offering up details, at least to me. I got the impression she was interested in someone, but she'd been burned a few times with dates so she was in the habit of not saying much. I think she was kind of embarrassed that she kept choosing guys who turned out to be losers." She glanced at her phone, then said, "Excuse me, I have to answer this text." She typed faster on her phone than I could, then looked up. "I have to go soon. Do you have a card? I could call you if I think of anything else."

"Sure." I gave her my card and thanked her again for her time.

She took a final bite into her mouth, then stood up with an apology. She took her tray and dumped it in a nearby trash can. "I hope this was helpful." She headed out the door with a frown on her face.

After she left, Olsen pointed at the counter. "How about some lunch? I might not get another time to eat."

"I hear that."

He ordered a roast beef sandwich, and I got a Southwestern soup with bread. We talked while we ate.

"If it took Jane half an hour to drive home from the restaurant, where did she go?" I mused.

"Somewhere far from home," Olsen said as he tackled his sandwich.

"Tres Hermanos? It's a popular new restaurant with great margaritas." Maybe I was grasping at straws, since I had just been there with Diane.

He nodded slowly. "That's what I would wonder."

"I have a team checking through our case notes," I said. "This may be something."

Olsen nodded. "You'll talk to someone at the restaurant?"

"Count on it," I said. "And I'll see what other restaurants are known for their margaritas."

"I'll let you take the lead on this, but you keep me posted."

"Absolutely."

He smiled grimly, and we finished our lunches and left. I'd no sooner gotten onto the highway than Spats called.

"I checked out Guerrero's alibi."

"And?"

The background noise told me Spats was driving, too. "I smooth-talked the woman he said he was with. As you can imagine, she doesn't want her name to come up. She said they were together on Tuesday night. She didn't want to give that up at first, but I worked on her a bit. And at the end of the conversation her kid came out and heard us talking about Tuesday night, and he blurted out that she hadn't been home that night, that she was out of town." I could hear the air quotes on his last two words.

"Did you get her busted?"

"Nah, the kid didn't know exactly what we were talking about."

"You think she was telling the truth?"

"Yeah, I think it's good."

"Hmm," I said. "Maybe Manny's off our list." Then I filled him in on my conversation with Vicki Ivers, but before I could say more, Ernie called. I told Spats I'd see him back at the station and answered the call.

"It's confirmed," he said. "I talked to another friend of Cherry's, and she said that Cherry had gone to Tres Hermanos the night she was murdered."

"Lisa Fernandez told me she and Cherry liked to go to places with a good happy hour, and Tres Hermanos fits the bill. And Jane Lasley could've gone to the same restaurant, although we don't know that." I told him what Vicki Ivers had said.

"I'll be damned. Oh, I chatted with Detective Walker in the Springs. His victim went out to dinner the night she was killed, only he has no idea what restaurant. We could interview her family and friends again. That'll take a while, though."

"Yes, it would," I said. "It's not likely she came up to Denver for dinner, but not impossible."

"Maybe our killer lived in the Springs before he moved up here."

"I'd love to find that out."

"In the meantime, I think it's time we paid Tres Hermanos a visit." Maybe my thought about the restaurant wasn't such a stretch after all.

I stared out the windshield. "I think you're right."

CHAPTER THIRTY-ONE

Ernie, Spats, and I walked into Tres Hermanos as a united front. It was five o'clock, happy hour, and the restaurant was crowded with people who were spilling out onto the sidewalk. We bypassed them and sidled up to the hostess, a woman I guessed to be in her early twenties, with dyed-black hair, plenty of piercings in her ears, and one on her upper lip. She gave us a warm smile, and I wondered if the piercing rubbed the inside of her mouth.

"Hello, seating for three?" she asked, her voice agreeable.

I shook my head. "Would it be possible to see the manager?"

She cocked her head to the side and nodded. "Is there something wrong? Did we not get you on the waiting list?"

I shook my head. "It's another matter."

"Oh, okay. Just a moment, please."

We looked around as we waited. I tried to spot surveillance cameras and didn't see any. The bar was packed, with both small booths and high tables full. The bartender raced back and forth behind a long wooden bar. A buffet was along a far wall, and people were filling plates with miniature tacos, chimichangas, chips, and salsa.

"They serve good food here?" Ernie asked.

"Where have you been?" Spats said. "It's one of the most popular restaurants in Denver."

"Denver's a big place," Ernie grunted.

I smiled. "Harry and I come here once in a while. I was a little surprised to hear that this was where Cherry went."

"It's a great restaurant," Spats said. "I've been here a few times with Trissa."

The hostess returned with a manager, a tall woman in a blue pantsuit and sensible, low-heel shoes. She was probably on her feet a lot. "I'm Rhonda McLean, the manager. What can I help you with?" She was shorter than I was, and slender, with delicate hands.

I stepped away from the hostess and showed McLean my badge. "I'm Detective Spillman. We're in the middle of a homicide investigation, and I have reason to believe the victim recently visited this restaurant. Could I bother you for a few minutes of your time?"

Her face fell, and she nodded. "Of course. Whatever I can help with." She glanced at Ernie and Spats. They both gave her deadpan looks. "What's this about?" Then she gestured. "Why don't you come back into the manager's office?"

We followed her away from the curious hostess, through the restaurant and into the kitchen. Several cooks worked furiously as food sizzled on stove tops and conversations in Spanish filled the room. More than a few people took notice of us. Rhonda escorted us down a short hall and into an office. It lacked decorations, with just a desk with a computer on it, some file cabinets, and a couple of bookcases filled with notebooks and papers. She sat at the desk and motioned for me to take a folding chair across from it. She waved at some plastic chairs in the corner, but Ernie and Spats shook their heads.

"What can I do for you?" she asked. She wasn't hiding the

slight warble in her voice. "I'll certainly do anything I can to help."

"Thank you," I said. "I appreciate your assistance. Were you working last Tuesday or Thursday nights?"

"Tuesday."

Before we'd left the station, Ernie, Spats, and I had printed out pictures of Cherry and Jane. I showed her the picture of Cherry. "Do you recognize this woman?"

She studied the photo and shook her head. "Should I?"

"She might've come in here Tuesday."

"We have a lot of people come in here every day," she said.

I nodded. "Do you have any surveillance cameras in the restaurant?"

"Well, we do." She faltered, seeming embarrassed. "Unfortunately it's an old system, and we only have one camera by the front door. I can queue it up now, if you'd like."

I looked at Spats. He spoke up. "Would you mind if I talk to some of your staff while you look at the video?"

Her response was slow. "Right now? During happy hour? I'm not sure I can do that."

"Why not?" he asked.

"Well, first, as you can see, we're very busy. And second, I think my employees are entitled to their privacy."

Spats nodded slowly. "Sure. I'd hate to do this. However, if we have to get a warrant, we will. And we look at your payroll and turn over our findings to the IRS."

The threat worked. Rhonda gulped. "You can talk to them. Please understand, they're working and it's a busy night."

"I'll be as little an intrusion as possible," Spats promised.

"Maybe I should talk to them first." She started to get out of her chair.

"It's okay, he'll be discreet." I gestured at the computer. "What can you show me?"

She sank back into the chair and watched Spats head out the door. Then she nodded for Ernie and me to come around the desk. She held the mouse and opened up the video software. It displayed a live view of the hostess area. "What night was this?"

"Last Tuesday night," Ernie said. "We think the victim was here sometime during happy hour. She may have been with an older man with dark hair, possibly some gray."

"Give me a second," Rhonda said. She worked the video for a minute, then touched the monitor. "This is that night, starting at four, when happy hour starts."

Ernie and I studied the screen. We only had one camera angle that looked down at the hostess area. The images were black and white, and not nearly as clear as I would've hoped.

"We don't capture everything," Rhonda said. "I keep telling the owner we should upgrade, but he hasn't done it yet. I'll go through the video."

"Can you fast-forward it some?" I asked.

She nodded. The video had a time stamp in the lower right corner, and the three of us watched the screen closely, Ernie and I alert for Cherry Rubio. Rhonda's phone rang, and she answered, spoke for a moment, then hung up. We continued to scrutinize the screen. When the time stamp read five-thirty, Ernie tapped the screen. "Wait! Is that her?"

Rhonda hit a button and the image paused. Ernie and I moved closer and scrutinized the screen.

"I think that's her," I concluded. "She came in alone."

Ernie nodded at Rhonda. "Let the image roll some more."

She complied, and we watched as Cherry talked to the hostess, then was led off screen, we assumed to a table. Ernie tensed.

"I'm sorry," Rhonda said, sensing his unease. "We just haven't upgraded the cameras to anything more than this."

"That's okay," I said. We watched the tape for a while longer, and saw Cherry leave.

"She's alone again," Ernie said.

I pursed my lips. "What about last Thursday night?"

"Sure," she said. "Hang on a second."

"She cued up the night when Jane Lasley was murdered, and we began watching that video as well. After a few minutes, I told her to stop the video. I wasn't sure, but I thought I saw Jane enter the restaurant. Like Cherry, she was alone.

"You think that's her?" I asked Ernie, not saying Jane's name in front of Rhonda.

"Hmm, hard to tell, but I think so," he said.

Ernie glanced at me with a frown. Then Jane went off-camera and was gone.

"I don't suppose you would know where those two women were seated?" I asked.

Rhonda shook her head. "There are a couple of sections in that part of the room, and a few wait staff working there. I don't have any idea where the women would've been seated, though."

I nodded, disappointed. We watched Thursday night's video until we saw Jane leave, alone as well.

"I'm sorry," Rhonda said again.

"That's fine," I said. I moved back around the desk, thought for a second. "If you don't mind, we'll also talk to some of your staff."

"Um, sure," she said, even though it was obvious she didn't mean it.

"How about a list of your employees?" Ernie asked.

She seemed to know we'd get it one way or another. "I can have a list for you before you leave."

"Thanks," I said.

I headed out the door, with Ernie behind me. By the time we walked through the kitchen to the dining area, Spats was near the entrance. Rhonda stepped past us and began talking to the wait staff, one at a time. By the glances at us, we could tell that she was letting them know we'd be asking questions.

"You talk to the cooks," I said to Ernie. "I'll talk to some of the wait staff and head into the bar." Ernie nodded his approval and went back into the kitchen. I started with a woman who was near the bar. She typed orders into a computer and barely gave me a second look.

"Excuse me," I said. "I'm wondering if you remember this woman. She would've been in the restaurant Tuesday night." I showed her a picture of Cherry.

She looked at it briefly and shook her head. "There's so many people coming and going, I can't remember them all, sorry."

I expected as much, but knew we had to try. "What about this woman?" I showed her Jane Lasley's photo.

She studied that, then said, "Possibly. What night was that?"

"It would've been last Thursday night."

"She's got pretty hair, but again, there's so many people in here."

"Did you see her with an older guy? If you take a break outside, maybe you saw him driving a Corvette?"

"Sorry, can't help you."

I tried a couple more of the wait staff, then went into the bar. The bartender who had served me the other night was there. I slid onto a stool, then motioned for him to come over.

"What'll you have?" he said, somewhere between pleasant and abrupt.

"I actually need a few minutes of your time."

He was reluctant. "I'm really kind of busy."

"I promise, just a few minutes." I tried for friendly. "I'm Sarah."

"Greg," he said reluctantly.

"How long have you worked here."

"A while."

"Where'd you work before?"

"Around." Not my business, he was clearly saying without actually saying it. He put his hands on the bar and stared at me.

I went on. "Have you seen either of these women?" I put both pictures down on the bar, then tapped Cherry's. "She was here last Tuesday night. And her," I tapped Jane's picture. "She was here Thursday night. Were you working those nights?"

"I don't know about them. The place is packed most nights, and the only time I really see people is if they sit at the bar."

He didn't really glance at the pictures, so I tapped them again. "Are you sure? Could you please look at them closely?"

He gazed at the photos, then back at me. He shook his head. "I don't know either one of them."

"And you were here both nights?"

"Yeah. I don't know them." The waitress I talked to came up and gave him an order. He glared at me. "I really have to get back to work."

I nodded and thanked him for his time. He hurried to the other end of the bar before I could ask him anything more. I sat and observed him, which made him uncomfortable. He kept eyeing me, a sneer on his face. Ernie finally emerged from the kitchen, and he and Spats talked to a couple of the other waiters, and then I noticed the waiter that had served Diane and me the other night. He was standing over by a soda station. I walked over, smiled at him, and introduced myself. "I suppose by now you've heard the questions we're asking," I said.

He nodded. "They said this is something about a murder?"

"Yes, two actually."

"You have some photos for me to look at?"

"I do." I held out the photos.

He studied them carefully. "They're pretty, aren't they?"

"Yes, they are. Or they were. Do you recognize either one of them?"

He put some thought into it. "I don't think so. How were they murdered?"

I sidestepped that. "Were you working the nights they were in here? Last Tuesday and Thursday."

He shook his head. "Just Tuesday. It was busy."

"You're sure?"

"Yeah, sorry." He shrugged. "Unless it's a regular customer or a big tipper. Then I remember them. Do you have any leads?"

"No," I said.

He glanced over his shoulder. "Sorry, I need to go."

I thanked him for his time, but he was already headed to a table with a tray of drinks. I joined Ernie and Spats at the entrance. Rhonda was waiting there. The crowds were growing larger, and the restaurant nosier.

"Was that helpful?" Rhonda asked.

"I'm not sure yet," I said. "Would you mind if we stuck around for a little while?"

She worked hard to keep her face neutral. "Of course, do what you need to do." She looked into the restaurant. The tables had filled up. "You'll have to find a spot in the bar. If you don't mind, though, I need to get back to work."

"Sure," I said.

I signaled for Ernie and Spats to go outside. We stood away from the entrance and talked.

"What did you find out?" I asked, suspecting what the answer would be.

"Nobody seems to remember either Cherry or Jane," Ernie said. "And no one remembers an older guy driving a Corvette."

Spats pulled at his shirtsleeve. "Yeah, the same for me."

"Yeah, I got the same thing, but the bartender was a little short with me." I stared at the entrance. "I know he's busy, but he didn't even really want to look at the pictures."

Ernie arched an eyebrow. "What do you think?"

"I'm not sure," I said. "It could be nothing. At this point, though, I don't want to dismiss anything."

"Why don't Ernie and I hang out here and watch for a while," Spats said. "We might see somebody hanging around who shouldn't be."

"Watch for any delivery people," I suggested. "There might be a regular guy who shows up, then picks his victims while he's at the restaurant."

Spats nodded. "You can go inside, watch the bartender for a while, see what you think."

"I was thinking the same thing. Text me with anything unusual."

The two of them walked to Ernie's car, and I went back inside. I strolled back into the bar and found a table in the corner. I sat back and watched. A waitress came over, and I ordered a martini which I nursed as I looked around. The wait staff was busy. They went in and out of the kitchen. They hustled food and drinks to tables. Lots of people were drinking alcoholic beverages, and the bartender was kept busy. He noticed me at one point and then seemed to avoid looking my way. He was good at what he did. He made drinks fast, and smiled and joked with the wait staff and the customers at the bar. After a while, I texted Spats and asked if they'd seen anything strange. I received a no. The waitress came back a while later to see if I wanted another drink, and I declined. Instead I switched to water.

"I'm curious," I said to her, "are there any regulars that you see coming in here?"

She thought about that for a moment as she tapped her pen on a notepad. "There are a couple of families that come in sometimes when I'm working." She glanced around. "But here in the bar? Not really. Keep in mind, I'm not here every night."

"Okay, thanks."

I watched the wait staff for a while longer, and the time

slipped away. Rhonda came by with a list of employees. She didn't seem too happy as she handed it over. I thanked her, and she walked off without a word. Harry called, and I texted that I would call him later. I finally decided it was time to go. I texted Ernie that I was coming outside. I left money on the table for my drink and walked out the front door. I could almost hear a collective sigh of relief from the wait staff. I went to Ernie's car, parked at the corner of the parking lot.

"I didn't see anything," I said. "The bartender noticed me, and then he seemed to be trying to avoid eye contact with me."

"Maybe he's been in trouble with the law," Spats said. "Having a cop hanging around would make him nervous. Did you get his name?"

"Greg." I held up the piece of paper Rhonda had given me. "I have the list of employees." I took a picture of it, then handed it to Spats.

"I'll check on him more tomorrow," he said. "It's late, and I need to get home."

"I'm going to get some detectives working on this list now," I said. "I'll have them check backgrounds of the employees and see what they come up with."

Ernie nodded. "We'll see you in the morning."

"That sounds good."

I walked away, tired and ready to go home myself.

CHAPTER THIRTY-TWO

He was furious. She had rejected him. Who did she think she was? He was a nice person, and perfectly deserving of her. He had been watching her, waiting for the right moment that never came. He wanted her badly.

The anklet was in his pocket, and he twisted it between his fingers. Normally that soothed him some, lessened the urge, but not now. He thought of the detective. The man she lived with was out of town now. No one in the house but her. He smiled at that. Now was the perfect opportunity for him to make a move.

He thought about her, and he reassessed his opinion of her. She really was attractive. She held herself a certain way, with a confidence that a lot of women he knew didn't have. It was sexy. And yet that dismissal of him. He couldn't get over that.

He stood outside and smoked. The more he thought of her, the angrier he got, and the impulse grew. He had to have her.

She would regret what she'd done to him.

CHAPTER THIRTY-THREE

As I drove home, I had that eerie feeling again that I was being watched. I kept an eye in the rearview mirror as I got on the phone and called Harry.

"Long day? You sound tired," he said.

"So do you. Did I wake you?"

"Just hit the sheets. Everything okay?"

"Yeah." I was in that mindset between thinking we were making progress on the investigation and thinking we hadn't figured out a thing. I told him about my evening at Tres Hermanos. He didn't comment much, so I said, "I'll let you get back to sleep."

"Thanks, hon," he said. "I'll see you soon. Love you."

"I love you too."

I ended the call, moody and irritated. I soon turned onto Grape and pulled my car into the garage. I checked the rearview mirror again and closed the garage door. I got out, listened for a second, and walked into the house. I took my gun and holster and set them on the counter, then called the station and talked to a detective on the night shift. I told him I'd email him the list of restaurant employees and asked him to get a team looking at the employee backgrounds. He said he'd get on it soon. I thanked him and ended the call, then looked out the back window for a moment. It was dark and quiet.

After another moment at the window, I fixed a drink and went into the living room. I put the drink on the coffee table, then slumped onto the couch and sat for a minute. I was weary, my brain fuzzy. On one hand, I felt as if we were close to finding a killer. Then I would change my mind, thinking the restaurant lead was nothing. So frustrating.

I finally sipped my drink and turned on some music. The Smashing Pumpkins. Good hard music for my mood. I took another sip and wished I could talk to Harry again. I was tempted to call him back, just to hear his voice, but it was late there. I was in the middle of my funk when the doorbell rang.

"Who the hell is it at this hour?" I asked nobody. I set my drink down and stomped to the door. I peeked through the peephole and got the shock of my life. Before I thought, I yanked open the door.

"Darren, what the hell are you doing here?" I blurted out.

He had a lascivious grin on his face. "Harry's out of town."

I could smell booze on his breath, and cologne hung around him like a dark cloud. He wore khakis and a blue shirt with one too many buttons undone, the hair on his head was slicked back.

"Darren–"

"Come on, let me in," he interrupted. "It's hot out here."

Before I could do anything, he brushed past me into the foyer. I looked past him to the street. "Did you drive here?"

He had already made it into the living room. "Of course I drove here," he called out. "In my Corvette."

I didn't see it on the street. "Where is it?"

"Does it matter?"

I walked toward the living room threshold. He stood in the

middle of the room and leered at me. "You know, you hurt my feelings the other day."

I stared at him, hands on my hips. "What are you talking about?" I pointed to the door. "You need to leave."

He glanced around and cocked his ear to the music. "Nice home. But Smashing Pumpkins? Really? I didn't figure you for alternative music." He laughed, then wagged his index finger at me. "You rejected me. I asked you to go out with me, and you weren't interested."

"I'm *still* not interested," I said firmly.

He studied me. "You're an attractive woman. You should update your online picture, you know, the one in your uniform. It's almost as bad as a driver's license photo."

It was a low blow, and I didn't respond to that. "Do you know how furious Harry is going to be?"

"Speaking of him," he said in a frustrated tone, "you shouldn't have told him about us. He wasn't very happy with me."

"Of course he wasn't. There's nothing between the two of us." I was silently running through how to get him out of the house. He'd had more than a bit to drink, and he wasn't taking no for an answer. I didn't want him driving. Call a taxi?

He took a couple of steps toward me. "Do you always sit in the back yard late at night?"

My jaw dropped. "How do you know that?"

Another Smashing Pumpkins song came on, the beat hard and loud.

"Do you spend your time thinking out there?" he asked. "Seems like a nice thing to do, although hot."

"You've been watching me?" I was furious and clenched my fist. I was about to belt him. "Darren, you have no business stalking me like this."

He took a couple of more steps toward me, his face eerily forceful. "You know, I get what I want. With all women."

I stared at him, my mind a blur. Things started going through my mind. Darren had a fancy car; he'd told me that the other night at the banquet. Cherry and Jane were said to have been dating an older man who had a fancy car, possibly a Corvette. Cherry's brother Chris had seen a Corvette down the street the night Cherry had been killed. I thought quickly about how the man they'd been with was tall with dark hair. It could fit Darren. And he'd said he'd been at Tres Hermanos the night of the banquet, the same night Cherry had been murdered.

I was suddenly uncomfortable as I looked at him. "What do you want?" I asked.

"You." His voice was low and husky, and dangerous.

I didn't like where this was going. I stared at him. Was he a killer? I swore under my breath. My gun was in the kitchen. How could I get it? Offer him a drink?

"What did you do after the banquet last week?" I raised my fists a little.

"What's it to you?"

"Just tell me."

He shook his head. "You don't need to know that."

"Why dodge my question?"

He narrowed his eyes. "It's none of your business."

I pointed to the door. "Darren, for the last time, you need to leave. There is nothing that's going to happen between us. I'll call you a taxi. There's a phone in the kitchen."

As he moved toward me, I moved back, farther down the hallway, toward the kitchen.

"Come on, Sarah. Let's have a little fun." His eyes danced with menace.

I whirled around and ran into the kitchen. I could hear him coming after me. I bolted around the island and grabbed my holster off the counter. I spun around as I pulled my Glock from the holster. I pointed it at Darren.

His jaw dropped. He started to move around the island, thought better of it, and raised his hands slightly. "What the hell are you doing?"

"Stay right where you are." I said. "You murdered those women."

He cursed. "What are you talking about?"

My hand shook more than I thought it should. "Cherry Rubio. Jane Lasley. Chelsea Baird. And how many women from Ohio? Why'd you do that to them?"

He stared at me, bewildered, for a long moment. "Who? What women? I have no idea what you're talking about." He put his hands on the island and leaned forward, suddenly sober. "I just wanted to go out with you, and you pissed me off." He jabbed a finger at me. "Nobody rejects me." The glare remained. "Who the hell are these women?"

"My investigation," I said, talking fast. "A number of women have recently been raped and murdered. One victim was interested in an older man who drove a Corvette. Like you. The victims were at Tres Hermanos, possibly with an older man. You said you'd gone there for happy hour before the banquet. And you've been watching me, haven't you? You think I'm your next victim?"

His eyebrows formed a thin, angry line. "You think I'm a murderer? Are you crazy?" He swore. "What the hell has gotten into you? I left the party with another woman. I can give you her name. I was with her all night. It sure as hell wasn't Cherry whoever you said."

"What about last Thursday night?"

"I was out of town that night. You can check my airline ticket, or ask Harry. He knows I was on a business trip."

"I ... uh ..." I didn't have an answer for that. My fear had led me to a wrong conclusion. I had completely blown it. I could chalk it up to stress, to sleepless nights, to whatever. He may have been acting like a total jerk, but I believed Darren. "Why do you keep pursuing me?" I finally asked.

He snorted. "Right at the moment, I'm asking myself the same thing. I just don't know why you want to be with Harry. I would've thought you'd see me as a good catch."

"And you don't like being rejected."

He shrugged, stayed silent.

"It's been a long night," I said. "Why don't you leave?"

"You want to lower the gun?" His tone was disgusted. "You've got a hell of a lot of nerve pulling that on me." He crossed his arms. "I made a mistake. I don't know why I'd be interested in you, especially when you think I could be a murderer." He appraised me with disdain.

I suddenly felt very foolish and felt heat on my face. I must've been beet red. I lowered the gun. "Darren, but you have to understand–"

"I don't need to understand anything." He threw up a hand. "You're not worth the time."

"Leave now." I stared at him. "I'll call a taxi for you."

Darren glared at me, turned, and walked down the hallway and out the door. It banged shut. I rushed after him and quickly locked it. I looked through the peephole. He was storming down the sidewalk. He flipped off the house and walked down the street. I opened the door and looked out. Down the block, Darren was getting into his Corvette. He started it, revved the engine and peeled away. The sound of his tires squealing would haunt me, the sound of my embarrassing mistake.

I went back inside and leaned against the door. What would my neighbors think? I didn't move for a moment as I questioned myself. Darren was right on one thing. How could I have assumed so much? What a rookie move, one that I hoped I could chalk up to being tired. Yeah, he was a schmuck for showing up at the house, and the same could be said for his lack of respect for Harry and me. That certainly didn't make him a murderer.

I walked on shaky legs into the living room and sat down. I dropped the Glock on the coffee table and picked up my glass, but didn't take a drink. *How could I have mistaken him for a killer?* I kept asking myself. The music pounded loudly, and I reached for the remote and shut it off. I thought through the conversation with Darren and wondered what he must've been thinking of me. I finally came to the conclusion that it didn't matter. It would still take me a long time to get over my embarrassment.

CHAPTER THIRTY-FOUR

I finally settled down from my encounter with Darren. But that feeling of being fooled wasn't going away easily. My drink was mostly water by now, so I went to the kitchen and tossed it down the drain. I refilled my glass with water, grabbed my phone, and plodded into the office. I sat for a minute at my desk and drew in a calming breath. I downloaded the employee list that Rhonda had given me, then emailed it to the detective at the station. When I finished, I got onto the internet.

I thought about calling Harry to talk to him about Darren, but on the East Coast it would be well after midnight, so I dismissed that idea. That conversation could wait until he got back. He was busy, and he didn't need to be dealing with Darren right at the moment. And because I'd pulled a gun on Darren, there was no way he'd be bothering me now. I'd handle the fallout from that later.

I checked the list of employees that worked at Tres Hermanos on Tuesday night. I eliminated the women, figuring there was no way the killer was female. I started first with the bartender, Greg. I checked the list, and was relieve to see there was only one Greg, last name Venable. He'd worked at the restaurant for ten months. I looked at his social media. He had a Facebook page, and the man in the pictures looked the same as the one I'd seen at the restaurant: sullen. He'd not posted a lot, and the ones I did see made me think he was an angry person. In one, he was threatening an ex-girlfriend, in another he was talking about a bar fight he'd gotten into, and that he was glad the police hadn't been called. It was too late to call Spats or Ernie, and I didn't want to go into the office at the moment, so I did a Google search on prison records and found Venable. He'd been at the Florence prison southwest of Denver for robbery. No wonder he hadn't wanted to share much. Of course cops asking questions would've made him nervous. Was he a killer though?

I jotted down a few notes about Greg, sipped some water, and moved on. The next male employee was a man named Freddie Herrera. He had pictures in cyberspace as well, only I didn't remember him. He was older, good-looking, with a strong jaw and a big smile. He'd worked at the restaurant for eight months. He was a college graduate and was also a teacher at a high school in Denver. I assumed he was working at the restaurant over the summer to make extra cash. He'd lived in Denver his whole life.

The next on the list was Carson Welch, who'd worked at the restaurant for only a few months. I checked for a Facebook page, but he didn't have one. Not terribly unusual, as younger people seemed to gravitate toward other social media sites instead. After a bit of searching, I couldn't find a social media presence for him at all. I went to a people-search site as I'd done with the others. He was listed as late twenties, and I found prior addresses for him. I scanned them, and my heart stopped. Carson showed a previous address in Colorado Springs, and he'd lived in Ohio before that. I checked the site more thoroughly and found that he'd lived there the previous summer. I swore as I stared at the monitor. Then I quickly went through the rest of the wait staff. According to the people-search site, no one else had lived in Colorado Springs.

My hand shook as I picked up my phone. I figured Spats could use all the sleep he could get, what with the baby, so I called Ernie first. After a few rings, he answered in a groggy voice.

"Sarah, what's going on? It's late."

"I think maybe I have our guy. Or at least a possibility." I couldn't get the words out fast enough. "His name is Carson Welch. He's worked at the restaurant for a few months, but get this. He lived in Colorado Springs last summer."

"You're kidding." Ernie was alert now. "Do you know where he worked down there? If we could find that, maybe we'd find a connection to other murdered women."

"I know. We'll have to check on his work history. I interviewed him earlier tonight, though."

"What'd you think?"

I gathered my thoughts. "He was quiet and didn't say a whole lot. He seemed upset about the women being killed, but he was interested, too."

"Like he was wondering what we knew."

"Exactly."

"Where does he live now?"

I looked on the internet. "It looks like he lives in a townhome south of Colorado and Florida Avenue."

"I know the area. Near that Home Depot."

"Right."

"He's worth talking to, even though it's late," Ernie said. "What's the address?"

I rattled it off. "How soon can you get there?"

A pause. "Give me half an hour."

"I'll see if I can get Spats up. He'll want to go, too."

"Yep." With that, he was gone.

I called Spats. It was time to pull him in. Like Ernie, he sounded groggy. As we talked, I heard the baby crying.

"I'm sorry to have bothered you," I said.

"That's okay. You wouldn't be calling unless something big is going on."

I filled him in on everything I'd discovered.

"You gotta be kidding me," he said, now wide awake. "He might be stalking women at restaurants? Man."

"I'm headed over to his townhome now."

"I'll be there in twenty minutes," he said.

I gave him the address as well, grabbed my gun and keys, and ran out the door.

Carson Welch lived in a townhome in the Virginia Village neighborhood, where the townhomes are older and have seen some wear and tear. The moon was behind hazy clouds, the street was bathed in eerie silver. I drove around the block and could see the back of the building. It was after eleven, and the streets were quiet. I pulled up to the front of the building. The units didn't have garages, and street parking was difficult at this time of night. I squeezed into a place down the block, looked around the street, and didn't see Ernie or Spats. I watched Welch's building for a moment. In the unit next door, a light was on in a window. Otherwise, it seemed quiet. I texted Ernie and Spats, and both responded that they were almost there. I texted the street and building layout to Spats and asked him to go around behind the building and watch. Soon I saw headlights turn the corner, and Ernie parked his car. I texted them both that the house was quiet, then told Spats to keep an eye on the back door, and told Ernie to meet me at the sidewalk near Welch's place. A moment later, we were standing in shadows at the end of the building.

"Let's knock on the door," I said in a low voice. "If he's there, we'll chat with him and see where it goes."

Ernie nodded. "Alrighty."

We went up the walk. I put my hand close to my gun and knocked on the front door. I tried the bell and waited a minute, then knocked. I looked at Ernie and shrugged. I rang once more with no luck. I called Spats. "See anything?"

"Nah, it's quiet back here. I don't see any lights on in his place."

"We can't force him to come out," Ernie said quietly. "If he's there."

I nodded. Then the door to the next townhome opened, and a woman with glasses peeked out through a crack.

"Hello?" I said to her.

"What's going on?" she asked cautiously.

I stepped over to her porch and showed her my badge. I pointed to Welch's place. "Do you know if he's home?"

She looked past me at Ernie, then shook her head. "I don't talk to him much."

I nodded. "Do you know much about Carson?"

Her gaze darted to me and Ernie and back. "Is he in some kind of trouble?"

"I'd just like to ask him a few questions," I said, careful not to tell her anything.

She shrugged. "Like I said, I don't talk to him much. He's kind of weird, keeps to himself. If you say hello to him, he doesn't answer back. He gives me funny looks, doesn't talk. So I gave up."

"How long has he been living there?"

She thought about that. "I guess about three or four months."

"You hear anything strange coming from his place?"

Another shake of the head. "It's quiet there, all the time. From that standpoint, he's a good neighbor. I think he works at a restaurant, makes pretty good money there. So his hours are a little different. He doesn't make much noise, so I don't care."

"Does he have a girlfriend?" I asked.

"I don't know. Maybe." She started to inch the door shut.

I whipped out a business card and held it out. "If you see him around, would you mind giving me a call? I'd just like to ask him a few questions."

She opened the door just enough to take the card, then quickly pushed it almost shut again. "I suppose so."

I thanked her, and she shut the door. I went back to Welch's porch.

"She ain't gonna call you," Ernie said.

I nodded. "Yeah, but I have to try."

I knocked on Welch's door again, and still no answer. We moved to the street and talked in low voices. "We're wasting time here."

"I'm not gonna be getting any more sleep now," he said. "Why don't I go to the office, see what else I can dig up on this guy. Maybe we'll find he's got a girlfriend or something, we can see if he's staying with her."

"I'll get a surveillance team to watch his place," I said. "And I'm going to watch for a while to see if he shows up."

"If you do see him, you call for backup." Ernie hefted up his pants and walked quickly back to his car. He seemed energized about things moving forward.

I went back to my car, called Spats, and told him what had happened. When I finished, he said, "I'll go join Ernie at the office, see what we can dig up on him. We need it fast. And let me know if you need to get a warrant. I can butter up a judge at an early hour."

I chuckled at that. "I'll be in touch."

I ended the call and stared at Carson's townhome. Where was he and what was he doing?

CHAPTER THIRTY-FIVE

His plans had changed. He wanted the detective, bad, but that wasn't going to happen. They were getting close to him, and it was too dangerous now. He snarled. The police must've thought him a fool, to expect that he'd go back to his townhome. He was smarter than that. He knew when they were asking questions at the restaurant that they would likely figure out who he was. It would only be a matter of time, and he'd have to run again. However, this time he was going to have his revenge. If he couldn't have the detective, he would do something better.

He fiddled with the anklet and watched the house. Faint light filtered out through the glass panes of the front door. At times the light flickered, as if someone were at the back of the house, watching TV. He looked up and down the street. The other houses were dark. Perfect. He put the anklet back in his pocket and eased open the car door. He quickly got out and softly shut the door. He listened. It remained still.

He walked down the block, then stole across the front yard. When he reached the side of the house, he headed around to the back. At the gate, he donned his mask. Then he took the knife out of his pocket.

CHAPTER THIRTY-SIX

As I scrunched down in my seat and watched Welch's house, I made some phone calls to arrange for a surveillance team to take over. It would take a while to get someone here, so I told them I'd wait. I didn't want us to miss Welch if he came home and left again. Once a team was on its way, I thought through everything we knew. I was almost certain this was our guy. I didn't see any way that it couldn't be. I let my mind percolate on all the information to see what I had. The light at the neighbor's house winked out. The street was peaceful.

While I waited, my mind wandered back to Darren showing up at my house. What had he been thinking? It took a lot of ego to think that I would want him over Harry, and just as much arrogance to believe he could judge Harry's and my relationship. My blood boiled thinking about it. I frowned. The crack about how my department photo looked like my driver's license picture. He wasn't completely wrong. I hated the photo on the department web site. But to say that to me was taking it to another level. I tapped the wheel, and then, something dawned on me. I sat up straighter. *A driver's license.* It has not only your photo on it, but your address. That's how Welch found where his victims lived. He was carding women, and he was using the information from the driver's licenses to find them. I swore. I thought back to when I was at the restaurant with Harry, how Welch had carded him, and how Harry had joked about it. Then something else occurred to me. Welch had waited on Diane and me, and he had carded us as well.

"Oh no," I said.

My mind pictured that evening with Diane. The waiter had seemed uncomfortable with her brusqueness, and I'd caught him staring at us. I'd attributed it to the intensity of our conversation. But, what if he was interested in us, saw one or the other of us as his next victim?

Had he been following me? Or, worse yet, Diane?

Panic overtook me, and my hand shook as I called Diane's house. It went to voice mail. I tried her cell, and she didn't answer that either. I left messages on both for her to call me right away. It was possible she was sleeping, but because she was on call a lot, she tended to answer. Why not now? I tried both numbers a few more times. No answers. I called her husband, Aaron, next. He was camping, and I couldn't reach him. I left him a message too, asking him to call, but I didn't expect to hear back from him. I jammed the key into the ignition and started the Escape. Then I called Ernie. He didn't pick up and neither did Spats. "Why aren't they answering?" I cursed as I peeled out of the neighborhood. My stomach roiled. I tried Ernie again, and this time he answered.

"What's up?" He didn't mince words.

"I might've figured it out. He's looking at driver's licenses. He's getting their addresses that way."

"What? Sarah, slow down."

"Welch cards the women at the restaurant. He has access to where they live. When Diane and I were at the restaurant the other night, he was our waiter. He watched us closely. I've tried calling her, but she's not answering. She said she'd be home all night. She's by herself. The family's gone camping. She was looking forward to it. She *always* answers or calls back, but I can't get hold of her. What if he went after her?"

"Where does your sister live?"

I quickly gave him the address. "I'm heading over there right now."

He cursed. "I'll meet you at her house. In the meantime, Spats is here. We'll get a crew to go over to your house and watch. You watch your back. Don't do anything without me."

"Get over to Diane's house fast. I don't want anything to happen to my sister."

I ended the call and tried Diane again. Still nothing. I stuffed my phone in my pocket and drove as fast as I could to her house. She lives in a ritzy neighborhood with big houses on big lots south of the Cherry Creek Mall. I soon turned onto her dark street. I raced down the block and into her driveway. I ignored Ernie's warnings and ran up the steps to the front porch. If she was in trouble, I didn't have any time to spare. I rang the bell and tried the doorknob. It was locked.

"Diane!" I called out.

Light from the back of the house came through rectangular panes in the door. I didn't see anyone. I pounded on the door and called out her name again.

Nothing.

I swore and stepped off the porch. I cupped my hands and peered in the front windows. Except for the light at the back of the house, it was dark. I started around the side of the house, and I called my mother. She answered after a few rings.

"Hello?" She sounded sleepy.

"Mom it's me, have you heard from Diane?" I said as I stared up at the second floor windows.

"Sarah, what time is it? Have I heard from Diane when?"

"I don't know. Earlier this evening. Do you know where she is? Did she decide to meet Aaron and the boys somewhere?"

"The last I talked to her was Sunday night." She was awake now, her voice clear. "She said she was going to enjoy some peace and quiet at home. And she mentioned she would be having dinner with you. What's going on?"

"She didn't call you today?"

"It's almost midnight. Why would I have heard from Diane?"

"I need to find her. Is there a way to get into her house? Do you have a spare key, or is there one hidden around here?" By now I had made my way around to a gate on the side of the house, and I let myself into the back yard.

"No, honey, I don't have a spare key. What's going on? You're scaring me."

I heard my father in the background, asking what was wrong.

"She may be in trouble," I said. "Try calling her cell phone, and if she answers, you tell her to call me right away."

"Sarah, I–"

"Just do it. I'll explain later."

"All right." She knew by the tone of my voice not to argue. "Is she hurt?"

"I don't know. I need to go Mom. I'll call you back."

I ended the call before she could say any more. By now I had come to the back porch. I drew my gun, crouched down near a glass patio table, and froze. The back screen door had been cut in an X pattern. I stepped up to the sliding glass doors and tried them. Locked. I looked inside. The TV was on, its silver lighting flickering off the walls. I watched for a moment and saw nothing. I pounded on the glass and called out Diane's name again, then peered up at the balcony to the master bedroom. It was dark. If she was there, she wasn't able to answer. I heard a car speed down the street and squeal to a stop, and I ran around to the front. Ernie parked his sedan behind the Escape, and he got out, moving with more agility than I'd seen in a while.

"Sarah, can you find her?"

I shook my head, frantic. "The back screen door is cut. He's here! We've got to get into the house!"

His face was steel as he raced up the sidewalk. He took the butt of his gun and hit one of the panes in the front door a few times until it cracked. Then he kicked at the glass with his foot. When the glass broke, he cleared a space with his gun, then carefully reached in and unlocked the door. We entered the house.

"Does she have an alarm on silent?" he asked.

I looked around for some kind of alarm panel. "I don't know." I raced for the back of the house, where the TV was on. Ernie followed. We entered the family room and saw the coffee table askew. I swore.

"Where's the bedroom?" Ernie asked.

I pointed, and we sprinted up the stairs.

"This way." I led Ernie down a long hall toward the master bedroom. The door was closed. We listened.

"I'm going to have some fun with you," Welch said, his voice low and creepy.

Ernie and I crouched down on either side of the door. He nodded. As I reached for the door knob, Diane screamed. I opened the door, and Ernie and I ducked into the room. In the shadows, I saw Diane lying on the bed, her pajama top ripped open, her breasts exposed, her hair disheveled. She sat up on the bed, clutching her throat.

"There." She pointed with her other hand. I looked to the far end of the room, and saw Carson Welch running out through a sliding glass door that led to the second-story balcony.

"Get him!" Diane said, then cursed as she pulled her top closed, her arms across her chest. I thought she'd never run out of swear words.

I looked at her, torn between wanting to help her and going after Welch.

Ernie hurried to the bed to check on her. "Stop Welch!"

I knew that, of the two of us, I was in better shape to chase him. I dashed to the balcony and peeked out. In the darkness, I saw Welch crossing the lawn. I ran out onto the balcony and yelled, "Stop!"

Welch ignored me and climbed over a fence into the neighbor's yard. I dashed to the railing, swung over it, and dropped to the ground. I hit hard, felt a stab in my ankle. I got up and raced across the lawn, ignoring the pain.

I reached the fence where Welch had disappeared and climbed over it. I crouched low and looked for Welch. The neighbor's yard was large, with towering oak trees and lots of flowerbeds. I didn't see him. My breathing sounded loud in the stillness. A porch light went on in the house, illuminating some of the yard. I watched for Welch, but didn't see him. Then I heard rustling at the other side of the yard. I limped in that direction, my gun aimed at the noise. In the corner was a large shed with its door partially open. I approached it carefully. When I reached the corner, I stood, waited, and listened. Nothing. Had Welch jumped the next fence?

The sound of a car racing down the street interrupted the stillness. I thought I saw movement in the shed, so I tiptoed toward the door and peeked inside. It was dark, and I couldn't see a thing. Then I heard a twig snap. I whirled around. Welch was standing at the far corner of the shed, a knife clutched in his hand.

"Drop the knife and put your hands up!" I backed up and raised my gun.

He took a step toward me. A trace of moonlight glinted off the knife. "You shouldn't have treated me the way you did." His voice wasn't as calm as I remembered it at the restaurant.

I took another step back. "What? What are you talking about?"

His face twisted up in anger, and he fingered the knife as he spoke. "You and your sister. I tried to be nice to you, offer you drinks, be polite to you, and you both treated me as if I didn't exist."

I pointed the gun at him, my hand steady. "Don't do anything stupid. We can work this all out. First you need to put the knife down. Now!"

He shook his head. "You'll pay, just like the others." He suddenly raced toward me, his eyes full of rage.

"Stop, or I'll shoot!" I shouted at him as I backpedaled. My mind raced, not wanting to pull the trigger, but not knowing how to escape him. "Stop!"

He screamed as he drew closer. I was keenly aware of my heart thudding in my chest, and my finger on the trigger of my gun. He raised the knife and slashed at me. I shouted one more time for him to stop. He drew close and leaped at me, the knife high.

I shot him.

CHAPTER THIRTY-SEVEN

Welch fell into me, and we both flew backward. We hit the ground hard and I lost my gun. He groaned, and his full weight was on me. His body odor overwhelmed me. I swore and pushed him off, then scrambled away, fearing what he would do next. I got to my knees and found the Glock. I picked it up and aimed it at him. He moaned once and lay still. I heard Spats yelling from somewhere as I gasped for breath, but my hand remained steady. Welch's knife was a few feet from him. I walked over, kicked it away, and turned to look at him. He wasn't moving. I approached with my gun on him, and nudged his leg with my foot. He still didn't move.

"Welch," I said.

Nothing.

Spats ran up, out of breath. "Sarah!" He stared at the body, then at me. "What happened? I got out of my car and heard you yelling, and then gunfire." He had his gun drawn as well. He turned on his flashlight, edged over to the body, and tapped him. When Welch didn't move, Spats bent down and felt his neck. "He's dead."

"I shot him," I said. "He leaped at me with his knife. I didn't have a choice."

Spats approached me, his face soft. "It's okay." I nodded mutely. "Sarah," he said. "You did what you had to do."

I nodded again, no words forthcoming. A uniformed officer ran up, his gun drawn as well.

"It was him or you," Spats said to me.

I took a deep breath, then turned around. "Diane! How is she?"

Before Spats could answer, we heard another voice.

"What's going on?"

We whirled around to see a man in a bathrobe, a baseball bat in his hand. He was probably in his fifties, his gray hair in disarray. The bat was cocked as if he knew how to deliver quite a blow. He saw Welch's body, and he backpedaled.

"Who are you?" Spats asked him.

"I'm Diane's neighbor, Fred Bartles. I live here."

Spats showed Fred his badge, then gestured at the uniformed officer. "If you could speak to this officer," Spats said to Fred. Spats nodded at me. "Go check on Diane."

I nodded and hurried across the yard. My ankle was throbbing as I ran through a gate and back into Diane's yard. The night sky was full of flashing red and blue lights as I crossed her lawn. As I approached the back door, another uniform stopped me. I showed him my badge and limped into the house. Diane and Ernie were now sitting on a couch in the living room. She'd put on a robe, and she'd combed her hair.

"Diane!" I ran over and knelt in front of her. Her face was pale, and she had a small cut on her neck, but otherwise she seemed okay, physically at least.

"He came into the house," she blubbered. "I didn't have the doors locked. I know you told me that I should, but I never lock the back sliding doors until I go to bed. I was up late, watching

TV. He cut the screen and slipped inside. I heard the door click closed and turned around to see him locking it. I stood up. He had a knife and he told me if I screamed that he'd kill me. The look on his face ..." She shuddered. "He ran up and grabbed me, put the knife to my throat. I couldn't get away. He was mumbling something about if he couldn't have the detective, he would have me. Sarah, I didn't know what to do."

"It's okay," I said. "You're safe now." She was a little shaky, but her emotions were moving from fear to anger.

Ernie patted her hand. "Take it easy."

"Where is he?" she asked.

I shrugged. "He's dead."

She ran her hands over her face, then through her hair. "I thought he was going to–" She didn't finish the sentence. "When he put the knife to my neck, I thought he'd hurt me, so I did what he said."

I reached to give her another hug, and she tensed, so I stopped.

"He forced me upstairs into the bedroom, then onto the bed." She coughed and went on. "I thought I was ... I was never going to see my family again." She broke down and leaned against me. Now I gave her a big hug and let her cry. I felt like crying myself, but held back.

"You're safe now," Ernie said.

Diane nodded, sniffled, and went on. "I didn't know what he was going to do. He was ranting and raving about his plans going wrong, that he wasn't going to jail. He was ... touching me." She rubbed her stomach at the memory, clearly indignant at the humiliation of it. She put a hand to her throat. "He had a knife on me most of the time. I didn't know what to do."

"Did he ... do anything else to you?" I asked in a low voice.

She shook her head. "No. I heard something–it must've been you –and I screamed. Then you two came through the door."

"In the nick of time," Ernie murmured.

I nodded and breathed a sigh of relief. A detective I vaguely knew came into the room. He would be taking over the investigation, which was okay with me. I was not telling anybody, but I was barely holding it together.

The detective sat down next to Diane, and he suggested she go to a hospital to be checked out. I overheard her protest and push back, said she was a doctor and she knew she was fine. In typical Diane fashion, she won the argument. She didn't get away without talking to him, though. He got her a bottle of water and a granola bar from the kitchen, then took his time and talked her through everything that happened. Ernie and I listened in, and her story the second time around matched everything she had told us. By the time she finished, an ambulance had shown up, and EMTs checked her over, even though she protested.

I finally stepped outside to call my mother and tell her we'd found Diane, and she was okay. I explained what had happened, and she said she and my father would come over. The EMTs checked me as well, and other than a twisted ankle that didn't need a hospital visit, pronounced me okay. Another officer took my statement. I went through everything that had happened, and how I had been forced to shoot Welch. The detective came out, listened and took notes, then had me go over the story again. The detective finished by asking me if I was okay. I nodded. Physically, I was. Mentally, I wasn't so sure. I kept picturing Welch as he came toward me with the knife. The crazy look in his eyes was burned into my brain.

I don't know how much time passed. Crime-scene techs arrived, and so did my parents. They were worried and distraught about Diane and me, but I let them focus on her. I wasn't able to say much at the moment anyway. Ernie and Spats were arranging for us to leave, and when no one was looking, I moved over by my car. No one could see me, and I bent down and threw up. I stayed bent over for a minute, then wiped my mouth with the back of my hand. I finally stood up and leaned on the car to steady myself. I looked up at the moon, so calm and peaceful in the sky. My nerves were jangled, my heart was still racing, and I didn't know when I would feel okay again.

CHAPTER THIRTY-EIGHT

Once we wrapped things up at Diane's house, Ernie, Spats, and I went back to the station. Rizzo was there, and he talked to me for a while. He was concerned about me, but in his usual calm way, he listened and nodded. He finished by assuring me of his support, both professionally and personally. Then he told me to go home and sleep. I drove home, my mind still abuzz. An internal investigation would be launched, and I'd be questioned again. An officer who kills a suspect would get a lot of scrutiny. I waited until I got home to call Harry, then I told him what had happened.

"Your sister, she's all right?" he asked.

"Yes. She's angry as a wet cat, but Welch didn't rape her."

"Thank god. And you?"

He wanted to know how I was doing. "I'll make it through this," I said. I finally said what I hadn't wanted to acknowledge. "I killed a man."

"I know. You had to."

"I guess."

A pause. "Try not to think about that now," he said. "There'll be time for that later."

"Uh-huh." I fought back tears.

"You sure you're going to be okay?" he said for the umpteenth time.

"I'll be fine."

"I'll catch the first flight I can get."

"Don't do that. You need to–"

"I'm coming back as soon as I can. Do you have to go into the station in the morning?"

"Yes. I have a report to write, and I'm sure more questions to answer."

"I'll see you there. No argument."

He made mundane conversation for a bit, clearly not wanting to say goodbye. He finally did, after telling me again that he loved me. I ended the call, then realized I hadn't even told him about Darren Barnes. That could wait for another time.

I took a long hot shower, drank too much Scotch, and laid on the bed. I stared at the ceiling and wished for sleep and calm. I saw neither the entire night.

Before dawn, I went into the kitchen and fixed coffee. I took a cup to the back yard and watched as the sky grew a lighter blue. I thought of Darren, and hoped he wasn't watching. If he was, to hell with him.

At seven, I went back inside and took a long shower to help me wake up. I got dressed, but skipped breakfast. I wasn't hungry. At eight I was at the station.

"How are you doing this morning?" Ernie asked. He was at his desk, typing on the computer.

I sat down. I stared at him for a moment, then said, "I'm tired, and my ankle is sore."

He knew I'd never killed anyone before and that it had to be taking a toll. I wasn't sure what to think. I'd had to kill Carson Welch. He'd left me no choice. That didn't make me feel any better. I didn't know how long the internal investigation would last, and I was sure I would have to see a staff psychologist. That was okay. I'm sure I would have things to talk about. I caught Ernie looking at me.

"Take all the time you need," he said.

I nodded and stared at my laptop.

A few minutes later, Spats walked in with donuts. He looked snazzy in a dark suit and tie.

"I thought we could use some of these," he said.

"Cops and donuts," Ernie said. "How appropriate."

Spats set the box down and Ernie got a powdered donut. He glanced at me and I nodded. He picked a glazed donut and handed it to me.

"Thanks," I said. I nibbled at it.

Spats sat down and glanced over at me. "Trissa and I had a nice conversation last night. Well, early this morning."

"Did you sleep at all?" Ernie asked.

Spats shook his head. "Not really." He held up a big cup of coffee. "That's why I need this." He looked over at me. "I think things will be okay. She's trying to understand, and so am I."

I smiled at him. "That's good news."

Ernie looked between us, seemed to know it wasn't anything he needed to comment on. He stuffed the rest of his donut in his mouth. "I'll get to working on my report."

I nodded. "So will I."

~

A week later, Harry and I were at dinner with Diane and her husband, Aaron. We chose a Chili's on Colorado Boulevard, far from the popular Tres Hermanos. Diane wore black leggings and a perfectly fitted top, and her hair was done a bit differently than usual. While we waited for our dinners to arrive, she talked about the investigation.

"What did they find out on that guy? I haven't wanted to look at the papers or anything, and I don't even want to say his name."

Aaron took her hand and squeezed it. "You do whatever you feel is right." Aaron's a big guy, and a bit stocky, with dark hair and eyes. He has a way with Diane that I don't. "It's taken her a few days to feel back to normal. She's still wary of the bedroom."

"Yes, I'm sure," I murmured.

"I was furious when I found out what had happened," he went on. "I think I broke every speed record to get back to Denver."

"I don't blame you," Harry said.

Aaron sighed. "We haven't told the boys too much. We don't want to scare them. Once Diane is in a better space, we'll tell them more."

I like Aaron. He's a good guy, surprisingly unpretentious. And he loves Diane and puts up with her in a way that no one else can.

"That makes sense," I said.

I glanced at Diane. She appeared fine, but she'd told me she had talked to a therapist, and that she might keep going to her for a while. I'd encouraged it, and knew that I needed to do the same.

"Yes, this hasn't been easy on Sarah," Harry piped up.

I loved him for that, loved the fact that he knew that it had been a rough week for me as well. I'd tried to act normal–whatever that was–and he knew I wasn't completely succeeding. The internal investigation had gone well: I'd been cleared of any wrongdoing in Welch's death. But it hadn't helped me that much.

"I wish I hadn't ..." My voice trailed off.

"You had every right to do what you did," Diane snapped. "Who knows what that maniac would've done to me?" Whatever trauma she had felt about the ordeal, she was dealing with it through anger.

"What did you find out about that guy?" Aaron asked.

"A lot more than we knew that night," I said. "Near as we can tell, he killed two women in Ohio, although I'm not sure we'll be able to prove it. He's most likely tied to at least a few killings in Colorado Springs last summer, and I think the DNA under Cherry Rubio's fingernails will match him, so he'll be tied to her death."

"What would possess a person to do that?" Aaron said with a shake of his head.

I shrugged. "He has all the makings of a serial killer. He came from a broken home, his mother was abusive, and he was a bed wetter. Those are some common traits of serial killers. He was very bright, but didn't do very well in school. He kept to himself."

"There's no excuse for what he did," Diane said.

We paused while the waiter brought our dinners.

"You're right," I said. "He fits a pattern, whatever that means. Regardless, who knows why serial killers do what they do."

"I'm just glad you're all okay," Harry said in an attempt to change the conversation.

"If we hadn't been at that restaurant, that maniac wouldn't have gone after us," Diane said. Aaron touched her arm. She almost said something else, then shut her mouth and ate her dinner.

I tensed up, and underneath the table, Harry put his hand on my knee. I stayed silent and smiled at Diane.

"I'm glad you're safe," I said.

"Me too." She was typically oblivious.

Dinner ended, and we left the restaurant. Diane gave me a perfunctory hug, and Aaron thanked me.

"Let's take the boys to a ballgame soon," Harry said.

"That'd be nice," Aaron said. He gave me a warm hug.

Harry and I watched them walk to their car and drive off, then we got in his car. He didn't start it right away, but turned to look at me.

"You handled the dinner with grace."

I stared out the windshield for a long time.

"Thanks," I said. "I'm not sure what to think right now. About Diane, about the case."

"Take all the time that you need." He smiled. "Your sister may never change, but you already have. I'm glad to see that."

I nodded. Things felt better between him and me. I was thankful for that. I pointed toward the road.

"Let's go home."

Turn the page to check out a sneak peek of *Deadly Guild*, Sarah Spillman Mysteries Book 3.

SNEAK PEEK

DEADLY GUILD, SARAH SPILLMAN MYSTERIES BOOK 3

Teddy: *The Guild will now come to order.*

She read the line on the computer monitor, then put her hands to the keyboard and typed.

Marilyn: *Marilyn Monroe is here.*

She'd chosen her favorite actress as her pseudonym. She loved old-time movies, and she loved Marilyn Monroe. Monroe carried herself as few other females did. She was sexy, sultry, and yet she played hardball with the Hollywood studios. People thought Monroe was dumb, but she was smart and tough. The woman nodded. Yes, that name fit her well.

Her house was quiet except for the classical music that played in her office. She looked at the screen. Other members of the Guild said their hellos. There was Brad Pitt, well, not *really* Brad Pitt, but someone who said he liked Pitt's movies. She assumed Brad was a "he," but for all she knew Brad could be a woman. The whole idea was anonymity. That was key.

Daffy Duck, Pete Rose, and Joe Smith were there. She wasn't fond of Daffy Duck. Daffy came across as arrogant. Pete Rose. "That was someone who loved baseball, and was a gambler," she thought with a laugh. Joe Smith was really going for obscurity. She had no idea who they all were, and they had no idea who she was. That was the way the Guild worked. They were in a secure online chat room, where no one would be able to identify them. They all had secure internet connections, untraceable. They all had money, enough to buy that kind of secrecy and safety.

Teddy Roosevelt, the leader, typed again.

Please agree to the Guild rules. Everything said here remains here. Do not talk about a member's actions or plans to anyone outside of the Guild. We are the group, no new members will be allowed. We all have the resources to make you pay. Do not break the rules. Your word is your oath.

She thought it was interesting that Teddy always started each recitation of the rules with a polite "Please," but ended the rules with a threat. She frowned. None of them needed the threat. If one of them talked, they were all vulnerable, and none of them wanted to go to jail. Or worse. So no one would say a word.

The monitor lit up with a round of yeses from the Guild members. The woman dutifully agreed to the Guild rules as well. Teddy went on.

Does Daffy Duck have a report for us?

The woman rolled her eyes as Daffy Duck responded.

Did you all see the report about a drowning near Parker a few days ago?

A round of yeses.

Daffy Duck: *That was me.*
Pete Rose: *Proof?*
Daffy Duck: *Check the paper.*

The woman opened a browser. As she was sure the others were doing, she typed in the newspaper and searched for a man who'd drowned. She found an article and quickly read it. Then she came to the pertinent section. A silver necklace with a fake ruby had been found at the scene. Jewelry with a red stone was the proof. Innocuous to most, but proof for the Guild. She went back to the chat room. By now, Brad Pitt had responded.

Marilyn: *It's right there. The proof.*
Teddy Roosevelt: *That's correct.*
Pete Rose: *You did it.*
Daffy Duck: *I was a bit afraid at first. I wasn't sure I could go through with it. But then I hit him over the head, and the rest was easier than I thought.*
Brad Pitt: *Way to go, killer.*
Daffy Duck: *Ha ha. I've thought about this for so long, wanted to know what it would be like to actually do it. Now I'm part of an elite group of people.*
Brad Pitt: *Like Teddy and me.*

The woman felt a twinge of jealousy. Daffy Duck now had a kill, like the others. She wanted to know how it felt. Before she could ask him about it, Teddy cut into the conversation.

The next order of business, who is next?

The woman stared at the monitor, waiting to see if someone else might respond. When no one did, she put her shaking hands to the keyboard and typed.

Marilyn: *Me.*

Her breath caught in her throat. She was committed now.

Teddy Roosevelt: *When?*

She pondered that for a moment. For days she had been thinking how she would do it. And she'd formed a plan that she was sure was foolproof, where she could not get caught. It was time to forge ahead. She typed her response.

Marilyn: *Tomorrow night. Watch the news after that.*
Teddy Roosevelt: *Wonderful.*

She picked up a crystal glass and took a drink of Scotch to calm her nerves. She had to go through with it now. That order of business finished, the conversation with Daffy Duck resumed.

Pete Rose: *Daffy, you're sure you were careful?*
Daffy Duck: *Of course. Don't insult me.*
Teddy Roosevelt: *Just like the others. With the correct precautions, there won't be any problems.*

The woman nodded at the screen. Yes, they were all exceedingly careful. They had to be, or their lives would be ruined. No one could have that. The irony of their victims losing their lives was not lost on her. But that was the price that had to be paid for the Guild members to experience killing. And she wanted to know. She finally asked Daffy Duck what she'd wanted to ever since he said he'd completed his task.

Marilyn: *How did it feel?*
Daffy Duck: *Incredible.*

~

Continue reading *Deadly Guild*, Sarah Spillman Mysteries Book 3, releasing early 2021: reneepawlish.com/DGwb

FREE BOOK

Sign up for my newsletter and receive book 1 in the Reed Ferguson mystery series, *This Doesn't Happen in the Movies*, as a welcome gift. You'll also receive another bonus!

Click here to get started:
reneepawlish.com/RF2

RENÉE'S BOOKSHELF

Reed Ferguson Mysteries:

This Doesn't Happen In The Movies
Reel Estate Rip-Off
The Maltese Felon
Farewell, My Deuce
Out Of The Past
Torch Scene
The Lady Who Sang High
Sweet Smell Of Sucrets
The Third Fan
Back Story
Night of the Hunted
The Postman Always Brings Dice
Road Blocked
Small Town Focus
Nightmare Sally
The Damned Don't Die
Double Iniquity
The Lady Rambles

A Killing

Reed Ferguson Novellas:

Ace in the Hole

Walk Softly, Danger

Reed Ferguson Short Stories:

Elvis And The Sports Card Cheat

A Gun For Hire

Cool Alibi

The Big Steal

The Wrong Woman

Dewey Webb Historical Mystery Series:

Web of Deceit

Murder In Fashion

Secrets and Lies

Honor Among Thieves

Trouble Finds Her

Mob Rule

Murder At Eight

Dewey Webb Short Stories:

Second Chance

Double Cross

Standalone Psychological Suspense:

What's Yours Is Mine

The Girl in the Window

The Sarah Spillman Mysteries:

Deadly Connections

Deadly Invasion
Deadly Guild

The Sarah Spillman Mystery Short Stories:
Seven for Suicide
Saturday Night Special
Dance of the Macabre

Supernatural Mystery:
Nephilim Genesis of Evil

Short Stories:
Take Five Collection
Codename Richard: A Ghost Story
The Taste of Blood: A Vampire Story

Nonfiction:
The Sallie House: Exposing the Beast Within

CHILDREN'S BOOKS
Middle-grade Historical Fiction:
This War We're In

The Noah Winter Adventure Series:
The Emerald Quest
Dive into Danger
Terror On Lake Huron

ABOUT THE AUTHOR

Renée Pawlish is the author of The Reed Ferguson mystery series, *Nephilim Genesis of Evil,* The Noah Winter adventure series for young adults, *Take Five,* a short story collection that includes a Reed Ferguson mystery, and The *Sallie House: Exposing the Beast Within,* about a haunted house investigation in Kansas.

Renée loves to travel and has visited numerous countries around the world. She has also spent many summer days at her parents' cabin in the hills outside of Boulder, Colorado, which was the inspiration for the setting of Taylor Crossing in her novel *Nephilim.*

Visit Renée at www.reneepawlish.com.

 facebook.com/reneepawlish.author

 twitter.com/ReneePawlish

 instagram.com/reneepawlish_author

Made in the USA
Coppell, TX
04 June 2021